The Moskowitz Code

The Moskowitz Code
by Joel Bresler

Tasfil Publishing, LLC
New Jersey, USA

Other Books by Joel Bresler:

Sunderwynde Revisited
Sunderwynde Revisited, Again
Letters to be Read in a Heavily British Accent

Chapter 1

It started with a sneeze.

It might have ended there, too, but for a simple matter of timing. Myron Moskowitz, "Mike" to the entire world minus one, happened to be on the phone with his mother when the sneeze in question ricocheted half-heartedly off the receiver.

"Myron? What was that?"

"What was *what*, Mother?"

"I thought I heard something."

"What do you think you heard?"

"It sounded like somebody sneezed."

"*I* sneezed, Mother. Perhaps that's what you heard."

"*You* sneezed? Are you sick?"

"Not to the point of requiring medical attention, if that's what you mean."

"How do you know? You're not a doctor. You *could* have been a doctor, if you'd have only applied yourself a little more at school. But you're not one, you know."

"Yes, Mother, I know I'm not a doctor. Thank you for reminding me anyway."

"Don't mention it. That's what mothers are for. So have

you seen the doctor yet? What did he say?"

"I haven't seen the doctor, Mother, so whatever he may have said, I would not have been there to hear it." He knew what was coming next.

"Well then, what are you waiting for? Make an appointment with Dr. Katz. You could be sick. There's something going around now, you know."

"What's going around?"

"How should I know? I only know that whatever it is, it's going around. Stop giving me such a hard time."

Celia Moskowitz, Myron, er, *Mike's* mom, was not so much a woman as she was a force of nature. Just under five feet tall (in heels) Celia was formidable far beyond anything her diminutive stature might suggest to the uninitiated. Her son was convinced she could move an entire mountain range with a wave of her arm, if she so desired. And if not actually move it, she could at least wear it down.

"And besides," Celia continued, "you could give whatever it is to that wife of yours."

Mike felt pretty confident that, given the amount of physical contact required to transmit "it," if there actually *was* an "it," his wife was in no real danger.

"That wife of mine has a name, Mother. You really ought to try using it occasionally."

"Christine. I mean, Jesus, what kind of a name is *Christine*?"

"It's a very nice name. A rather popular one, too."

"Well, I never knew anybody named Christine. There were never any Christines in *my* old neighborhood."

"To their great fortune, I have no doubt."

"Ha, ha, Mister I-just-got-one-over-on-my-poor-old-mother. So, will you go to the doctor?"

"I'll consider it."

"Enough with the consider, already. Just do it."

"All right, Mother," sighed what was once the Himalayas.

Whether through Celia's incredible powers of suggestion or just an unfortunate consequence of basic immunology, Mike's sneeze soon metamorphosed into something considerably more inconvenient. The "it" that was going around, perhaps. Whatever it was, it was beginning to seriously interfere with Mike's ability to perform functions he normally took for granted, such as breathing. Left to continue on its current path unabated…well, the prospect was not a happy one.

Still, Mike waited until there was barely any trace of audibility remaining in his larynx before finally breaking down and calling Dr. Katz's office. Fortunately, the receptionist had plenty of experience listening to barely-audible sick people, and grasped the situation immediately.

"It's going around," she said.

"So I've heard," Mike croaked back.

"The doctor is booked solid, but for Celia Moskowitz's son I'm sure we can find a way to squeeze you in sometime this afternoon." She was packing it all in in a few days anyway, so she could afford to be accommodating.

Frankly, Dr. Katz's receptionist was just grateful the appointment wasn't for Celia herself. Mike would have understood.

He arrived at the office early, just on the off chance that the squeezing-in might occur sooner rather than later. That had never happened before, but there was, he reasoned, always a first time.

And while there *was* always a first time, today was not going to be it. Mike waited an interminably long while, feeling the disease progressing in stages as his butt progressively warmed the chair. He was convinced his temperature had been climbing an additional degree every thirty minutes or so, by which reckoning it was probably hovering somewhere in the neighborhood of 117 degrees Fahrenheit by now . He could also feel his brain, eyeballs, and sinuses being sucked deeper into his skull, and wondered how much further they could possibly go before seeking refuge in another, larger body cavity.

It was just as he was fading into a disease-induced state of euphoria that the office nurse called out his name.

"Mr. Moskowitz?"

Mike was beginning to enjoy the disease-induced state of euphoria, and thus did not feel particularly compelled to answer her.

"Mr. Moskowitz?" the nurse asked, somewhat more insistently this time.

He was still just enough on this side of the euphoria to pull himself back, which he did with a deep pang of regret.

"Mr. Moskowitz?"

"Present and accounted for."

"Glad to hear it," the nurse said, with a nursely smile. "Would you please walk this way?"

Mike felt far too under the weather to suggest that, if he could walk that way, he probably wouldn't need to be there. He followed her back to an empty examination room where he was invited to make himself comfortable. He felt far too under the weather to respond to that one, too.

His wait here was not quite as long as it had been prior to being summoned, but to Mike it definitely seemed that way. There was no euphoria to break up the monotony this time, however. He was stuck with his present reality, which under the circumstances was not proving to be an especially good one.

Eventually, the doctor could be heard shuffling around outside the door, and eventually plus one minute later, he joined Mike inside the room. Dr. Katz made a beeline for the small desk facing a wall perpendicular to the examination table on which his rather pitiful patient was presently perched.

The doctor then began typing on a keyboard connected to a small PC, which were the sole articles on the desk. Mike wondered what the guy could possibly be typing already since they hadn't even acknowledged one another yet.

After about two minutes of frenzied data entry, the doctor broke the ice.

"Mr. Moskowitz, how nice to see you. How have you been?"

"Is that a trick question, Dr. Katz?"

"Well, obviously, you're sick. But other than that, I

mean. How's your mother?" He continued typing away.

"Why, she was just complaining that she hasn't seen nearly enough of you lately. She's thinking of scheduling an appointment just to pay a social call."

"Um, hmm." Still typing.

Just as Mike thought: obviously not paying attention. He should have gotten at least a prairie dog out of that one.

"So, Mr. Moskowitz, what seems to be the trouble?"

"How should I know? I'm not a doctor. Just ask my mother. She'll tell you."

Dr. Katz thought he'd just take Mike's word for it.

"Okay, then. Why don't we start with the symptoms? Run them down for me." Dr. Katz continued typing into his computer.

Mike ran down a laundry list of symptoms, to which Dr. Katz occasionally added an "Ah?" or an "Um hmm." Once or twice he even threw in an "I see."

"It's going around," Dr. Katz said.

So, Mike informed his physician, he'd been led to believe.

The doctor prescribed a course of antibiotics, a decongestant, one or two other similarly palliative pharmaceutical items, and suggested a few activities that might also help improve Mike's sense of well-being. His fingers never once let up off the keyboard.

As the doctor was about to finish the consultation by entering in the appropriate diagnostic codes, he turned to Mike and, *still* tapping away, wished his patient a swift return to health.

In the miniscule span of time that Dr. Katz's attention

was directed away from his computer screen, what should have been a right ring finger keystroke was instead delivered by a left pinkie. Or maybe it was the other way around. In any case, what the doctor thought he had entered and what was, in fact, actually recorded, wound up being two entirely different things.

On a college term paper, a typographical error of this nature would have probably been circled once in red pencil and then completely forgotten about.

On Myron Moskowitz's permanent electronic medical record, however, it was not going to get off quite so easily.

The following month, when the insurance payment for Myron "Mike" Moskowitz's visit arrived at his doctor's office, the check was in an amount considerably higher than what was typical for treating whatever it was that had been going around. The figure showed up again on the practice's monthly financial report, where it was circled once in red pencil and then completely forgotten about.

His illness ran its course with almost embarrassing rapidity, leaving Mike mildly ashamed of himself for wimping out and running to the doctor practically at the first sniffle. It was all his mother's fault, he decided, which was his fallback for a lot of things. And the fact that he was generally right made coming up with other excuses largely unnecessary.

There was no denying that Celia had a special gift for

infiltrating virtually every nook and cranny of her son's life. It would not have been surprising to learn that black magic figured into it somehow. Come to think of it, that would probably have explained quite a lot. If insinuating oneself into other people's lives could be considered a form of kung-fu, Celia Moskowitz would have been the discipline's undisputed master.

Interestingly, this had not always been the case. Young Mike (even Celia called him that back then) had been as free a spirit as one could possibly hope to be when saddled with a moniker like Myron Moskowitz. It was only after he had left for college that Celia, feeling her maternal grasp slipping away, began truly playing to win. Mike had, to some extent, been under that doll-sized thumb ever since.

Well, *almost* ever since. There were those few, happy years when he'd managed to escape the pressure of that undersized, opposable digit, beginning when he had first met Christine. In those blissful days, Mike had remained mostly oblivious to anyone and anything that was not either Christine or the ground she so angelically floated over. He would even have considered writing poetry, if only it could have been called something else. Mike had always maintained that the reason most people cringed whenever *poetry* was mentioned was due entirely to the word itself. A bit of brand-management, he believed, would do wonders for what was, basically, a pretty decent little art form.

As the scales gradually fell from his eyes, however, they were replaced by images of Celia. By themselves, these would have been easy enough to ignore. Unfortunately, the images were also accompanied by the sound of her voice, which rendered any chance of escape somewhere on the order of trying to elude death. In Mike's imagination, that voice was either offering hyper-critical opinions about his judgment, in a Monday-morning quarterback sort of way, letting him know what *she* would have done in the same situation. Which, of course, she would never have gotten herself into in the first place. Or asking seemingly innocuous questions in a manner calculated to leave Mike second-guessing everything he ever believed or thought he knew. At best, his mother could only be put off for a little while. Like the guy in the original black hoodie, however, in the end resistance would always prove futile.

Mike assumed it was Celia's uncanny powers of suggestion that had turned what had likely been only a minor blip on his constitutional radar into a wicked case of the flu. He was grateful, at least, that she had probably never heard of Dengue Fever or Bubonic Plague. The world, he felt, was undoubtedly a great deal safer for it.

He derived some satisfaction from the knowledge that, despite exceeding even her usual, exceptionally high standards of contact avoidance, Christine had somehow managed to come down with whatever was going around, too. Now there, he thought, was an instance when the word *poetry* seemed altogether appropriate. He was referring, specifically, to its use in the term, *poetic justice*.

Chapter 2

The matrimonial Moskowitzes were seated in opposite corners of their communal living room, each apparently engrossed in a paperback. Mike's nose was buried in a contemporary history of Second World War atrocities in Poland. Lately, it seemed to require something of this magnitude for him to escape the mind-numbing minutia of his own, everyday life. Christine was engrossed in a best-selling volume on the subject of empowerment for women, a genre she had recently been devoting a considerable portion of her available reading time to. The television was turned on quietly for background, just in case either Moskowitz momentarily forgot themselves and attempted to have speech with the other.

"Mike?" asked Christine, shattering the library-like atmosphere of the room.

"Hmmm?" answered the addressee, trying not to interrupt his reading.

"Honey, how much is that life insurance policy for?"

"What life insurance policy would that be?" asked Moskowitz male, trying to bury his nose even deeper into his book. He could guess where the conversation was headed and hoped that a conflagration along the lines of the destruction of downtown Warsaw would soften his own impending artillery attack.

"Didn't you have a million-dollar life insurance policy?"

"If you already knew the amount, why did you ask?"

"You still have the policy, don't you?"

"No."

"*No?* Why not?"

"Because," Mike closed his book on his index finger, "the term ended and the premiums went up like, ten times what they were before. I decided not to renew." He had a premonition that not even the rape of the Polish countryside could help him escape what was coming next.

"So we have *no* life insurance? What happens if you die?"

"Well, let's see...if you believe in Heaven and Hell, there's one potential scenario. Otherwise, I'll either become worm food or contribute to global warming. The choice will pretty much be up to you."

"I mean, what happens to *me?*"

"Well, again, there's the Heaven or Hell option, and frankly I have my own theories on how that one would go. Then –"

"Mike..." Drawn out as long as humanly possible without losing its intended target.

"How do *I* know? I mean, I'll be dead, won't I?"

"Don't you care what happens to me after you're gone?"

"Who says I'll be the first one to go? And in any case,

you have my promise: I'll take just as good care of you when I'm dead as you've taken of me while I'm alive."

"You're such a pig. I can't imagine why I ever married you. I could have married a doctor, you know."

"Don't you start that, too."

"It's true. I should have listened to your mother."

"*My* mother?"

Yes. She kept insisting her son had no business marrying me."

"I don't think you quite gleaned her meaning."

"I'm sure I gleaned it perfectly. She was certain our getting married was a big mistake."

He had to score a point to Celia for that one. Or else it was that spooky power of suggestion thing of hers at work once again.

Mike went back to his book, but found that he had inadvertently pulled his finger out and lost his place. He flipped through the pages attempting to relocate it, but all those Luftwaffe bombing sorties tended to blend together, rendering the task pretty much a hopeless one.

Christine, having just finished a chapter on women taking their futures into their own hands, was not about to spend the rest of her husband's life, and hopefully an even longer thereafter, without the assurance of a little financial security. She knew, however, that this was not a battle she was likely to win without considerable reinforcements. This meant placing a call to Celia, whose methods she was coming to, if not actually like, at least appreciate on a purely strategic level.

Not being one to let a minor tactical retreat keep her

from getting the last word in, Christine mumbled the word *pig* under her breath and went back to her chapter on dealing with personal issues in a more detached, professional way. Mike stopped his own page flipping at the story of the Russians beating the enemy back from the Polish capitol, immersing himself so thoroughly that he would have sworn he could hear rifle shots. It was, however, only the sound of Christine gnashing her teeth.

"**W**hat's this I hear about you not having any insurance?" asked Celia, in her most accusatory tone of voice. "How can you not have insurance?"

"Wait–let me guess. You've been talking to that wife of mine, haven't you?"

"That wife of yours has a name, you know. And yes, Christine *did* happen to call me. She wanted my advice."

"*Your* advice? Are we still talking about *my* Christine? Wow. How long have you been waiting for that one?"

"Ha, ha, Mister Smart-aleck. Admittedly, it did seem a little long in coming. But she was practically in tears."

"You didn't really fall for that, did you?"

"Of course not. But just because she was bucking for an Academy Award doesn't mean she was wrong."

"So, what did you tell her?"

"I told her she didn't deserve you."

"Ah. Like you've been saying ever since we announced our engagement."

"No, *not* like I've been saying ever since you announced your engagement. Now *she's* the one who deserves better."

"And they say that a boy's best friend is his mother!"

"Yeah, I saw that movie, too. Now *there* was a son!"

"As I recall, that son *killed* his mother."

"Yes, but such *devotion!*"

Two days later, Mike called a friend of his who was in the insurance business.

"Todd? Mike Moskowitz. I need some life insurance."

"I thought you weren't going to give your wife the satisfaction."

"Things change. No, on second thought, they don't. That's why I need the insurance."

"Let me guess: you've been talking to your mother again, haven't you?"

"Do they sell insurance for *that?*"

"Not through us, they don't. So, do you want a million dollars?"

"That depends. Can I have it now?"

"Sorry. Gotta die first. Hardly seems fair, I know."

"My definition of fair has become increasingly open to interpretation lately. So how much is this alleged benefit supposed to cost me?"

Todd quoted several companies' rates at Mike's previous level of coverage. While they were all significantly lower than what his last policy had threatened to jump to, they still seemed far too high where Christine was concerned.

"What have you got for half-a-million?" he asked.

Todd pulled up a few more quotes, all of which sounded far more reasonable to Mike considering what the money would be going toward. Whether the lesser amount would satisfy Celia, however, remained another matter. Of course, none of this would even be an issue if Mike could somehow manage to outlive the two of them. He made a mental note to stop off and pick up a bottle of vitamins on his way home from work.

A plan underwritten by the Itinerant Life & Casualty Company was settled on. The necessary on-line forms were eventually completed. Then Todd reminded Mike that the nasty, acidy bile-like taste in his mouth to the contrary, he was doing the right thing.

"Oh, good. I feel *so* much better now."

Todd mentioned that someone from Itinerant Life would be contacting him to schedule the requisite pre-insurance physical, and the two made plans to get together in some recreational capacity in the very near future.

As it had after running to the doctor, Mike's self-esteem was stinging a bit from having succumbed so quickly to his mother's will. He took some consolation knowing he'd only given in to fifty percent of the insurance, which, coincidentally, was about as much chance as he could hope for of earning the Celia Seal of Approval. Oh well. He could always lie. With any luck, by the time anyone found out he'd be safely out of harm's reach. Hopefully in Heaven, though he'd settle for becoming worm food or atmospheric ash. As a final stop along this thought track, Mike wondered if it hurt much when your widow beat the living snot out of your already lifeless corpse.

He did tarry briefly at a vitamin shop on the way home from work that evening. The breathtakingly beautiful sales clerk sent him home with supplements for treating conditions that probably didn't even exist, really. Yet Mike knew he'd be back to buy them again.

Early the following week, Mike received a call from an Itinerant Life & Casualty Company nurse to schedule the pre-insurance physical he'd been warned to expect. He was in no hurry, even when she pointed out that his loved ones would not be protected until the exam had been successfully completed. This news did absolutely nothing to increase Mike's sense of urgency in the matter. But the nurse had wide experience in dealing with procrastinators. Claiming to have produced a calendar, she made quick work of her reluctant client.

"Oh, and by the way, we'll need copies of all your medical records for the past ten years," she said. "So if you could please contact any healthcare providers and health insurers you may have dealt with over that period and arrange for those authorizations, it would be extremely helpful." And before Mike could ask if this could wait until after the physical, she added: "*Before* the physical, please. Thank you so much." She had, as previously noted, a wide experience in dealing with procrastinators.

"Anything else?" asked Mike, hoping the answer was no.

"Nope. That'll do, Mr. Moskowitz. May I call you Myron?"

"If you must, though only my mother calls me that. I prefer Mike."

"Okay, Mike then. I look forward to meeting you in person." She always said that, and on exceptionally rare occasions, she even meant it.

Chapter 3

Mike hung up after his conversation with the Itinerant Life & Casualty nurse, and silently uttered a minor curse. The description of which may well be verse, but his disposition had gone from bad to worse.

Homework! Not only was he about to be paying for an insurance policy he didn't want, *and* facing the prospect of being poked and prodded by a complete stranger in the bargain; now they expected him to do *homework*! Mike picked up the phone, prepared to call Todd and cancel the whole thing, but then carefully set it down knowing that was never going to happen. Somewhere Celia nodded her head approvingly.

Mike pulled a pen and a small notepad out of a drawer and wrote down the date and time of his impending physical. He next tried to think of any healthcare providers he may have had contact with over the past ten years. Ten years! That seemed like an unreasonably long period of time. Anything that serious would have surely killed him by now, wouldn't it? And what if he forgot someone? Would they take points off, or something? Raise the premiums? Turn him down altogether?

He began making a list:

1. Dr. Sherman Katz.

Sherman! Who names a kid that, anyway, Mike wondered, until he remembered that someone had once named him Myron.

1. Dr. Sherman Katz
2. Shortshrift Urgent Care Center. That was the time he jabbed himself in the hand with an Xacto knife while opening a walnut. And he didn't even *like* walnuts.

That was it. Oh, aside from the dermatologist who removed that (fortunately) benign skin thingy a few years ago. He probably wouldn't have even bothered with it really, except for where the unusual growth had happened to be located. Mike remembered paying cash for that particular office visit, not wanting even his insurance company ever finding out about it. He decided to leave the dermatologist off his list.

This left only his health insurers, of which, in the past ten years, there had been two. The first went out of business after its entire C-suite of executives was convicted of fraud, money laundering, and an apparent disregard for the spirit of sound business practices. The RICO statutes had been invoked once or twice, Mike seemed to recall. And then there was one.

He made the requisite requests to release his medical records to the Itinerant and settled back to fully savor his dread of the impending physical examination itself.

Deep within the labyrinthine bowels of the Itinerant Life & Casualty Company's corporate offices, there existed a cubicle. Actually, there existed literally *hundreds* of cubicles, but only one of these was occupied by a particular individual whose job it was to review the medical histories of the firm's life insurance candidates. For identification purposes, we will simply refer to this person as "Jackie," since that was her name.

Jackie had been scrolling through the day's complement of electronic medical records on her computer screen. This was the very sort of thing Jackie did as a matter of course, rarely encountering anything that was not mind-numbingly predictable. As for interesting, Jackie could count the number of times anything truly interesting had popped up in the past eight years on one hand.

Until now, that is. Hand number two had just been called into service, courtesy of one Mr. Myron Moskowitz.

Jackie sat with eyes transfixed on her computer screen in baffled concentration, having been shaken out of the torpor in which she normally sat staring at it. The cause was a diagnostic code she had never before seen; and while she was pretty sure she had never before seen it, Jackie was somehow entirely certain that, whatever it was, it could not possibly bode well for one Mr. Myron

Moskowitz.

She pulled out the code manual and verified that the diagnosis on Myron Moskowitz's chart actually was both one she had never encountered and one which, indeed, did not bode well for Mr. Moskowitz. She was confused, which was ironic since, as an insurance company employee, she was generally the one doing the confusing. Jackie rang for her supervisor.

"Couldn't this have been handled in an email, Jackie?"

"Sorry. This one has *voice* written all over it."

"Sounds serious. Okay, what have you got?"

Jackie deftly delineated the diagnostic dilemma. Her supervisor demurred.

"Wasn't that wiped out in, like, the late eighteen-hundreds?"

"That's what *I* thought," replied Jackie. She wasn't sure if this was true or not, but she didn't want to appear ignorant. Especially with a review coming up just around the corner. "Maybe it's come back, like in Outer Mongolia or somewhere."

"Or maybe," suggested the supervisor, "someone made a typo. It *has* been known to happen, you know. Why don't you call the doctor's office and double check?"

Which Jackie duly did. Dr. Katz and his nurse were both out at that moment. So their newly-hired receptionist, enjoying a spate of confidence on this, her second day on the job, checked the *Moskowitz, Myron* file and verified that the vexatious sequence of digits matched the ones on the patient's chart to the letter. Or number, as the case may be.

Jackie thanked her, rang off, and called her supervisor.

"Yep, it's the right code."

"Who did you speak to at the doctor's office? Was it the nurse?"

Jackie hadn't remembered to ask. I mean, it wasn't like this sort of thing came up every week, or anything. But with the aforementioned review just around the corner, she thought it best that she not mention this tiny oversight to her supervisor.

"Yes, that's right. The nurse."

"Hmm. Okay. Why don't you push that application off to the side for now? I'll need to check with Underwriting and find out what they want to do with it. I'll let you know as soon as I do. By *email*."

Jackie pulled up the next electronic medical record. The torpor didn't return until the one after that.

Slightly less deep within the labyrinthine bowels of the Itinerant Life & Casualty Company corporate offices there existed a department full of quietly eager men and women who knew the answer to the question: *What does an actuary do?*. This was the firm's Underwriting Department, where highly trained specialists sat around and tried to guess when prospective policy holders were likely to die.

Such might seem like a fairly morbid vocation to those whose livelihoods are not directly linked to the probable longevity of relative strangers. Those in the profession, however, liken their work to fantasy football: weighing the probability that their players will score a certain number of points in any given game against the risks of those same players getting injured, traded, or scoring fewer points than that idiot Josephson from Accounting's team somehow pulled out of their spreadsheets last weekend.

It was to this department's general number that the aforementioned supervisor, whom we'll call "Judy" (since that was *her* name), placed her next call.

"Underwriting."

Judy identified herself and asked to speak with one of the underwriters.

"Couldn't this have been handled in an email?"

"No. This one has *voice* written all over it."

"Must be serious. Hold on, I'll see who's available."

Judy was transferred to a guy named Matt, who sounded as if he might be in the very early stages of puberty. As Jackie had done a few minutes earlier, she now deftly delineated the diagnostic dilemma to Matt, adding that she hoped his department could offer some guidance. She placed exaggerated emphasis on the *his department* part, knowing from experience that the more important she made people feel, the more helpful they were likely to be. This was especially true for underwriters who, even though they wielded a lot of power insurance-wise, tended to be a bit awkward when it came to dealing with anybody who wasn't either a probability or a statistic.

"Ah, yes. Last reported case was in nineteen-oh-two, in the southern region of Upper Volta. Prior to that, it was believed to afflict one person in every sixty-two million, seven hundred and thirty thousand, approximately, though there is the likelihood that at least a few of those cases may have been misdiagnosed. Long incubation period, but always fatal, eventually. But then, so is life, right?" Matt said, in a voice showing obvious signs of cracking. "It's probably just a typo."

"No typo," replied Judy. "We checked."

"Was the applicant anywhere near Upper Volta? That might be important."

"Important to *what*?"

"Good point. Forget I asked."

"Done. So, what do I do with the application?"

"Beats me. Medical science has come a long way in the past hundred years. Maybe it's no longer invariably fatal. Is he being treated for it?"

"I don't know. I didn't think to ask. I can look into that."

"Do, and let me know what you find out. This could have ramifications actuarially."

"You mean, 'actually'?"

"No, *actuarially*. I may need a new table."

"With matching chairs?"

"Huh?"

"Never mind. I'll keep you posted."

"Via email."

"Goes without saying."

"That's *it*?" Mike asked the Itinerant nurse, who, it turned out, was not a nurse at all but rather a cross-trained phlebotomist.

"Almost," she replied, snapping off a pair of latex-free

examination gloves. "I just have a few more health-related questions, and then you'll never have to see me again!"

Mike was mildly disappointed by the prospect. There was something both commanding and sexy about a woman brandishing hands sheathed in latex-free gloves...

"Mr. Moskowitz?"

"Huh? Oh, right. Questions. Well, fire away."

She had been given a list of, frankly, *bizarre* questions to ask Mr. Moskowitz, and was told to make them sound as normal and routine as she possibly could. Based on the questions, she feared this was going to be easier said than done.

"Okay, Mr. Moskowitz–"

"Mike."

"Okay, Mike. Have you experienced any unusual medical symptoms recently?"

"Define unusual."

This was already getting tricky. She had been expressly instructed not to put any words in the applicant's mouth. Did clarifying count?

"Why don't you just tell me what symptoms you've experienced in the past, oh, six months or so? That ought to cover it."

"Well, let me see. I had the flu a few weeks ago."

"The flu? Are you sure?"

"That's what my doctor called it. It was going around at the time."

"And what were your symptoms?"

Mike described them.

"Anything else?"

"No, not that I can recall."

"No, say, bleeding from your eyes, ears, or through the pores in your skin?"

"I think I would have remembered those."

"And *do* you remember those?"

"Um, no."

"Okay. What about organ failure?"

"What *about* organ failure?"

"Have you had any?"

"Not that I'm aware of."

"That's good to hear. Has there been any unexplained, major hair loss?"

"This sounds like a list of possible side-effects from a pharmaceutical commercial. Are you sure this is just routine?"

"Positive. I ask these things all the time. Sometimes two or three times a day, depending on how busy we are. Now, hair loss…?"

"I can account for every follicle."

"Terrific. Last question: have you recently been anywhere near Upper Volta?"

"Upper Volta?"

"Yes. It's a country in West Africa."

"I know what it is. Or what it was—it hasn't been called that in decades. Why do you want to know if I've been to Upper Volta?"

"Or *near* Upper Volta. One or the other."

"What does that have to do with anything?"

"Just routine. So?"

"No, I have never been within a continent of Upper

Volta or whatever it is nowadays. Hadn't planned on it, either. Do you think I'm missing anything?"

"I'm sure I couldn't say. Thanks, Mr. Moskowitz. We'll be getting back to you soon, I have no doubt."

"It's Mike. So what do you think? Am I going to live?"

"If you were, you probably wouldn't be buying life insurance now, would you?"

Mike wasn't quite certain how he should take that. But, since the cross-trained phlebotomist was smiling when she said it, he figured she was just being witty. He was half right.

Internal email exchange at Itinerant Life & Casualty Company:

> *Matt:*
> *Applicant Moskowitz, Myron (as discussed) not currently being treated for any rare or pre-sumed extinct diseases, nor is he exhibiting any symptoms of same. Last seen by personal physi-cian approx. three weeks ago, told he "had the flu." Please advise re: actions to take on this application.*
>
> *Judy --------*

> *Judy,*
> *Obviously, he's still in the incubation period,*

though by my reckoning he should have been dead weeks ago. Doctor probably just doesn't have the guts to break the bad news. Hate when they do that - wastes everybody's time. I recommend stalling for as long as possible. Either it will cease to be an issue, if you know what I mean; or we will have to reevaluate.

    Are you free for lunch next week?

    Matt

Chapter 4

A couple of weeks went by following Mike Moskowitz's insurance physical without any word from the Itinerant Life & Casualty Company. This was fine with him since, for reasons already mentioned, he was in no hurry to be insured. As far as Mike was concerned, he had satisfied his end of things the moment he'd placed the call to Todd's office. If he died in the meantime...oh, well.

He had, in fact, achieved a certain degree of amnesia about the matter when his friend telephoned for an update.

"Mike? Todd. How're you doing?"

"Can't complain. What's up?"

"Mike, have you spoken with anyone from Itinerant in the last few days or so?"

"No, not since my physical."

"Well, I hadn't heard from them either, so I called. They passed me around to five different people before guy number six told me I needed to talk to you. Any idea why?"

"Beats me. Maybe guy number seven was at lunch. Is that unusual?"

"Very. Itinerant is usually pretty quick when it comes

to processing new applications. Was there anything, oh, out of the ordinary that came up during the physical?"

"You mean besides asking me if I'd been to Upper Volta?"

"*What?*"

"The cross-trained phlebotomist who examined me asked me if I'd been anywhere near Upper Volta recently, apparently unaware that there's no such place anymore. Obviously, a keen knowledge of geography is not one of the Itinerant Life & Casualty Company's stricter job requirements."

Todd assumed his friend was being a smart-ass.

"Well, do me a favor: if you hear from them, let me know. Okay?"

"You got it. Hey, if they turn me down, will you write me a note for my mother?"

"Sorry. My own insurance specifically excludes *Death by Celia Moskowitz*. It's right there in between *Acts of God* and *Death by Suicide*. You're on your own. But think positively."

"I was."

Three days later, Todd phoned again.

"Mike, you've got to call the insurance company."

"What have I got to call them?"

"I'm serious. Apparently, there's some sort of problem."

"Problem?"

"Yeah, and they won't tell me what it is. They said

they'd only talk to you directly."

Mike's first thought was that he should have mentioned the dermatologist.

"Did they give you any kind of hint?"

"Nope. Nothing. Said they couldn't divulge confidential health information."

If this was about the dermatologist, at least that part was good news.

"All right. Who do I call?"

Todd gave him the name and direct-dial number of his contact at Itinerant Life & Casualty.

"And tell him I said 'hi,'" Todd added.

"Didn't you just talk to him?"

"Well, yeah."

"Then wouldn't that be just a little redundant?"

"Just call him! And call me right back, okay?"

"Will do." As long as it isn't about the dermatologist, that is.

He dialed the number Todd had given him and, as expected, was sent straight into voice mail. As was *not* expected, the message was answered right away.

Before Mike could explain the nature of his call, however, the Itinerant guy launched into a series of questions obviously designed to ensure that Mike was, in fact, the correct Myron Moskowitz. Apparently, there'd been a run of them or something recently.

With his identity firmly established beyond all reasonable doubt, he was informed that, regretfully, his application for a five-hundred-thousand-dollar life insurance policy had been turned down.

"Was it because of that business with the dermatologist? I mean, if it was, he assured me that it was a just one-time thing, and never posed any real danger or anything. It was just cosmetic. I could get a note."

"No, Mr. Moskowitz. There's nothing here about any dermatologist. But you might want to have a chat with your primary care physician. You see, according to our records, you've been diagnosed with an extremely rare and, inevitably, mercilessly fatal disease. Statistically speaking, Mr. Moskowitz, you should have already experienced your own excruciatingly painful demise weeks ago. I could describe how it will probably end for you, if you'd like."

Mike had to digest this for a minute. Other than a little stiffness first thing in the morning, he had actually been feeling pretty fit of late. He'd attributed it to the vitamins.

"Perhaps another time. Look, isn't the fact that I'm still clinging to this mortal coil proof that there's been some kind of mistake? If I really had—whatever it was you called it—shouldn't my nose at least be running?"

"You can't even imagine."

"There, you see? And here I am, completely devoid of symptoms. Not a single ache, pain, bodily fluid issue. Nada."

"Your symptoms, when they *do* finally appear, will, I'm told, hit you in every part of your body more-or-less at once. Fortunately, you'll probably be dead long before any of them become too inconvenient."

"You don't consider death inconvenient?"

"In your case, not so you'll notice, no."

Based on what he'd just been told, there was probably some truth to that.

"Look, Mr. Moskowitz, the person you should really be talking to about this is your doctor. It looks like, let me see, a Dr. Katz?"

"Right. Katz."

"Well, call Dr. Katz. And I'd do it really soon, if I were you." Then, eager to end the conversation on a slightly more positive note added: "Oh, and tell Todd I said 'hi.' After you talk to Dr. Katz, that is."

"It'll be the second thing I do."

The very first thing Mike did was to try to reach Dr. Katz. But as luck, or the lack thereof, would have it, Dr. Katz had chosen that particular week to be on vacation. Mike asked to speak with the office nurse. Apparently she, too, was on vacation, prompting Mike to wonder briefly if there existed a Mrs. Katz. In any case, further enlighten-ment on the state of his *own* affairs was going to have to wait.

Celia was unimpressed.

"If you *really* wanted to, you would have found a way to do it."

"It wasn't up to me, Mother." If it had been, none of this would have ever come up in the first place. "There was obviously some sort of mistake, and I can't correct it without talking to Dr. Katz first. Which, as I've already told you, I can't do since he's on vacation."

"And why shouldn't Dr. Katz take a vacation?"

"There's no reason for him not to take a vacation, Mother. But that's not the point."

"Doctors work hard. Not that you'd know that from personal experience, although as I've said many times, you could have been one. Besides, it's very stressful being around sickness and death all day. *You* try doing that sometime!"

"Are you volunteering?"

"Always the comedian. Anyway, all I'm saying is, the man deserves a little well-earned time off once in a while. Dr. Katz is practically a saint!"

"He took his nurse with him."

"What! That's terrible. He's a married man. He should be ashamed of himself. Men! Such pigs."

"Still, unlike me, he *is* a doctor."

"Doctor, shmoctor. He should be ashamed of himself."

"St. Porky."

"What was that?"

"Nothing, Mother."

Todd, at least, had been concerned.

"You should probably have that looked into," he told Mike.

Chapter 5

Dr. Katz eventually returned from his vacation, as did his office nurse. They were at once so totally slammed with patients that the two medical professionals found it necessary to schedule even their own bathroom breaks in advance. This was not a particularly desirable way to arrange that sort of thing, especially if you did not actually need to go to the bathroom when it was your turn, or, worse, if you actually *did* and it *wasn't*. Suffice to say, the pair was far too busy to field any phone calls from patients, let alone return one anytime in the foreseeable future.

Their nascent receptionist, new as she was to her vocation, could sense that Mr. Moskowitz was clearly a man with a high sense of urgency about him. She would have probably sensed this even if he *hadn't* called the office every thirty to forty-five minutes, being, as she believed of herself, unusually attuned to the needs of her patients. (It is notable that, with fewer than two weeks' tenure in her current capacity, she had already begun to view the practice's patients as her own.) The next time Mr. Moskowitz called—and she had no doubt he would again—she planned to be ready to render all the assistance she could without violating too many serious policies and/or procedures.

To that end, she took the initiative to pull the MOSKOWITZ, MYRON file and set it on her desk alongside her telephone. This was not the sort of thing she ordinarily did, or was even supposed to do. But this was clearly, for Mr. Moskowitz at least, one of those times that tried men's souls. Not that she would have put it quite that way herself, but that was her general understanding of the situation. Heck, the doctor might even give her a raise for taking such exceptional care of her patients. Note that easily misapplied possessive pronoun again.

After about an hour of her eye wandering over to the buff, manila folder each time the phone rang, she commenced to staring at it, until the urge to pop open the flap became nearly a biological one and much too powerful to ignore. The thought was doubly thrilling since, first, she had never read a patient's complete chart before; and second, because she was pretty sure she wasn't really supposed to. She could not remember whether it had ever been expressly forbidden, but it was a bit like a tree falling in the forest: no witnesses, no unpleasant commotion.

She flipped open the front cover, took a quick peek at the first page, and then just as quickly closed it again. Coolly rotating her head three-hundred-and-sixty degrees (not at the same time, obviously), she could detect no sign that her recent activity had been at all observed. So she did it again, only this time with the intention of perusing the contents.

It would have been impossible to read the MOSKOWITZ, MYRON file in its entirety without attracting at least *some* attention, but what little information she could make out appeared wholly uninteresting. She'd have gone as far as to say it was exceptionally boring but for the fact she had already lost too much interest to take her *lack* of interest in Mike's medical history to that next level. When the patient called again, she told herself, she would simply offer to take a message.

Up until this point in the narrative it would be forgivable if the reader had passingly presupposed Mike Moskowitz to be a gentleman of leisure, or to have granted the *of leisure* part and left the *gentleman* bit to be determined later. This was, in fact, not the case. Mike, like most of us ninety-nine-percenters, found it necessary to toil for his daily bread. Specifically what he did in pursuit of a livelihood is not of any consequence insofar as it affected events. He was not a doctor, as his mother would have been quick to point out; and he did not, as a rule, lift any heavy boxes, at least not professionally. Beyond that, the reader is free to contrive any vocation for him that sounds reasonable. It is about time the reader started pulling a bit of the load around here, anyway.

As a perquisite of his employment with (fill in whatever company name you like), Mike was eligible to participate in an employer-sponsored health care plan. This he took advantage of, though, as we have seen, only sparingly. It had been his intention to continue doing so with equal monotony until the distant end of a long and, presumably, fruitful career.

That had been *his* intention, at any rate. But one morning, while he was still waiting for Dr. Katz to return one of his innumerable telephone calls, Mike's presence was requested in the office of the head of the Human Resources Department.

As anyone who has ever worked for a living knows, being called to the Human Resources Department is generally considered something to be avoided. An audience with the department's head honcho is doubly to be avoided, since this is scarcely ever a harbinger of good things to come. Such a summons is, in fact, almost invariably a portent of the sort of news one would rather not know, particularly if the holidays are coming up. The holidays were *not* coming up, as it happened, but the bad omen factor was still pretty formidable. Mike expected that, whatever fate Human Resources might have in store for him, he wasn't going to like it very much. He was not disappointed.

"Mr. Moskowitz!" intoned the Head Human Resources Honcho, extending his hand to complete the greeting. "How nice to see you again!"

The HHRH's repertoire of greetings was fairly limited, and he tended to fall back on that one a lot. This was especially unnerving to employees who could not recall ever having seen the Head Human Resources Honcho in person before, and particularly so for those who suspected his summons meant they would probably never set eyes on him again.

"Thanks. You really should invite me down more often," Mike replied. "I'd almost forgotten what you looked like."

"Yes. Well. On that subject...I suppose you're wondering why I asked you here."

"You mean it wasn't just to shoot the breeze, share a bit of *auld lang syne*, that sort of thing?"

"Ha, ha, yes. No. The fact is, Mr. Moskowitz, something has come up which is, shall we say, *concerning*?"

"Okay. Let's."

"I'm sorry?"

"Let's say it is, as you put it, *concerning*."

The HHRH paused for a moment to regroup. So far, the meeting was not progressing in quite the way meetings like this were supposed to, and certainly not like it had in rehearsal. Admittedly, the rehearsal had failed to include any nettlesome Moskowitzes.

"Mr. Moskowitz, I fear this conversation is straying rather far afield from its intended destination. As I was beginning to say, a matter has arisen which is generating some concern among our senior-most management."

"So you'd mentioned. Or started to, at any rate"

"Quite. And I suppose you would like to know what it is that is causing them, er, *us*, such concern?"

"No."

"Pardon?"

"No, not really. Truth be told, I would be perfectly happy to remain blissfully ignorant as to whatever it is that has come to the concerned attention of our senior management, and simply continue doing my humble part in maintaining the status quo."

"I see. It is, however, the very status quo you refer to which is presently in jeopardy of becoming, well, status *un*-quo. Thus, here we are."

Yes, thought Mike. Here we are. "Ah. In that case, I suppose you really ought to fill me in, then."

"I have been attempting to do just that for the past, oh, seemingly forever," sighed the HHRH. "May I continue?"

"By all means."

"Very well. The situation is this: as you know, the company provides certain extras above and beyond one's basic salary for the benefit of its employees—"

"And generous they are, too," Mike added, figuring a little obvious gratitude might be worth a point or two, in the event he might find himself needing one.

"We believe them to be, yes. Anyway, as I was saying, among these extras is what we consider to be exceptionally comprehensive health care coverage."

Suddenly, Mike thought he had a pretty good idea about where this was going. His initial spasm of relief, however, quickly gave way to anger, annoyance, and a pressing desire to engage Dr. Katz in a ten-minute, no-holds-barred cage match. And he wasn't even aware there *was* such a thing as a cage match.

"As I was saying," the HHRH had a habit of saying, *as I was saying* more than he strictly needed to, "the health coverage we provide our employees is, we believe, an important part of the overall, er, *employee experience* for all who work here. Would you agree with that, Mr. Moskowitz?"

Mike was about to say: *call me Mike, please,* but thought better of it.

"I suppose," he said, instead. "Especially for those employees whose health weighs heavily on their minds. Though, come to think of it, if you're *that* worried about your health, you're probably not getting a lot of work done. I mean, that sort of thing could become pretty distracting, don't you think?"

The Head Human Resources Honcho had budgeted what he felt would be sufficient time to conclude his business with Mr. Moskowitz. He hated being wrong nearly as much as he hated having his schedule seriously screwed with. After all, he had not risen to his present level of the corporate stratosphere to be toyed with by a member of the comparatively rank-and-file. He decided to come straight to the point.

"The point is, Mr. Moskowitz, this benefit, which is so important to so many, is at serious risk of being taken away, and, I may add, because of you."

"Me?" Mike asked, aiming his fingertips in the direction of his torso and trying to appear simultaneously innocent and confused.

"Yes, Mr. Moskowitz. You."

"But I don't understand." Yeah. Right.

"I won't beat around the bush, Mr. Moskowitz. According to our plan administrator, you are a very sick man."

"That's funny. I feel perfectly fine."

"Be that as it may, those with access to your relevant medical files are strongly of the opinion that the cost of

your impending care will substantially exceed the financial resources available for the entire company. And while
I am not privy to all the gory details—you should pardon
the expression—I'm told that, if all the treatment options
in the world were placed at your disposal, the effort would,
ultimately, come to naught."

"*'Knot'*?"

"To *naught*, Mr. Moskowitz. As in, nothing. Nada.
Bupkis, if you prefer. In other words, despite the most
vigorous applications imaginable of both science and
technology, all the king's horses and all the kings men
couldn't put you back together again. Am I making myself
clear?"

Mike decided that this had gone far enough.

"Look, I can explain. This is all part of one huge
misunderstanding. It's a computer error. That's all it is."

"They warned me you might say something like that.
Everyone does, apparently."

"This type of thing comes up that often?"

"Frankly, I never thought to ask. Regardless, in matters
such as these we invariably prefer to rely on the experts.
And the experts were crystal clear: you are in the singular
position of either creating or averting a major catastro-
phe."

Aha, thought Mike. Here it comes.

"Mr. Moskowitz, to put it bluntly, we are hoping you
will rise to the occasion and, er, take one for the team."

"*Come again?*"

"Take one for the team, Mr. Moskowitz. A small,
personal sacrifice for the sake of the greater, corporate

good."

"The greater, corporate good part I think I get. It's the small, personal sacrifice portion I'm still a trifle vague on. What exactly did you have in mind?"

"We in senior management have discussed the matter in great detail, and we believe unanimously that the noble thing would be for you to, er, somehow remove your case from the benefit pool. Before things become irreversibly out of hand, that is to say."

Mike *knew* he wasn't going to like any meeting he was called into by Human Resources.

"Define 'remove.'"

"Oh, the standard definition. You know, take yourself out of, withdraw, cease to be a part, extricate…shall I go on?"

"No, I think I get the idea. And in what manner do you see me taking myself out, withdrawing, etcetera, etcetera?"

"Yes, well that part's somewhat tricky. We had briefly entertained the notion of terminating your employment –with a suitable out-package, naturally."

"Naturally."

"But then there would be certain inconveniences such as Continuation of Benefits and possibly one or two other issues of a decidedly legal disposition to contend with. Ditto, your simply resigning from the company on your own initiative."

"Not to mention the fact that I would never resign from the company on my own initiative."

"Hmmm…we hadn't really taken that possibility into

account. Still, it's all academic anyway, since that's not really an option. The only solution, as we see it, is for you to take early retirement."

"Early retirement?"

"That's right. We would like you to retire, Mr. Moskowitz. Effective immediately."

"A little premature, isn't it? I mean, my most productive working years are still well ahead of me."

"Not according to our plan administrators, they aren't, no."

"Well, they're wrong!"

"I applaud your positive outlook, Mr. Moskowitz, misguided though it may be. Still...there it is."

"Look, I can straighten this out. Just give me a few days before you go scheduling the party and requisitioning the gold watch. Okay?"

"Neither are practices we engage in these days, I'm afraid. But I understand. Do what you feel you must, but do it fairly instantly. Tomorrow, as they say, is promised to no one. And for someone in your position, Mr. Moskowitz, even the prospect of this afternoon is looking decidedly shaky."

Mike could take a hint.

Chapter 6

He had been dogging Dr. Katz for over a week. The office receptionist had developed what she began to think of as her "Mr. Moskowitz voice." This was something akin to the one most grown-ups use when addressing other people's errant ten-year-olds. It was usually preceded by what she had come to regard as the "Mr. Moskowitz sigh." Still, the doctor was up to his ears in sick people. As a result he had so far failed to respond to any of Mike's attempts to reach him.

After his rather awful little *tête-ê-tête* with the Head Human Resources Honcho, however, Mike turned the heat up another notch. He began leaving messages with words like *attorney*, *State Medical Board*, and *Bolivian hit squads*, to no further avail. Mike eventually pulled out the final weapon in his arsenal and threatened to get his mother involved. Whether it was the Celia Ultimatum or just a case of better timing, Dr. Katz promptly returned that phone message.

Mike's initial attempts at explaining the problem to Dr. Katz were somewhat tortured. Still exasperated over a triple-whammy of recent events, conversations he could have happily gone without, and a generally astronomical sense of frustration with the guy on the other end of the line, words poured out of his mouth more quickly than his brain could effectively organize them or his lips form themselves into proper vowels and consonants. Dr. Katz threw in an unusually high complement of *ah, um hmm,* and even *I see* interjections.

Eventually, Mike wound himself down.

"So, do you understand?"

"Um, well, frankly, no, Mr. Moskowitz. I mean, for a moment there I wasn't sure if you were actually speaking in any recognizable form of language. Would you mind going over it again, only a little more slowly this time?"

Being largely out of steam, Mike walked Dr. Katz through the scenario once more, this time in what was undeniably the King's English and, in consequence, with a great deal more lucidity. Breaking the important bits into verbal bullet points didn't hurt. Bullets somehow seemed appropriate to what Mike had felt like giving Dr. Katz anyway.

"Hmmm, well, obviously there has been a mistake someplace."

Mike didn't know quite how to respond to that without rupturing an important blood vessel.

"Probably a coding error. They happen all the time. Well, of course, not all the time. Some of the time, though. Let me check into it and get back to you."

Mike, knowing better than to let a caught fish off the hook quite so easily (or a caught Katz, either, come to that), said he would prefer to remain on hold while the physician looked into the matter now. As in, *right* now. Celia's name was mentioned.

"As you wish. I may be a few minutes."

He was. When the doctor finally got back on the line, he admitted that the error had, in fact, occurred on his end.

"It must have happened on your last visit. I'm surprised nobody caught it sooner."

Mike replied that people seemed to be catching it all over town. "You could say it's going around," he threw in, just because he could.

"We can probably get this straightened right out."

"*Probably?*"

"I'm almost certain we can. Though, of course, since it's the end of the day on a Friday, and Monday is one of those silly bank holidays, it may take a little while."

"Take as long as you need, as long as it's no more than seventy-two hours. After that, you can explain to my mother how you single-handedly cost me my career."

Dr. Katz could take a hint, too.

Deep within the labyrinthine bowels of the Itinerant Life & Casualty Company's corporate offices there existed a cell. Not the living-thing type of cell, of which, within the labyrinthine bowels of the Itinerant Life & Casualty Company's corporate offices there presumably existed gazillions of the little buggers. Rather, this was a cell of the small-group-of-a-larger-group variety, comprised of fully-assembled human organisms. That those human organisms were *themselves* comprised of billions, or possibly even trillions, of cells is neither here nor there. And frankly, the topic has already become tiresome on a cellular level.

As with most entities of its ilk, the cell's members shared a likeness of both mind and purpose. In their particular case, this one centered around the idea that, as unfair as life was when simply left to its own devices, it tended to become exponentially worse any time an insurance company entered the picture.

Specifically, the group took great umbrage at the way insurance companies wagered on other people's well-being, while at the same time rigging the odds to tilt like a drunken British soccer fan in their favor. One particular source of revulsion was the Underwriting Department, with its actuarial tables and matching chairs, which the cell was convinced granted its Caesar-like thumb-up or thumb-down to things solely on a whim. They made a point of never associating with Underwriters or inviting them to any of their parties. This helped explain, at least partly, why the cell was still together: facts were much less likely to creep in and spoil any otherwise good rallying points that way.

The Itinerant cell had counterparts at health insurance companies, hospitals, and even the odd specialty clinic. The various cells would occasionally get together as a tissue for clandestine meetings, picnics, and parties, none of which they ever invited anyone from Underwriting to.

Their involvement in the case of Myron Moskowitz, however, began down in the labyrinthine bowels of the Itinerant Life & Casualty Company's corporate offices.

One of their number, code named "Jackie," had stumbled upon the case in the course of her work, and had duly reported the situation through the proper cell channels. Inquiries were made across the underground network, and an image began to emerge of an everyday, average Myron who was in the process of being seriously screwed over due to what was probably just a stupid typo.

It should be noted that the typo hypothesis had not been universally embraced within either the Itinerant cell or their larger network. There were many of those who, deep in their hearts, truly *wanted* Mr. Moskowitz to have somehow contracted this rare and brutally fatal Upper Volta disease, believing that his having it rendered him an even more tragic and sympathetic figure. The typo faction believed that the other guys were just being typically overdramatic. Besides, screwed was screwed, no matter how you got that way. Apparently, however, there is always some room for degree.

The two sides did agree in principle on a couple of things: if Myron Moskowitz needed expensive and potentially fruitless medical treatment, they would find a way for him to get it; if not, they would find a way for him to get even.

Dr. Katz's nurse phoned Mike toward the end of the next business day.

"Mr. Moskowitz? Hi, it's Dr. Katz's nurse. The doctor had asked me to call your insurance company and look into this little, er, *misunderstanding.*"

"What? It wasn't important enough for him to call them himself?"

"Yes, well, that really isn't his thing, you know? I mean, he's a brilliant diagnostician and everything, but we really encourage him to leave the business-side of things to others. Saves us all a lot of confusion and, well, damage-control, if you know what I mean."

"Yes, my wife has the same idea about me and laundry."

"I'm sure she does. Anyway, I phoned them this afternoon, and, well, it was an interesting conversation."

"Okay, I'll bite. Interesting how?"

"Interesting like, *Twilight Zone* interesting."

"You're too young to know about *The Twilight Zone*.

"Not too young to watch it on reruns. But old TV shows aside, this was one strange conversation."

"It's one strange situation. For me, at any rate. So, what did they say?"

"They said you don't exist."

"Killed me off already, have they?"

"More like you were never born in the first place. They have no record of you ever having been in their system."

"Obviously a glitch in their system."

"Not according to the person I spoke with. They pride themselves on that system. Said it's never gone down, ever. Not even a hiccup in the entire time it's been online. That's why they're fairly certain you don't exist. Never have, as far as they're concerned."

"But didn't they just pay you for my last office visit?"

"I mentioned that. He denied it."

"What do you mean, he denied it?"

"He denied it. Said it never happened. I told them the date, the reference number, the account number...even the check number. He said there were no such numbers."

"Not even the date?"

"That one, he gave me. The rest, though, he said I must have made up. Or else I had the wrong insurance company."

"Are you sure you had the *right* insurance company?"

"Should I tell you the same thing I told him, or just answer *yes*?"

"Got it. So, what should I do?"

"I'd suggest calling the company yourself. You certainly couldn't do any worse than *I* did. You want the guy's number?"

"He's probably the *last* person I should talk to. Give me the number of the mailroom, I'll start with them. Somebody there has to know exactly what the hell is going on."

"Maybe. I wouldn't hold my breath, though."

"Thanks for the expert medical advice."

"Not at all. It's what they pay me for."

Chapter 7

Early the next morning, Mike busied himself making essential preparations in advance of dialing the number Dr. Katz's nurse had given him. He assembled a variety of snacks and beverages, which were then strategically arranged across the better part of the living room coffee table. He gathered his half-finished detective novel, a book of Sudoku puzzles, a two-month-old copy of *The New Yorker*, and the cable television remote. He dumped them all in a pile on the sofa, dumped *himself* in a pile on the sofa, and then un-dumped himself once again the moment he realized that he'd forgotten to bring the phone.

Mike managed to sample a bit of everything except the Sudoku before finally getting a live human being on the line who was even modestly capable of grasping what he wanted. This individual could not help him directly, but managed to send Mike to the first of three other individuals who could not help him directly, either. The fourth transfer was a charm, though, however dubious: Mike was connected to the guy Dr. Katz's nurse had spoken to about him yesterday.

"Yes, my name is Myron Moskowitz, and—"

"No it isn't."

"I beg your pardon?"

"No, it isn't."

"But I only said—"

"You said your name was Myron Moskowitz. And it isn't. It couldn't be."

"What are you talking about? Of course it could be. And, as it happens, it *is*."

"I know for a fact that it isn't. There is no such person as Myron Moskowitz. I should know. I've researched the matter quite extensively. In fact, if one could be considered an expert on something that never existed, I would be he. Him. Whatever."

"Yes, well, that's what I wanted to talk to you about. I—"

"I was just discussing this very subject the other day. Or was that yesterday? Hmm. Anyway, some woman called and wanted to tell me something about this Myron Moskowitz non-person. It was a short conversation, as you can imagine, seeing as there's no such animal."

Mike wasn't entirely sure how to take that. "On what, exactly, are you basing this conclusion?"

"Why, I checked the system, naturally. I always rely on the system. If a person exists anywhere, if there is any record about them at all, it's in the system. Therefore, no record, no person. Q.E.D."

"Do you even know what that means?"

"Er, no. But somebody in a TV show I watch a lot says it all the time, and I think I pretty much get the gist. The bottom line is there is no Myron Moskowitz. So whoever you may be, it couldn't possibly be he. Him. Whatever."

"I see. Then, how about a Mike? Got any Mike Moskowitzes in that system of yours?"

"Let me check. Would this be a Mike Moskowitz who's currently alive?"

"Yes."

"No."

"I see." This was going even further nowhere than Mike could have possibly imagined.

"Then let's just say, for the sake of argument, that there really *was* a Myron Moskowitz, a living one, that is, and he suddenly became ill. What should he do?"

"How ill?"

"Just ill."

"But *how* ill? It makes a difference."

"Look, ill enough, all right? He exists, he's sick, and he's convinced that he's protected by insurance through your company. What would he do?"

"Go to the doctor, I should think. Or an urgent care center or hospital, you know, depending."

"Right. So he does that. When they ask, he produces his insurance card. It says that his name is Myron Moskowitz, he is insured with your company, and while it is not exactly a Cadillac health plan, it's not exactly a Yugo one, either. What happens next?"

"Is he at the doctor's, urgent care center, or hospital?"

"He's at the ...oh, never mind! It doesn't matter! What happens about the insurance?"

"Nothing happens."

"Nothing? What do you mean, nothing?"

"I mean, nothing. The guy doesn't really exist, re-member?"

Dr. Katz's nurse had grossly understated this fellow's capacity for driving someone out of his mind.

"Well, thanks. You've been *extraordinarily* helpful."

"No problem. That's what they pay me for."

While Mike had been thus engaged with Mr. Helpful, two calls had been placed to his number. Both callers elected to take advantage of the available voicemail service, and had left brief messages for him. Both messages succeeded in getting Mike's attention.

The first was from the Head Human Resources Hon-cho, congratulating Mike on his retirement and wishing him many happy years of separation from the company. That voicemail ended with a reminder that he would no longer be eligible to participate in the company's health insurance program, and, once again, wished him the best of luck and all of that sort of thing.

If this message evoked a certain emotional reaction in its recipient, it was nothing compared to the one that fol-lowed. The second voicemail, in addition to being brief, had the added quality of also being a little weird.

"Mr. Moskowitz," it began. "You don't know me, so my name will be unimportant. It's Dan, by the way, but like I said that probably won't mean anything. While you don't know anything about me, however, I happen to know quite a lot about you."

After a brief pause, the voice, or Dan, if the caller was

to be believed, continued: "Not, you know, in a stalker-kind of way. I didn't mean to sound...you know..."

There was the sound of a throat clearing, and the message continued.

"As I was saying, I know all about your recent, ah, circumstances, and I wanted you to know that you are not alone. There are people out there, here, that is, who want to help you, who *will* help you, and who are trying to help you even as we speak. As *I* speak. You get the idea. Anyway, you'll be hearing back from us very soon. I can't say exactly *how* soon, of course, but it should be soon. Soon*ish*. There are things in the works—wheels within wheels, as it were—and there's no telling how long it will take to...well, suffice it to say that it shouldn't be *too* long before you hear back from me again. Me, or somebody like me. Though maybe not exactly like me. It may even be a woman, who knows? So, um, goodbye, then." Followed by the inevitable clicking-off.

In the re-telling, that last message wasn't really all that brief, after all.

Mike allowed himself about thirty seconds of stunned confusion before shifting his attention back to the larger issue of his supposed retirement. Could they really *do* that? Mike was nowhere close to retirement age—well, not *that* close, at any rate, and not according to *his* definition, certainly. There had to be a law about this somewhere. He'd have to consult an attorney, which, when you got right down to it, he probably should have done when this whole business came up in the first place. Unfortunately, Mike didn't have an attorney of his own. Maybe

Todd would loan him one of his.

Mike desperately wanted to call the Head Human Resources Honcho. But try as he might, he could not figure out exactly what he'd say or how he'd even begin saying it, assuming he was somehow able to get the HHRH on the phone. He was decidedly still up in the air about whether to fight being forcibly retired, or find out just how much the company was willing to fork over to him for never gracing their hallowed halls again.

And it really was a toss-up. The more he thought about it, the more the latter idea seemed to acquire a whole host of new merits. Getting paid for *not* doing something seemed a pretty novel concept to him, one which could even be considered intriguing, in a way. Liberty with positive cash flow...unencumbered time...hanging around all day in the comfort and privacy of his own home...with Christine...

Something had to be done to nip this retirement nonsense in its stride before it trod a single further step. Suddenly, it appeared to Mike, there wasn't a nanosecond to lose.

He knew, however, that this was not a battle he was likely to win without considerable allied reinforcements. And while others, under similar circumstances, would have called in the cavalry, Mike instead picked up the phone and called in Celia. After all, a boy's best friend is his mother. Right?

"**U**pper What-a?"

"Upper Volta. It's a country in Africa. At least, it *used* to be a country in Africa. It's called something else now."

"So, did you already know that, or did you have to look it up?"

"I already knew that. But forget about Upper Volta. It's not germane."

"Not German? I thought you said it wasn't African."

"Oh, say goodnight, Gracie!"

"You're too young to know what that means. For that matter, so am I."

"Mother, have any of the more vitally *important* parts of this conversation crossed the heavily-guarded border of your conscious mind up to this point?"

"Yes, Myron, I get the idea. I may be old, but I'm not completely senile yet."

Sotto voce: "Wanna bet?"

"What was that?"

"I said, 'no, not yet.'"

"I'm not deaf, either. Don't ever forget it, sonny boy."

"Okay, so your hearing and mental capacities are still fully functional. How absolutely marvelous for you. But what do you *think*?"

"About what?"

"Mother!"

"I mean, what do you want me to tell you?"

"How do I get out of this? I need your advice!"

Celia just sat and stared absently at her son, lost in seemingly blissful reverie.

"Mother?"

"You really *do* need my advice! And your wife needed

my advice the other day, too! I feel almost like a mother again!"

"Yes, but Mother—"

"Shush! Let me savor the moment just a little longer."

Mike gave Celia her moment. He had nothing better to do.

Seated around a table in the farthermost corner of the coffee-based beverage emporium which served as their de-facto headquarters were several members of the Itinerant Life & Casualty Company cell. They were uncharacteristically quiet, their silence broken only by occasional slurping noises as they disinterestedly took sips of coffee beverages with very silly names. Every now and then one of them would lift his gaze from the table as if about to say something; but, apparently thinking better of it, would instead lower his eyes with a look of impotent muteness.

This sort of thing can only go on so long before somebody speaks, even if only to suggest that it might be time to leave. But they had each ordered the largest size coffee drinks available, and with the price of these things being almost as absurd as their names, the group was understandably reluctant to abandon any of them in such early stages of consumption.

The object of all this non-attention and non-conversation was Dan, who had only a few minutes earlier hung up after a rather awkward attempt to reassure one Mr. Myron Moskowitz that he had nothing to worry about. The problem was voicemail, which had always been something of a brain-eraser whenever Dan encountered it.

"I told you, you should have written it down."

"I didn't have to write it down. I could say the whole spiel in my sleep."

"Too bad you happened to be awake, then. What *is* it with you and voicemail, anyway?"

"I have no idea," answered Dan. "I just freeze up. I mean, I think I'll handle it just fine, and then that beep goes off and it's like some perverse chemical reaction takes over my cerebellum or something. Suddenly, I'm just dumb."

"Suddenly?" said all three of his companions. The quartet went back a long way.

"Funny. So, do you think I blew it?"

"The taking-you-seriously factor's probably not terribly high right about now, so, yeah. But we'll try again later. He'll probably be home tonight. But, just in case: we write it down this time. Agreed?"

"Agreed," the other three replied, in near-unison.

Celia had volunteered to call the Head Human Resources Honcho on her son's behalf, and Mike was half-tempted to take her up on it. He decided instead to put his final stab at resolving this himself in the form of a letter, sent Registered Mail so that it would at least inconvenience someone.

Two days later, the letter landed on the HHRH's desk, where it inadvertently took the brunt of a particularly catastrophic coffee spill.

Chapter 8

Three of the four cell members departed their de facto coffee shop headquarters, leaving the fourth nursing yet another extremely expensive and equally silly-sounding processed coffee concoction. They reassembled at the apartment of an altogether *other* cell member, a young woman named Jackie, with whom the reader will already be familiar. The three went to Jackie's partly because she'd been the one who had alerted them to the Myron Moskowitz situation in the first place. Mostly, though, they went there because they thought Jackie was kind of hot, in a geeky sort of way.

"Let's have Jackie make the call," suggested someone improbably called Kermit. "He may take it more seriously if it's coming from a girl. Woman. You know, a female."

Dan wasn't so sure. Besides, he wanted a chance to redeem a little of his self-respect after such a disastrous first performance.

"I'm not so sure," he said. "And besides, I'd really like a chance to try again. I kinda flubbed things up earlier."

The trio of people-who-were-not-Jackie debated the relative merits of the two candidates. Dan's elongated, whining "pleeeease," however, ultimately secured for him their official endorsement.

"But this time *write everything down first!*"

This he did, with enough input from the committee to push the hour well past dinner and to a point teetering on the edge of too-latedness. It was no sooner than the last scripted word had been officially agreed upon by the majority when Dan grabbed for the phone and dialed the Moskowitz's number. Mike picked up on the third ring.

"Mr. Moskowitz? I hope it isn't too late." The last part was ad-libbed, generating looks of disapproval from his counterparts. "This is Dan again. I left a message for you earlier?"

It took Mike a moment to recollect that someone alleging his name might or might not have been Dan had left a rambling and barely coherent voicemail for him recently, and it very well might have been that morning. It had been a pretty long day.

"Uh, huh," he managed, finally.

"Mr. Moskowitz, we, my associates and I," another ad-lib, which he slipped by apparently unnoticed, "believe that you have been the victim of a pernicious medical record."

Mike considered the proposition for a second, but conceded that pretty much summed things up.

"We know you've been denied life insurance, your employer has cancelled your healthcare coverage, and you have in all likelihood been severely traumatized by the implication that your body is on the verge of some horrific, irreversible vapor lock."

Mike gave him two out of three.

"And just how," he asked, "could you possibly know all that?"

Dan's script co-authors had somehow failed to antici- pate this particular line of inquiry and were momentarily stymied for a comeback.

"We have sources," volunteered Jackie, *soto voce*.

"We have sources," said Dan.

The rest just nodded their approval.

"Evidently. But who *are* you? I mean, in both the collective *and* the individual sense?"

This line of inquiry they *had* anticipated.

"We are avengers," Dan replied.

"I see. And do you wear costumes? Prowl the city by night in masks and capes?"

"Not *that* kind of avenger, Mr. Moskowitz. Though some of those we have helped in the past would probably regard us as superheroes."

This caused the guys to silently high-five each other, and Jackie to pantomime gagging and projectile-vomiting. In a geeky-cute sort of way.

"Too bad. Masks and capes would have made this conversation far more interesting."

Jackie was beginning to like this guy.

"So, how exactly do you capeless crusaders intend to make yourselves useful?"

"We've already been working some of our magic," Dan half-boasted.

"Enlighten me."

"Well, for starters, the Myron Moskowitz—uh, the

Mister Myron Moskowitz with the Scarlet Diagnostic Code, is systematically being phased out."

"So I've noticed."

"No, no, I mean the *computer* Myron Moskowitz. *You're* not actually being phased out. I mean, *are* you?"

"Depends on who you ask, I suppose." This went a long way toward explaining why his health insurer of many years had no record of his existence. "Couldn't you simply change the code or something?"

An excellent question, which somehow must have eluded everyone in the cell in a decision-making capacity.

"Um, yeah, well, that would be against the law," Dan answered. He had no idea whether this was true or not, but he rather hoped it might be. Otherwise, someone would be looking a little foolish when he brought the subject up at their next Big Meeting, and that someone would probably be himself.

"And tampering with other people's computer systems *isn't?*"

"Well, technically, yes, I suppose it is." Dan did not like the direction this was going. And if the shaking heads and waving arms of his associates was any indication, neither did they.

"We're on the side of the angels here, Mr. Moskowitz," Dan asserted. He had heard that line about seven hundred and fifty times over the years, but never dreamed he might one day be called upon to use it. "Besides, what we take out we always put back in, eventually. Well, most of it, anyway. I mean, that diagnosis will be gone, but the rest of it'll still be there. That is, unless you don't want—"

"No, the diagnosis will be more than sufficient, thanks."

"Oh? Okay. Good. Um, this may take a little time, though. It's not as easy as hacking into some dinosaur-era school computer and changing your grades. Not that I've ever, you know..."

"I understand."

"Oh, ah, good. Good. So, we'll keep you posted, then."

Mike said he'd appreciate that.

"You went off the script!" Kermit exclaimed, pointing an admonishing finger at Dan.

"Oh, shut up!" the others exclaimed, pointing admonishing fingers at Kermit.

"Who was that?" Christine asked as Mike climbed into bed.

Faced with the choice of a lengthy explanation involving things he did not want his wife to know about or lying outright, Mike replied: "Political survey."

"You shouldn't answer those, you know. They'll just keep calling, and before you know it, they're asking for money."

"Probably want me to get out and vote, too. Like that would ever do any good."

The resurrection of Mike's medical history was taking an

excruciatingly long time. He had begun to think that the caller allegedly known as Dan might have been a phony, though there were two things which kept him on just the right side of credibility. The first was that Dan somehow seemed to know an awful lot about him; and the second was the near-certainty that, if the call was a prank, the caller would presumably have sounded a lot more be-lievable. That superhero line alone was far too stupid not to be sincere.

He was a little ashamed of himself, however, for put-ting so much faith and hope in such a strange prospective Samaritan; but his own attempts at correcting the problem had effectively run headlong into an unrelenting brick wall, and at the moment he'd been fresh out of better ideas. The way Mike figured it, he had nothing to lose by giving someone else a crack, even if that someone turned out to be a bit on the cracked side himself.

Unbeknownst to Mike, the cell's intentions on his be-half, while of the purest, had run headlong into an unre-lenting brick wall of their own. This was owing, as it frequently is these days, to an unforeseen computer glitch.

It was like this: in attempting to re-launch Myron Moskowitz into the virtual universe, they had found the system resolutely unwilling to cooperate. The procedure had started out very much along the lines of business as usual. A replacement file had been painstakingly created; the data assembled in a nice, orderly fashion; the I's were all dotted and the T's were all crossed.

The computer, however, was having none of it.

"Dot your silly I's!" it seemed to leer. "Cross your

stupid T's! See if *I* give a RAM!"

They had tried all the usual tricks: logging on as higher-ups, whose passwords for some reason were always their birthdays; poking their virtual noses into system back doors; and even going about the procedure the proper way. But the network was acting like a bouncer at one of those exclusive nightclubs that didn't allow people like themselves inside.

Still, they kept trying.

Chapter 9

About once a month or so, barring any major scheduling conflicts (of which there inevitably were several), the leaders of the various cells like the one at Itinerant Life & Casualty—the nuclei, if you will—came together for what they called *the Big Meeting*. This was something of a misnomer, since the clump of nuclei thus assembled was not an especially large one. It *was* exclusive, however. Not only wasn't anyone from Underwriting ever invited, nobody else was, either.

The grand purpose of the Big Meeting varied depending on whom you asked. But it was there that individual cases were presented and considered, and where discussions of those currently in progress could take place. And, of course, there was beer.

They had just finished discussing the status of a woman whose husband had tragically expired mere hours after his overlooked life insurance policy had done likewise. A digit was adjusted, and the relieved widow, now in Aruba, was settling quite happily into this new phase of her life with a younger male companion she had met on an internet cougar-connection website.

The meeting next moved on to the issue of Myron Moskowitz. To say that the nuclei were not overjoyed to be doing so once again would be stating the matter with the sort of polite, professional detachment few of them were, in fact, capable of just then. Even with beer.

"Why are we still talking about this?" asked one of the reigning nuclei. "This Moskowitz guy keeps coming back around like a bad penny."

He had to explain the reference to a piece of physical coinage. It was a young crowd.

Dan was there representing the Itinerant Life & Casualty cell. With the exception of Dan himself, the decision to send him there this time had been received unanimously. He restated the problem.

"Still? This seems like it's been going on since around the Nixon administration!"

The speaker had to explain who Richard Nixon was. It was a *very* young crowd.

They covered the standard catalog of *Have you tried...* questions in record time, then launched straight into the *How about...* ones. When the opportunity to offer any new suggestions finally came up, no one had any.

"So, this Myron Moskowitz has just been flapping in the breeze for *how* long now?"

The answer brought a chorus of concerned *hmmms* from the clump.

"Any way we could make this whole debacle simply disappear?"

"We've already made *him* disappear. The only question now is: how do we get him back again?"

This met with general grunts of agreement from the floor, though not all were entirely certain what it was they were agreeing to.

"Well, we created this mess. We might as well clean it up."

This also met with general grunts of agreement from the floor, sans any uncertainty.

"And Dan, we expect *you* to find a way to get it done."

The grunts of agreement this time shook the rafters.

As to the case in question, Mike was experiencing something of a bi-polar retirement.

He didn't want it. He didn't mind it. It made him frustrated and angry. It could easily become habit-forming. In other words, the story of Mike Moskowitz's life at this immediate juncture read a lot like the beginning of *A Tale of Two Cities*.

He didn't really miss his job at all. If anything, *not* doing his job made him realize the absolute futility of having ever done his job in the first place. He was well to be out of it.

The *idea* of his job, however, was proving to be an altogether different kettle of fish. Mike deeply resented the apparent ease with which his career had simply been yanked out from under him after all those years of dedicated service, the relative futility of his entire work history notwithstanding. Granted, his former employers were paying him surprisingly well under the circumstances, but that was only because they fully envisioned every one of his vital organs imploding simultaneously without so much as a how-do-you-do. Mike wondered how long their generosity would hold out if he failed to die up to their expectations.

He had, as yet, not mentioned any of this to Christine. Initially, Mike held off in the hope he would have everything worked out before filling her in on the situation became an unavoidable necessity. Then the two of them could enjoy a hearty laugh before retreating to their respective paperbacks and their respective pieces of living room furniture. As more time went by, however, he *still* hoped he could have everything worked out before filling her in became an unavoidable necessity. By now, it had turned into a kind of game: seeing just how long he could keep his wife from noticing something was up before she noticed he was doing it.

On the other hand, Celia, being Celia, was not making the game any less challenging. After all, what sort of mother would she be if she didn't nudge (pronounced *noodge*) her offspring to make the most of himself? And that son of hers could certainly *not* be accused of taking the bull by the horns as far as his own success was concerned. No, Myron definitely needed his mother now, maybe more than ever.

This thought brought a lump to her throat. At least, she hoped it was the thought, and not something more serious. She did not want to have to see Dr. Katz, who was very much in the doghouse with her these days.

Celia decided that the situation demanded a firm, motherly hand. She usually decided this, since she had never really mastered the fine art of butting out to any significant extent and was a firm believer in sticking with what you know. Besides, one did not move mountains, or even wear them down, merely by dropping hints. This was especially true when one stood just under five feet tall, in heels.

And anyway, her son had practically *begged* for her assistance, which was a license to meddle if ever there was one. She covered the standard catalog of *Have you tried...* questions in record time, then launched straight into the *How about...* ones. Everything obvious, she discovered, had already been done. A lot of not-so-obvious had, too, reinforcing Celia's belief that, if Myron had only applied himself a little more when he was younger, he would probably be a brain surgeon by now. The kind of brain surgeon, she might add, who did not let himself get into this sort of *mishegaas*.

The dilemma required a good bit of thinking, which, beyond a certain point, was not what even Celia would regard as her strongest suit. She quickly found herself completely out of her depth. Not being one to allow a little thing like not knowing what to do stop her from telling her son to do it, however, she decided to tap into the one re-source Jewish mothers can always count on for sympathy and support: other Jewish mothers.

She knew her son would never approve, of course. So? When did he ever? Celia recalled some of the numerous occasions when she had been shamefully unappreciated by her very own flesh and blood throughout the years. By a strange coincidence, her list of grievances could have been sung, measure-for-measure, to the Gilbert and Sullivan tune about a policeman's lot not being a happy one.

She called her good friend Linda, just to talk about the weather. They both agreed that the weather was far too important a topic to discuss over the telephone and made a date to rendezvous at their usual haunt. Said haunt was a cafeteria-like establishment where the women could sit around for hours without feeling the least bit compelled to order anything. This was especially appreciated on those occasions when they didn't really feel like buying so much as a cup of coffee even by way of only pretending to patronize the place, which for them was most of the time. And, to make absolutely certain that they would be subjecting the weather to every conceivable point of view, Linda recommended asking their mutual friend Shirley to join them. Celia thought they'd have plenty of points of view to discuss without Shirley adding her two cents; but after some debate, she wearily conceded the invitation.

Today, the ladies uncharacteristically *did* order food and beverages to wash it down with. That was not out of any sense of obligation to the management, but rather because it was lunchtime and none of them had taken the usual precaution of grabbing a bite to eat before heading out to the restaurant.

"So, what's new?" asked Linda.

Shirley gulped down a mouthful of salad just in case the question might require her to reply. She was pretty sure it wouldn't, being half rhetorical and wholly directed to Celia (who had, after all, called this meeting), but you never could tell.

"What's to be new?" Celia answered. "At our age, what's *left* to be new? At least, that we'd still be alive to talk about."

"We're not *that* old, yet. We know older. Besides, you're as young as you feel."

"Is that supposed to be comforting?"

"You're right. Whoever thought that one up was either too young to know any better or too far out of his senses to know any better. Comes out the same either way."

The happy, depressing banter continued for another ten or fifteen minutes before Celia came to the point. More accurately, it continued for another ten or fifteen minutes before Celia began that slow, circuitously laborious conversational path that would, ultimately and eventually, come to the point. One simply did not rush these things, especially when one is still digesting.

"Hey, here's a funny story for you," she began. "A friend of mine you don't know—"

"How do you know?"

"What do you mean, how do I know?"

"How do you know we don't know this friend of yours?"

"Trust me, I know. You don't."

"We might. Shirley and I know a lot of people ourselves. You don't know everyone we know."

"And *you* don't know everyone *I* know. This is one of them, okay? Take my word for it."

"We believe you, but you shouldn't always just assume that we don't know something. Or someone. It's always possible we do."

"Enough with the assume, already! It's like talking to my son, for crying out loud! Now, may I continue, finally?"

"Sure. Go ahead. Continue."

"Thank you. So anyway, this friend of mine *whom you don't know* has this son..."

Now that Linda and Shirley knew exactly who Celia was talking about, they gave her their undivided attention.

"So, my friend's son had this funny thing happen to him."

Celia gave her friends the *Reader's Digest Condensed Version of Myron's Adventures in Blunderland*, up to his forced retirement at a spry-enough age when he could conceivably take serious advantage of all the extra free time. She made it clear, however, that he was instead thoroughly displeased about the arrangement, prompting Shirley to observe, not originally, that youth truly was wasted on the young. Linda and Celia nodded in agreement.

"So, what's the big *megillah*?" asked Linda. "If he doesn't want to stay retired, he should just go out and get another job. It's not as if they took his identity away from him or anything."

"Well, as a matter of fact..." Celia set her friends straight on that point.

"Could be a problem," agreed Shirley.

"Yeah, but it could be an opportunity, too. Like, if he thought to embezzle first."

"My, er, friend's son wasn't brought up that way. Though I'll bet he wishes in hindsight that he'd thought of it."

"You always think of those things afterwards, when it's too late."

They lamented that this was invariably so.

"So, your, er, friend's son doesn't like being the Invisible Man?"

"And why should he like being the Invisible Man?"

"I'm just saying, if he did, it could maybe help him to see himself through."

"He was never very good at seeing anything through," Celia nearly confessed. "At least," she added quickly, "so his mother tells me."

"Has he tried—"

"Whatever it is, he's tried it."

"There you go assuming things again. For all you know, we may have an idea or two he *hasn't* tried yet."

"Fine. Yes, you're right. I'm assuming again. Shame on me! So what were you going to say before I so rudely assumed?"

Linda and Shirley rattled off a list of *has he trieds*, every one of which he apparently had, before giving up.

"Told you," Celia felt entitled to say.

"Hmmm," they all thought. This was tough one.

"Maybe his mother could bring him back into the world," offered Shirley.

"She already did that once," said Celia. "At this point, she probably couldn't survive the labor. And the delivery? It's too unbearable to even think about."

"Yes," agreed Shirley, pushing the remainder of her lunch aside at the image that had suddenly planted itself inside her head. "What I meant, though, was something not quite so traumatic." Or unappetizing.

"You—I mean, *she*—could start getting his name out everywhere. Sign him up for things. Get his name on mailing lists. Register him at hotels and reunions, whatever. Like that guy in *North by Northwest*, what was his name...George Kaplan!"

"There was no guy in *North by Northwest* named George Kaplan. Everybody only thought there was."

"Exactly."

Celia digested this little strategy, and the longer she ruminated, the more she liked it. She was glad she'd insisted on dragging Shirley along.

Chapter 10

"Looks like you're the big mail winner again, today," Christine informed her husband. "Three magazines; subscription information for the ballet and opera societies; a chance to win a cruise for two to some island nobody's ever heard of; the 'complimentary trial pass you requested' to the gym up the street; two—no three—credit card applications, and your membership cards for the NRA and that retired people's organization. Did you buy a gun?"

"It's crossed my mind a couple of times recently," answered Mike. "But, no."

"Then why did you join the NRA?"

"I did not join the NRA."

"You must have. Why else would they send you a membership card?"

"You'd have to ask them. I know—why don't you shoot them an email?"

"You're so clever." Meaning no, you're not.

"And what about this other one? Did you retire recently and forget to tell me?"

Mike choked on God-only-knows-what, since just then he was neither eating nor drinking anything. He began to cough uncontrollably, making his conspicuousness inescapable when the one thing he wanted most in the world at that moment was not to be conspicuous at all.

"Here. Do you want a glass of water?"

Mike was not sure how pouring water down an obstructed gullet could possibly improve the condition, but he took the offered glass and poured away despite his better judgment. Miraculously, as he did so the hacking stopped completely.

"Thanks," he said in a sort of gasp. "This seems to have helped." He looked at the glass and took another sip, considered the merits of taking yet one more, and instead dumped the remainder into the sink.

"Are you going to live?" asked Christine, sounding very nearly concerned.

"If I'm not careful," Mike replied.

Today's postal offerings were typical of what he'd been receiving regularly for the past week. He couldn't say how, but obviously he had managed to find his way onto somebody's mailing list. Somebody who believed in sharing. The only entity he *hadn't* heard from yet was his college's alumni office; but at this rate, it was only a matter of time.

Mike stood over the wastepaper basket, individually dropping pieces of today's postal offerings to their eternal rest. Goodbye, ballet subscription! So long, NRA! Opera Society...we hardly knew ye.

He was about to jettison the complimentary gym pass when he hesitated, setting it off to the side instead. Heck, he thought, he definitely had enough free time these days.

No reason not to put at least some of it to good use. Besides, you never know, he just might have an opportunity to take his shirt off in front of somebody again someday. A few bench presses and a curl or two probably wouldn't hurt.

Dan and his cellmates were feeling gloomy.

They still had not figured out a way to re-insert the Myron Moskowitz file, sans his last diagnosis, back into the System. This was seriously disconcerting, since up 'til now they had rather prided themselves on their technological acumen. Abject failure in one's self-declared métier was undeniably a major kick in the pants. They had also violated their own version of the Hippocratic Oath, having now caused more harm than they had originally set out to remedy. A *lot* more, if they were being completely honest. And they were now officially out of ideas.

"Let's be logical," tendered Kermit. "Maybe we've just been looking at this all wrong."

"What are you talking about?" Dan asked, somewhat severely.

"Well, think about it," replied Kermit, as if they'd done much of anything else lately. "Up to now, we've only been looking at things from *our* perspective, from the inside out. Maybe it's time to start attacking this from the outside *in*."

"Kermit, what the *hell* are you talking about?" asked Dan again, his severity now diluted somewhat by a mild curiosity.

"Wait," said Jackie, jumping in. "I think Kermit may be on to something."

The others highly doubted it. But being hot, even in a geeky sort of way, carried no small amount of influence with this crew.

"If I understand Kermit correctly, which is frankly pretty scary in its own right, maybe it's time to get Mr. Moskowitz more involved in his own re-integration."

They weren't convinced, but did we mention that Jackie was kinda hot?

"All right, we'll try it," said Dan who, being completely devoid of any alternatives, was game for just about anything. "How do you propose we do it?"

"Let's put him together with some of the other cells, guys with access to other computers," Jackie threw against the wall. "People with different ways in than we have. I mean, what have we got to lose?"

"It's a thought," agreed Dan. "Okay, what else?"

"We could start signing Mr. Moskowitz up for things. Museum memberships, frequent flier programs. Get his name in every computer on the planet."

Heads nodded.

"Great idea. Do it. And leave no mailing list unturned."

The meeting broke up and the group headed over to their regular caffeinated-beverage-serving haunt. Their usual table, however, was already occupied by someone with an ear-mounted cell phone and a laptop, so they were forced to plant themselves and their refreshments in another part of the establishment. Feeling slightly out of place in this new and unfamiliar piece of real estate, the conversation never gathered enough momentum even to languish and, ultimately, die away altogether.

Little mention has been made up to now on the subject of how Mike had been whiling away the hours of his reluctant retirement. He had, since somewhere around the third or fourth day, been dividing his time in nearly equal measure among three modes of existence. These could roughly be characterized under the headings of activity, inactivity, and something that was neither one nor the other.

It was while passing time in this latter mode that Mike could generally be found contemplating his options for the other two, and thus could be considered either actively inactive or inactively active, depending on whether one tended to see the glass half-full or half-empty.

The bulk of his activities, at least during the week, had the overall design of keeping Christine from noticing that he was engaged in them. So far, he seemed to have kept things well below the spousal radar. There'd been a few close calls, of course, as there inevitably would be, but Mike somehow always managed to choke his way out of them. If there'd been an old war wound, it would have likely chosen at least a few of those occasions to start acting up again. He was pretty sure his wife hadn't caught on to him yet, though he knew it was always good policy to assume nothing wherever wives were concerned. The moment you've become convinced that you're safely out of the woods is the same moment the arsenal of matrimonial

ICBMs have locked on target and begun their descent.

A typical day for Mike included leaving the house at the usual work-departure hour, dressed in the usual work attire. He would drive off in the usual direction until he was far enough away to avoid being recognized by anyone he or, more importantly, Christine, knew. Then, just short of the old firm's parking lot, he would veer off into a strip mall hosting, among other things, a trendy coffee emporium. By pure coincidence, the strip mall was not very far from the corporate offices of the Itinerant Life & Casualty Company, and the table at the back Mike generally favored was the Itinerant cell's own little home-away-from-home.

By another coincidence, or maybe not, this was the typical sort of behavior a lot of newly-retired guys favored over sleeping in and hanging listlessly around the house. Denial sells a great deal of coffee.

Once fully caffeinated Mike would next head over to the neighborhood gym where he took advantage of their complimentary, temporary membership offer. The place was fairly quiet by the time he got there, being, as it was, between the before-work crowd and the fitness-for-lunch bunch. Mike had come up with that one himself. The abundant accessibility of equipment and instructional staff enabled him to strike a significant blow for healthful exercise, and he ended each session wondering why he hadn't taken up getting in shape years earlier. Then he'd remember he'd had a full-time job, and as soon as he found another one the word *cardio* wouldn't appear again anywhere in his vocabulary until after his first heart attack. Or possibly not even until after his second heart attack. Knowing this, when the club pressed him to splurge for the full-blown membership package, Mike remained politely non-committal.

The immediate post-iron-pumping period would typically be devoted to vigorously replacing all the calories his morning's exertions had vigorously burned off. This was part of Mike's strategy. It would not do to appear too buff too quickly, or Christine might begin to notice. Unlikely, of course, since she had not looked at him that closely in years. Yet it was still enough of a possibility to bear paying attention to.

Lunching required an extra degree of ingenuity since Mike still wanted to avoid any contact with potentially nosy acquaintances, but he found eating at the same few restaurants all the time could get old very quickly. This left only several hundred other food service establishments for him to choose from, a fact which, unfortunately, did not make the daily task of picking one appreciably easier.

It was only after lunch, however, in the interval between settling his check and arriving back at home at an hour when Christine would be expecting him, that Mike was really forced to be creative. He needed places to go and things to do, and ideally ones that did not cost very much. He *was* retired, after all. Celia had graciously offered to keep him company over at her house, but so far hell had not frozen over yet, pigs had still not gotten the hang of self-propelled aviation, and Mike could always come up with a better alternative. Admittedly, this included hanging around coffee shops a great deal. But on the bright side, it meant he now had something concrete to blame his increasing nightly insomnia on.

Finally, his evenings were largely devoted to sorting through the stacks of applications, promotions, brochures of all shapes and description, and whatever else you can think of that found its way through his mail slot. The daily delivery had become so overwhelming that the local postmaster briefly entertained the option of giving the Moskowitz's address its very own zip code. Nine digits and all.

The phone rang.

"Mr. Moskowitz?"

"I certainly hope so."

"Um, hi, Mr. Moskowitz. This is Dan. Remember me?"

"Well, let me see...there was somebody calling himself Dan who talked to me about a month or so ago. Said something about fixing a little problem I was having. *That* Dan?"

"Um, yeah. I mean, yes. Same Dan. So has anything, um, changed since the last time we talked?"

"Nope. Same Dan. Same problem. And how have things been going with you?"

"Oh, I'm, uh, you know, okay. Anyway, the reason I'm calling—"

"Wait, don't tell me—let me guess. You've solved the problem and my life is going to get back to normal again?"

"Well, um, no."

"Ah. Then, you've realized the situation is hopeless, and you're giving up. Am I getting warmer?"

"Not exactly. But I *do* have an update for you."

"I see. Then, by all means, fill me in without further delay."

"Right. Well, it's like this. We, my, er, associates and I, have called in the cavalry."

"And here I thought you were finished horsing around."

"Huh? Oh, right. Good one. No, no horsing around. We've brought in some other experts."

"Experts? Like the way *you're* experts?"

"Absolutely. Better, even, in some ways. And they have access to different computers than we do. I really think they can help."

"So why waste time talking to me? Sic the different experts with their different computers on the scent and call me back when you can say: 'Problem solved, Mr. Moskowitz! Go in good health!'"

"Um, yeah, well, it's not quite that simple, Mr. M. You're going to have to meet with them, help them reconstruct your history so they can put you back in the system. Or put a new you in the system, with all the same information as the old you. The current you. You know what I mean. Everything except that weird diagnosis. By the way, has anybody figured out that you haven't died yet?"

"If they have, nobody's mentioned it lately. So, it sounds like I don't have much choice in this."

"You sort of do. I mean, if you were thinking about

maybe starting a new life somewhere under an assumed identity or something, now's your chance."

This was the first intelligent thing Dan had said up to that point.

"Intriguing possibility. But let's start with getting the old Mike Moskowitz back online. If I change my mind and want to disappear again, I'll know whom to call."

"And is this Mike Moskowitz any relation to you?"

"No. Mike and Myron are one and the same, to everyone but my mother. And please don't get me started on my mother."

"No worries there. So, will you meet with our guys?"

"Just tell me when."

A date was set, with Dan promising to phone back with a location as soon as he had one. Mike replaced the receiver and attempted sleep, but found that he was once again one large java over his limit.

Chapter 11

The agreed-upon meeting place, which had apparently been agreed upon without any input whatsoever from Mike, turned out to be the parking lot of an old, abandoned drive-in movie theater. Mike hadn't realized there still were such things as drive-in movie theaters, abandoned or otherwise. So if nothing else came out of all this, he consoled himself, at least he'd have learned something.

The Moskowitz Mobile was first on the scene, leading Mike to wonder if he had not, in fact, been sent on some wild-goose chase. That would have been most annoying, particularly in light of the adroit verbal tap dancing he'd had to do to get out of the plans Christine insisted he had already made with her. Mike did not remember committing to anything, but that was not unusual. He rarely committed to anything, and when he did, he hardly ever remembered it.

His wild-goose-chase concerns were soon alleviated, however, when other vehicles gradually began showing up. Cars, motorcycles, and even a couple of bicycles pulled into the lot and planted themselves alongside denuded speaker posts, none of them within spitting distance of Mike. Instead, the newcomers spread themselves out across the lot and sat waiting, as if for the start of a date-night double feature that would never be run. A classic slasher film, perhaps followed by something with vampires or zombies. A few of the bloodier cult favorites sprang readily to Mike's mind.

Thinking about slasher movies reminded Mike that he was essentially alone in the middle of a concrete nowhere, surrounded by people he did not know and who, so far, were not going out of their way to appear overly neighborly. The cars were a little intimidating, the motorcycles even more so. Then his eyes took in the bicycles, and any apprehension he may have been nurturing vanished into thin air. For, try as one might, it was impossible to look scary standing astride a bicycle. Especially when there's Spandex and silly headgear involved.

As if on cue, heads began turning around, eventually gravitating toward Mike's direction. Had they been zombies, this would have been really creepy.

One of them, a youngish-looking man, separated from the group and started walking over to Mike's car. His arms were not stretched out in front of him and he did not walk with the pronounced side-to-side gait one normally associates with the undead, and his eyes lacked that certain zombie-like stare. Mike observed these things with an embarrassing degree of relief.

"You must be Mr. Moskowitz," he said, in a voice that was clearly un-undead. Or would that be un-un-undead?

"I used to be. Lately, though, I'm not too sure."

"Close enough for government work, as my grandpa

used to say. So, um, welcome. I'm Dan, the guy you talked to. I'd offer you something, but I doubt anybody remembered to bring anything. Well, one guy probably brought beer—he usually does. But if so, it'll only be enough for himself. He keeps insisting that he doesn't want to contribute to anyone else's delinquency, but I think he's just kinda stingy."

"Just as well. Coming home reeking of beer would blow my cover story to smithereens. So, is this your brain trust?" Mike asked, waving his hand across the horizon of people. The horizon waved back.

"Yep. That's them. Us. If you'll come on over, I'll introduce you."

Dan led Mike to an abandoned concession area near the large wall that had once done duty as a movie screen.

"You guys come here often?"

"Some of them do. I can't for the life of me figure out why, though."

"Some things are best left to the imagination," suggested Mike.

"Or not," countered Dan.

The group assembled, introductions were duly made, and the situation was explained to Mike in more detail than he'd imagined possible.

"So, basically," he summarized, addressing Dan, "This whole fiasco is all *your* doing?"

"Well, technically, Mr. M., this whole fiasco was your *doctor's* doing."

"Dr. Katz," someone interjected, in the event Mike had somehow forgotten.

"I—we—only screwed up after the fact, when we tried to put you back in the system. Oh, and by the way," Dan added, sounding contrite. "Sorry, man."

Mike nearly launched into an animated diatribe on how *sorry* wasn't exactly going to cut it after everything he'd been put through. But one look at Dan's genuinely remorseful visage and the diatribe died away.

"Thanks," was all he said.

Someone stepped forward and addressed Mike.

"The trouble is, it's almost impossible to create a new human being within the system right now. There are lots of security things in place that weren't there a few years ago—all kinds of cross-checking databases, verifying and re-verifying. Even things we're not supposed to know about that wouldn't fool a mentally-challenged twelve-year-old have been thrown in. It's supposed to make it harder for people to set up false identities or something. Anyway, it's a real hassle."

"Sounds harder than it is to create a *real*, new human being. Although you could say that the process of conception is remarkably similar to what's been done to me."

Mike had to explain what he meant by that, and he immediately regretted it. Strangely, only the women found the analogy funny.

In an act of almost Herculean patience, Mike recounted as much of his personal life as he could remember, traveling nearly far enough back in his childhood to require getting his passport stamped. His audience appeared terminally disinterested in anything that could not in some way, shape or form have involved a computer, and the ones that operated with punch cards didn't count. Mike hadn't fully appreciated before just how much of his time on Earth had been spent in the Punch Card Era.

The plan, as it was explained to him, was to find at least one computer somewhere in the world that had a Myron Moskowitz in it, and preferably the correct one. They would then somehow figure out a way to "remotely extract" said Myron from that computer, transfer it, or him, as it were, to the main network, bring the information up to date, and *voila!* They'd be rolling in Moskowitz.

To Mike, this was beginning to sound like the plot to one of the older James Bond movies, but he was in way too deep by now simply to get up and walk away. Besides, he'd always rather liked all those older James Bond movies. Even the ones with Roger Moore.

In the final analysis, it was determined that Mike had had far less computer-involved activity than was considered normal outside the Third-or Fourth World. Even lumping the Third World into that mix was by way of being slightly generous. But the experts vowed to do everything in their power to put the virtual Myron back where they had found him, and everyone went on their merry way. Everyone, that is, except for one guy on a bicycle, who stuck around a while longer to finish his beer.

Chapter 12

Had Salvador Dali himself conceived the scene at the Moskowitz's dinner table the following evening, it could not have been more surreal than it seemed to Mike, who found himself smack dab in the middle of it.

That he and Christine were dining together was not exactly unusual. That Christine was animatedly engaging in conversation was *somewhat* unusual. That she was doing so with Celia was extremely unusual. And that Christine had been the one to invite Celia over for dinner in the first place, was downright bizarre.

As if to throw yet another melting clock onto the canvas, the two women were getting along as though they actually liked one another. And, as if *that* wasn't enough, they were, for the first time in their history, in complete agreement.

The subject on which the two Moskowitz women were seeing eye-to-eye was seated at one end of the table, such that neither Moskowitz *femme* was forced to watch him squirm while unwittingly being discussed in the third person. So engrossed were they that, had the object of their discourse spontaneously combusted, they would not have discovered the charred remains any sooner than dessert. Mere throat clearing? Forget it.

What had precipitated all this was the observation by Christine that her husband had clearly not been himself lately. Longer than lately, as a matter of fact. Not to put too fine a point on it, Mike was acting strangely even by Mike standards, which in her mind was really saying something.

If it sounded more than a bit out of character for Christine to show signs of even noticing any change in her husband's behavior, let alone experience genuine concern about it, this was only because one did not fully comprehend the depth of her attachment to him. True, she had shut and bolted the door on her husband emotionally and physically eons ago, but it still felt like they belonged together. She might even go so far as to say she still loved Mike, though of course not out loud and certainly never in front of him.

Those whose natures lean toward the cynical side might consider it much more likely Christine had convinced herself that her husband was up to no good, and her sole interest in the matter was in ferreting out precisely what that no-good something might be. This explanation would not be an entirely fair or even accurate one, despite the liberal sprinkling of grains of truth seasoning the suspicious sentiment. After all, if she truly didn't care, she probably wouldn't at all. Care, that is.

It would have been a fairly simple matter to ask Mike directly, at the breakfast table, say, or while watching TV together on an evening. But Christine dismissed the direct approach out of hand on the assumption that the conversation would go approximately like this:

She: "Mike, are you up to something?"

He: "No."

And that, as they say, would be that.

The situation, as she saw it, called for a strategy, one that was highly clever and just a little bit sneaky. *I Love Lucy* sneaky. Not mean or ill-spirited or anything. Just, well, *sneaky.* And clever, too, naturally.

Which was when Christine had had her brainstorm. Without passing *Go* or collecting two hundred dollars, she phoned her mother-in-law with an invitation to dinner. Celia could wring a confession out of the most recalcitrant offender with nothing more energetic than a sulk. Add a few lines of guilt-inducing soliloquy to that mien of absolute disappointment, and anyone on the receiving end didn't stand a chance. Mike, despite knowing nearly every trick up his mother's sleeve, would be a sitting duck.

Celia herself already had a fairly strong inkling about what was troubling her son, having been thoroughly inkled directly by the source himself. She was surprised, however, to learn that he had not yet shared any of it with his own wife. But upon further reflection she conceded that, under the same circumstances, she probably wouldn't have, either. Christine just had that effect on people.

Still, dinner invitations from her daughter-in-law did not grow on trees, so Celia decided to go and play along. She could keep Mike's secret as long as he could, or at least until she could find some way to use the information to her personal advantage.

The meal itself was tasty if not overly creative. Christine had made chicken—or what was far more likely, had bought one already prepared from the nearest supermarket—and had complemented the entree with a disproportionate number of side dishes. Most of these Celia could identify immediately, though there were a couple of grain-like things she did not recall ever having seen before. This was unusual for someone who, in her lifetime, had sampled more than her share of unusual foodstuffs. But their presence at the table showed at least a little initiative and—dare she say it?—effort on Christine's part, so the older woman was willing to give the younger a Brownie point or two for trying.

Celia had barely swallowed her first bite of drumstick when the meeting was called to order. Not in so many words, that is to say, but if Christine was making any attempt to camouflage her agenda, she was not making a very convincing job of it.

"You know, Mom, we don't see nearly enough of you these days," Christine began.

Celia had just addressed the aforementioned drumstick.

"In fact," she continued, "I think Mike, in particular, could really stand to spend a little more time with you."

Celia tentatively lanced a small mound of foreign, grain-like substance with her fork, but quickly withdrew the utensil before it had time to make any definite commitments. Her eyes searched the dining room.

"Okay, so where is it? Where's the camera?" she asked, smiling knowingly.

"What camera, Mom?"

"The one for *Candid Camera*, or, that other thing, What's-it-tube."

The same thought had occurred, albeit fleetingly, to Mike.

"There's no camera here," Christine assured her in-law, and conveniently re-commandeering the conversation. "It's just that Mike's been acting like he's at loose ends lately, and who better for him to confide in than his mother?"

Celia's eyes searched the room again.

"Is that a trick question?"

The conversation, such as it was, took off from there, Christine unabashedly engaging while Celia attempted unsuccessfully to negotiate bites of chicken leg.

There are, in this vast world of ours, individuals for whom the answering of one question with another question can, it if happens often enough, drive them clear out of their skulls. It was fortunate that none of these happened to be in the neighborhood of the Moskowitz's dining room that evening. For, had there been, the resulting conflagration would have undoubtedly made the morning papers.

Mrs. Moskowitz-the-Younger kept trying to get Mrs. Moskowitz-the-Elder fired up by asking a series of questions—prepared well in advance—which, directed at any lesser mortal, would be guaranteed to stir the pot. The latter Mrs. Moskowitz, no lesser mortal she, would then respond to Christine's questions with questions of her own—improvised on the spot—designed to keep the other woman talking long enough to give Celia a chance to make a dent in her dinner.

Needless to say, this back and forth of parry and dodge did not advance either woman's objective one iota. It eventually occurred to Celia that the path of least resistance, not to mention optimal nutrition, might simply be one of general acquiescence. And she was right: once started down that road, the aforementioned drumstick was quickly dispatched, as, too, were its various plate-mates.

The rest of the discussion may be summarized as follows:

Christine: "Mike's been acting strangely lately."

Celia: "He's *always* acted strangely. So, what else is new?"

The sixty-two minutes or so it took for these conclusions to be drawn were sometimes intense, frequently lively, and bordered on the cruel and unusual for Mike, who was forced to endure the entire performance in the hapless role of mute spectator.

There was, however, one small glint of silver lining in his otherwise cloud of gray. Celia, demonstrating a hitherto unobserved degree of self-restraint, had so far done an admirable job of not spilling the proverbial beans. If she could somehow get through the rest of the evening with the better part of valor still intact, Mike thought, he could very well develop a whole new respect for the old bird.

Christine, however, was determined not to make this task a particularly easy one. She was, in a word, relentless. She was also, in another word, desperate. Inviting her mother-in-law to the house for dinner and carrying on a conversation with her, questionable though most of it was, were not things the Christines of this world did lightly. To go through all of that and come away empty-handed, fell somewhere between disappointing and devastating. Christine did not intend to go down without a fight. The small glint of silver lining in *her* otherwise gray cloud was the knowledge that she had not actually had to cook anything.

One by one, Christine exhausted everything left in her arsenal. She baited. She cajoled. She used humor, though not very well. Finally, the extreme border of her patience having been breached and invaded, Christine stood up and blurted out: "For God's sake, Mike! Are you up to something?"

"No," came the seated reply.

And that was *almost* that. Celia did manage to get in an "I told you so," first.

Chapter 13

"**W**hat a kerfuffle!" Dan did not say. What he *did* say was considerably less suitable for younger ears and sounded marginally like *custard duck*. "And all because of a stupid, mistyped medical diagnostic code. The Moskowitz Code. Sheesh!"

He did not really say that last word, either.

The silver lining in Dan's otherwise much darker cloud was the minute twinge of exoneration he felt in knowing that the brain trust, as Mr. Moskowitz had referred to them, were not faring any better. Their subject had somehow managed to elude more databases than they'd even thought possible in this digital day and age. Which was particularly odd, since he had also somehow managed to get his name onto virtually every mailing list in the galaxy. Unfortunately, being on mailing lists was not especially helpful. Not to anyone, really.

The other cells had, separately and unsuccessfully, replicated everything Dan and *his* cell had tried, also unsuccessfully, to do themselves. This was, in effect, a tech-geeky way of asking, "Are you sure?" and finding out, after wasting a considerable amount of time and effort that yes, you were.

The new hands had then launched the aforementioned massive database hunt, with the equally aforementioned lack of joy. The only success of note came from adding Myron Moskowitz's name to the two remaining mailing lists that had hitherto been overlooked by both Celia and Kermit. They were big believers in being thorough.

Finally, they had come around to Dan's strategy of getting Mr. Moskowitz more involved in his own restoration. Someone suggested starting with a visit to Dr. Katz's office, since that was where the pernicious Moskowitz Code had begun its life of typographical mischief. If nothing else, it might at least get the idiot who'd accidentally wiped out all of the guy's records off the hook for a while. And, like so many bad ideas that had come before and after, it had sounded like a pretty good idea at the time.

Mike failed to follow the logic when they tried to explain it to him. But in the spirit of suffering absolute futility absolutely, he scheduled an appointment anyway. He arrived at Dr. Katz's office a solid ten minutes before he was required to, and announced his presence to the receptionist. Sort of.

"Table for four, please, and not a booth, if you can help it."

The receptionist instinctively looked around for the three other members of the party, before recollecting that this was, in fact, a doctor's office and not a restaurant. She remembered this just as she was about to reach across the desk for menus.

"Do you have a reservation? I mean, an appointment?"

J. Bresler

Probably works cheap, Mike thought.

"Yes. The name is Moskowitz. *Mike* Moskowitz."
Shaken, not stirred.

"*Myron* Moskowitz?"

"Only to my mother."

"Here," she said, handing him a clipboard with a form
attached. "Could you please fill this out? Oh, and can I see
your insurance card?"

This was Mike's first clue that things might get a little
complicated.

"Um, I don't have one."

"No worries," the receptionist reassured him, using an
expression Mike had long thought the world would be
much better off without. "I can look it up. Who's your
insurer?"

"Um, I don't have one of those, either. Which kind of
explains why I don't have a card, I guess."

"You don't have insurance?"

She didn't miss a trick, this one.

"Yes. No. No insurance."

"Not even Medicare?"

"Sorry. Too young."

"Then, who are we supposed to bill?"

"You can bill me." Mike was careful to enunciate the
word *bill*.

"I don't think we can do that. I mean, I've never seen it
done before, just billing the patient directly."

"Sure you can. It'll be just like in the old days, before
there even *was* any such thing as insurance. A guy went to
the doctor, the guy paid the doctor. Sometimes with things

102

other than money, like chickens."

The receptionist could not imagine that sort of thing ever happening, especially nowadays. For one thing, she knew Dr. Katz's fee just for scheduling a basic office visit, and it certainly wasn't poultry.

"You mean, you're going to pay the entire thing *yourself*?"

Like he thought. She didn't miss a trick.

"You sound like you've never heard anybody say that before."

"I don't think *anyone's* ever heard anybody say that before."

"Ah. A new experience for you, then. How exciting! So, we're good?"

"*I'm* good. I'm not so sure about you, though. And I can't let you see the doctor without filling in the insurance information first."

"Don't let me stop you."

"But there's nothing to fill in."

"Of course there's something to fill in."

"What?"

"'NONE.'"

"I can't do that."

"Why not?"

"The computer won't let me."

Welcome to my world, thought Mike.

"Just tell Dr. Katz I'm here. I'm sure he'll see me. And if not, I'll be happy to send my mother, instead. She has insurance."

The young woman did not understand what that could

possibly have to do with anything, but in spite of her confusion, or perhaps because of it, she quickly retreated down the corridor leading to the examination rooms. She returned a few minutes later with Dr. Katz in tow.

"Mr. Moskowitz! How nice to see you," he said, more to the other occupants of his waiting room than to Mike. "Did you ever get that business, you know, straightened out?"

"Well, no, actually. That's what I'm here to talk to you about."

"Why didn't you just phone? I wouldn't have put you to all this trouble." Again, smiling to the waiting room audience.

"Because of caller I.D."

"I don't understand. What about caller I.D.?"

"Apparently, you have it."

"Oh, um, I see." He didn't see. "So, how can I help you?"

"For starters, is there any place other than the reception desk where we can talk?"

The packed waiting room's worth of patients was eyeing the two men with interest, the exchange being considerably more engaging than any of the magazine offerings.

"We could go to my private office, I suppose," offered Dr. Katz. "Would you mind waiting out here for a few minutes? I have several patients in various stages of undress I need to attend to first, and I wouldn't want to leave them out in the cold, so to speak."

Mike looked out at the waiting room. The waiting

room looked back at him.

"I think I'd rather wait in your private office, if it's all the same to you," Mike replied. "I promise not to steal any pens or anything."

The doctor laughed uncomfortably. It wasn't all the same to him, but he smiled and agreed in spite of himself.

"Of course. That will be fine. Lily here will show you the way."

With that, Dr. Katz turned and walked briskly back to his several patients in their various stages of undress. Mike wondered if his physician realized the irony of having anything called lily associated with his medical practice. Probably not, he guessed.

Mike was escorted to a room he'd never noticed before on any of a multitude of previous visits, an oversight he attributed to his usual preoccupation with whatever symptoms and sufferings had conspired to send him there.

The room had the look and general ambiance of an old study. Its centerpiece was a large desk of some heavy, darkly-stained wood—Mike had never been able to tell oak from mahogany or walnut—with two identical, leather-upholstered chairs at the bow and a much grander leather desk chair astern. The walls weren't paneled, but their reddish-brown-beige paint temporarily gave one the illusion of another, less chrome-and-glass era. Mike could understand why Dr. Katz might want to keep this little sanctum all to himself.

He helped himself to one of the chairs and set about making himself comfortable, figuring that *a few minutes* in doctor-speak meant that he was probably going to be there awhile.

The chair, however, was determined to make the notion of comfort a mere pipe dream. Shift and settle though he might, a suitable position seemed always just outside his posterior's grasp. When the idea that standing would undoubtedly be a more comfortable alternative to anything Mike could conceivably do involving that particular chair, he formally abandoned it in favor of its identical twin.

This did not prove to be a trade upward, however, being, as it was, an exact duplicate of the one he'd just rejected in its stead. Mike was beginning to wonder how he was going to arrange himself until Dr. Katz showed up when his eyes settled on the grand, comfy-looking tush depository directly across the desk.

He knew he probably shouldn't. After all, there was a reason that somebody had placed a large, heavy wooden desk in his path. A boundary, beyond which interlopers proceeded at their own peril. It would almost be a violation of Dr. Katz himself, the man who had attended to his family's ills for so many years, the physician who, with a single careless, absent-minded, unconscionable keystroke had sent Mike's very existence down a deep, dark virtual black hole...

Mike did not even bother walking around. Instead, he deftly climbed on top of the desk and rolled himself, butt-first, into the seat of honor.

This would have been a comically opportune moment for Dr. Katz to stroll in. But if the key to successful comedy is timing, Dr. Katz would never have made it as a professional comedian, being, as he perpetually was, late.

Mike had already settled back in relative comfort and was in the first stages of boredom when Dr. Katz finally arrived.

Actually, this is not completely true. Mike had, in fact, already entered the *second* stage of boredom and was distractedly picking at things on the desk in front of him when Dr. Katz finally arrived. Good timing, again, was not the physician's strong suit.

"Mr. Moskowitz! There are extremely confidential items on that desk!"

"Really? Where?" Mike looked around, but could not find any.

The two men maintained an uncomfortable eye contact for about twenty seconds, before the doctor took a seat in one of the visitors' chairs. He found this arrangement unpleasant in a number of ways.

"So, what can I do for you, Mr. Moskowitz?"

Mike brought Dr. Katz up to speed on his recent history, after first insisting that the doctor call him Mike. Mike nearly said, "Call me Mike, Sherman," but he stopped himself in time. The glare piercing into him just then definitely did not belong to a Sherman.

"An unfortunate state of affairs, certainly," Dr. Katz agreed. "But I don't see where I can be of any assistance. My expertise is strictly corporal. The virtual is the domain of a different set of experts entirely. Even Lily, my receptionist, can run rings around me in any matter involving computers. And she is far from the sharpest scalpel on the tray, if you get my meaning."

"I don't foresee any MacArthur grants in her immediate future, no," Mike conceded. "However, Lily notwith-standing, I believe what I have in mind will be right up your alley. I'd like you to create a new, electronic patient file on me."

"What's the matter with the *old* electronic patient file I have on you?"

"There isn't one anymore. It was destroyed in the fire, so to speak."

"So, how would my creating a new file help your sit-uation?"

"Because, once it exists, you could, sort of, submit it around."

"To whom, exactly?"

"Well, my insur..." The first flaw in his great plan suddenly reared its ugly head.

"You mean, your insurance company? According to what you completely flummoxed my receptionist with, you haven't got one. Don't take that wrong, by the way. My receptionist flummoxes practically at the drop of a hat."

"It's probably just as well nobody wears hats nowa-days."

"I've been known to make the same observation my-self."

"Look, couldn't you just email it to a few places 'accidentally'? By the time they'll have figured it out, I'll have been processed and put back in the system."

"Sorry. No can do."

"Why not?"

"Patient privacy laws. They can be pretty brutal about that sort of thing. A breach like that could have serious repercussions."

"But *you started all this!*"

"I did not, Mr. Moskowitz, remove anything from anybody's computer file that I was not directly responsible for causing to be there in the first place. Someone else gets to enjoy that dubious distinction."

"Well, what if I got my mother involved?"

"Not even your mother could ever induce me or anyone in my employ to break the law. She'd simply be wasting her time."

Dr. Katz smiled broadly, and if he could have, he'd have given himself a high-five. As far as he could remember, and he had a superb memory, this was the first time he had ever scored against the Celia Moskowitz Defense.

"Dr. Katz, are you sure there's no way at all to get me into your computer system?"

"Hmmm, let me think...I know! We're going to begin sending out a patient newsletter in the next few weeks. I could see to it that you get put on the mailing list."

Not without the Post Office putting out a contract on you, thought Mike.

"I think that's a wonderful idea," he said.

Chapter 14

Even retirees take vacations.

"A vacation from *what*?" asked Celia, doing that very expressive thing she did with her left eyebrow. If this had been a silent movie, the audience would have known exactly what emotion she was trying to convey. And, if this had been a silent movie, Mike would have probably been enjoying the conversation at least a little more than he presently was.

"It's just a vacation. People take them all the time. Christine's been itching to get out of town for a few days and now seems like a good opportunity to get away."

"Why does now seem like such a good opportunity for a vacation?"

"Because it's off-season, and I'd have no trouble getting the time off work."

Celia's eyebrow shot up. It was her right one, this time.

"Would you mind repeating what you just said?"

She really *is* going deaf, Mike thought. "What? About this being a good time to take a vacation?"

"No, the other thing."

"Oh, about being able to get off work?"

"Yep. That one."

"Things are usually pretty quiet at the office around now, and everybody else will have probably used up most of their PTO days. Time off will be pretty easy to get."

"Time off?"

"Right."

"From work?"

"Where else?"

"Myron, you don't work."

"Yes, mother. I know that."

"Then, what's all this about getting time off? I mean, who would you even ask?"

"My boss."

Celia wanted to choose her next words very carefully. This was a bit of a challenge for her, since she had never done it before. "Son, I know you've been under a lot of strain lately, but have you gone completely out of your mind?"

Admittedly, not the most spectacular of first efforts.

Mike was too confused by the question to be at all offended by it.

"What do you mean?" he asked.

"What do you mean, what do I mean? There is no job. No boss. No one else's PTO to work around. What's that word? Delusional. Yes, that's it! You're delusional!"

"Of course I'm not delusional!" Mike countered, with less emphasis than the exclamation mark might imply. "I have to talk like this. I have to *think* like this. If I don't, I'll slip up in front of Christine."

"You *still* haven't told Christine?"

"Well, I can't very well now, can I? She'll want to know why I didn't say anything sooner, and that's all she'll want to talk about on our vacation."

Delusional, or just nuts? Celia wondered.

"Myron, you're walking a slippery slope with that wife of yours," Celia warned, wagging a child-sized finger. "She's a clever one. I'd be doing you a favor if I sent her an anonymous letter, only I don't know how to spell 'anonymous.'"

"Or even *be* anonymous, as far as that goes."

Not long after this episode of Quality Time with Celia, Mike went online and, after looking up a bunch of things he'd had no original intention to, navigated to the website of a popular discount airline. He did so laboring under the misguided belief that he was about to make the necessary travel arrangements for his and Christine's upcoming get-away. This belief was short-lived, however, due in no small measure to a Transportation Security Administration technicality mandating that any person attempting to book a flight on a commercial airline must, in fact, really exist.

Mike entered all the requisite personal data required by both the carrier and the law, providing everything short of a DNA sample. But when he hit the confirm button, instead of a pair of bona-fide boarding passes popping triumphantly up onto the screen, he was presented instead with a message stating that his transaction could not be processed.

He tried again, then yet again, then again once more.

The website, however, merely greeted each new attempt with a resoundingly adamant *No Sale*.

As Einstein is believed to have noted, doing the exact same thing over and over again but expecting to get a different result does not look particularly impressive on a fellow's MENSA application. Still, Mike took one more shot at it anyway, just in case, before hunting down the nearest telephone and dialing the toll-free customer service number.

His on-hold time was well within the limits of his patience, and the woman's voice at the other end of the line sounded cheery and capable. Mike was practically optimistic.

He explained the difficulty he was having in coaxing his boarding passes out of the company's online reservation system, and the voice—Mike had immediately forgotten its name—promised to help. Mike's optimism ratcheted up one full notch.

"I'm sorry about that. Now, let me make sure I have this right," the voice said. "That was Moskowitz: M–O–S–K–O–W–I–T-Z. Myron: M–Y–R–O–N?"

"That's right," Mike replied. R–I–G-H-T, he didn't add.

She confirmed his social security number, date of birth and credit card information. Mike confirmed she'd gotten every last detail down correctly.

"Ah, well, Mr. Moskowitz, I think I see why the website wouldn't allow you to complete your reservations."

"And why is that?"

"Because, apparently, and let me just check one more

thing here...yes...apparently, Mr. Moskowitz, there's no such person as, well, you."

Mike had been afraid she was going to say something like that.

"The computer can't verify your identity. No identity, no getting on an airplane. Are you sure all the information you gave me was completely accurate? It's easy to trans- pose a number or two. Heck, I do it all the time. Well, not exactly *all* the time. In fact, not really ever, come to think of it. Were you reading from the card, or going by memory?"

"The card," he lied. "What about my wife?"

"Would that be Christine? She's good to go. Any chance she'll be willing to travel without you?"

The second she gets wind of this, Mike thought with some dread.

"No. It's together or nothing."

"I see. Well, sorry I couldn't be of more help. Oh, and Mr. Moskowitz?"
"Hmmm?"

"Thank you for being a member of our Frequent Flyer Program. We really appreciate your business!"

Mike felt a smack right between the eyes.

"Hey, wait a minute! How can I be—"

But the voice had already moved on to the next cus- tomer.

"Train?"
"Yep."

"We're going by train?"

"Um hmm."

"Why are we going by *train?*"

"I thought it would be something different. You know, see the country. Make the trip more of an adventure."

"But what's wrong with flying? We'd get there quicker and have more time for sightseeing and things."

"We fly all the time. Besides, when was the last time you were on a train?"

"Back in college. There was an extended farm family from Italy taking up most of the coach section. I still have nightmares. And we *don't* fly all the time. We never go anywhere."

"I was speaking figuratively. C'mon, it'll be fun!"

Christine doubted it. But the close quarters might yield some clues as to what was up with Mike these days. She had not forgotten her recent dinner with Celia.

"The train, then," she said. "Don't they usually run in the middle of the night?"

"I don't know. Maybe. Why?"

"There won't be a lot of country to see in the dark."

"There'll be plenty of country."

"I know there'll be country. I'm just not sure we'll be able to see much of it, that's all."

"Well, at least there'll be more scenery than you'd get on a cruise ship. Night or day, it probably all looks pretty much the same."

"True, but at least on cruise ships there's unlimited food and booze."

"Trains have food and booze, too. Haven't you seen

North by Northwest? They were on a train."

"That was a whole, other era ago, back before every-thing fun became illegal."

"When did you suddenly become such an expert on fun?"

"I know about fun. From books."

That made sense to Mike, oddly. Anyway, Christine seemed on board with the train idea, or at least wasn't re-sisting very hard, and Mike could recognize a good time to change the subject when he saw one.

The appointed day came, if one can regard a two-thirty a.m. departure time *day*. The Moskowitzes officially launched their vacation and then promptly fell asleep, having not bothered attempting to grab even a single wink before leaving for the station.

There was not, as Christine had anticipated, much to do in the sleeping compartment of an American passenger train that did not involve close physical contact. Christine mainly divided her time between reading and trying to bait her husband. She occasionally directed her gaze to the world outside her window. While what rolled past tech-nically qualified as scenery, none of it would have chal-lenged even the most limited of landscape artists. Another characteristic of American railroads, Christine realized, was their tendency to be placed far away from anything in the least bit vista-worthy. By the time their train finally reached the end of the line, she truly was in need of a va-cation.

And spending a single conscious minute more than absolutely necessary inside a hotel room with that spouse of hers did not show up anywhere on the agenda. Staying in the same room—well, she supposed she had to do that. But after being cooped up with Mike for what felt like an eternity, Christine was not about to submit to such inescapable proximity again without a very large gun pointed at her, and possibly not even then.

Mike, of course, had had no problem with the whole experience, and could not understand what all the fuss was about. Typical, really.

The first few days of genuine vacation consisted of the sort of hyperactive touristy-things that people unaccustomed to regular holidays usually look forward to going back to work from. There were sightseeing tours, sightseeing non-tours, shopping, shopping, and more shopping. This appeared to have a therapeutic effect on Christine, if not accomplishing the same for Mike, but he continued tagging along almost dutifully. He was particularly impressed by how much his stamina had improved since taking up strenuous exercise, and decided that, if the complimentary trial gym memberships he kept getting in the mail ever dried up, he just might have to plunk down the dues money and join one in earnest.

But enhanced stamina notwithstanding, it is well-nigh impossible for even the most ardent excursionists to maintain too frenetic a pace for too long. There are generally only so many things to see and do, for one thing. For another, once the inevitable fatigue factor kicks in, folks tend to remember exactly what it is they went on vacation to do. By that point, the idea of a little down-time starts sounding pretty darned good.

J. Bresler

Christine hit the wall somewhere around the middle of day four. She had shopped 'til she dropped, and now wanted only to find some quiet place where she could lick her wounds and recharge her batteries. Loafing about in the room was out of the question, just as a matter of principle. Fortunately, the hotel offered a rather nice pool area for the benefit of its guests. Christine selected poolside as an ideal spot for performing some serious lounge-lizarding.

She was sunk deeply into a chaise and taking a quick survey of the terrain when she noticed a man in either shorts or swim trunks striding purposefully toward her. The sun was at his back, and thus was in her eyes as she glanced over in that direction, rendering the man's facial features undistinguishable. From what she could see, however, Christine could tell that, whoever he was, he took pretty good care of himself. His bearing was confident and he had the tapered physique of a guy who made a point of having things like tapered physiques. As he came closer, Christine could make out the shapes of well-conditioned shoulder muscles and the tasteful hint of a six-pack.

One can only imagine, then, what her first thought was upon realizing that this strange man, who pulled up the chaise right beside her, was Mike.

Her second thought was about how characteristically inconsiderate it was for him to buff himself up like that and not tell her, his own wife, and that she had to find out on the street the same as everybody else. Yet another isolated piece in the jumbled-up jigsaw puzzle that was Mike

118

Moskowitz.

Somewhere around the fifth or sixth thought Christine began seeing a pattern and came up with a potentially plausible explanation for it all. And the more thoughts she dumped onto the pile, the more they seemed to lead to only one possible conclusion: Mike had a bimbo.

Suddenly, it all made sense. The puzzle pieces all fell neatly into place. A few of them did, at least, and Christine was able to snip, twist and wedge most of the others in until they fit too, approximately.

She was stunned. She was appalled. Hadn't she been the very model of a perfect wife to him all these years? Well, maybe not, she conceded. But still, she'd given Mike the best years of her life, or so she reckoned. Besides, they were *married*, for Chrissake! Didn't that count for *any-thing* anymore?

"Do you want to have dinner here at the hotel, or find a restaurant in town somewhere?" Mike asked innocently.

"What?" Christine answered, rather more loudly and animatedly than she probably would have had her mind not been otherwise engaged.

"Dinner. Would you like to eat it here," Mike gestured toward the ground with his left index finger, "or at a res-taurant out there somewhere?" he asked, enunciating de-liberately and waving a hitchhiker's thumb back over his left shoulder.

"Why are you asking me about dinner? I haven't eaten lunch yet! Why are you so interested in where I have dinner?" Again, with a greater degree of both animation and volume than was strictly called for under the circumstances.

This was not quite the reaction Mike was either expecting or prepared for when he'd broached the subject. It would be putting the matter mildly to say he was taken somewhat aback and, therefore, nearer the mark altogether to say that Christine's little outburst nearly sent him flying out of his chair. It had a similar effect on the occupants of every other chaise lounge in the immediate vicinity. Fortunately, these were few and generally untroubled by such things as heart conditions or severe nervous disorders.

Mike froze, wondering just what he might have done wrong. The subject of dinner had never been a particularly passionate one during the main course of their relationship. So unless his wife was feeling unusually weight-conscious that probably wasn't it. And, he reasoned, if Christine *was* feeling unusually weight conscious, why would she be sprawled out on a chaise by a pool in a bathing suit?

Perhaps he had startled her, he thought, until he remembered she had watched him approaching for a good minute or more. Ditto for accidentally waking her. Hormones could also be a possibility, but he'd been out of touch with those for so long he'd largely forgotten what a hormone looked like.

Whatever it was, Mike decided that at least one person's quality of life would be temporarily improved if Christine was left alone for a while. With that in mind, he quasi-gymnastically extricated himself from the chair and proceeded to head back in the direction from which he'd come.

"Where do you think you're going?" Christine asked.

"The hotel has an exercise room. I thought I'd take advantage of it," Mike replied. "Maybe work up an appetite for later," he could not resist adding.

Christine was on a quest for a comeback when it dawned on her that the last thing she wanted Mike to do was anything that would improve him in any way, shape or form. *Especially* in shape or form.

"Wait! Don't go!" she urged. "I'm sorry I snapped at you just now. I don't know what got into me."

Hormones, Mike concluded. He turned around, hesitated for one barely perceptible instant, and then re-installed himself on the chaise.

Christine continued. "I was thinking about something, and um, I, uh, you know, must have been in that weird, in-between state of thinking and, um, not thinking. I think."

"Must have been important. What were you thinking about?"

"Oh, nothing, really."

Mike looked skyward. The sun was not yet high enough to have caused a sufficiently serious case of sunstroke. He'd just stick with his original diagnosis until a better one came along.

The conversation returned to more normal levels of volume, animation and general banality. Mike was aware that Christine seemed to be looking at him an awful lot, and, unless he was very much mistaken, with a rather peculiar eye. He may have only just been imagining the peculiar eye part, though. She was also smiling a bit too aggressively, and without a great deal of obvious sincerity.

What Mike could not see was the internal combustion engine driving his wife's thought processes at that moment. Christine was not sure exactly how she was going to handle what she was by now very much convinced she knew. But there was still another day and a half of vacation and one very long train ride home to come up with a game plan.

And if that didn't work, there was always Celia.

Chapter 15

Within the architecturally-un-noteworthy edifice which, for so many years, had served to keep Mike Moskowitz's former employers out of the rain, one suite of offices sat apart from the rest of the building. It was here that the firm's most senior executives arrived for work each day. The conventional wisdom held that the reason this select group was kept in quasi-isolation was to prevent the more rank-and-file employees from annoying them all the time. As usual, the conventional wisdom got it completely wrong. The company's senior-most executives had, in fact, been placed safely out of the way in order to keep *them* from annoying everyone else all the time.

At the far end of the suite sat a strategically-sized conference room. It was not too big, since it rarely ever hosted more than a few people at any one time. Yet it was large enough and apportioned in adequate style to leave visitors from the outside suitably impressed. Internally, it had been dubbed the Hibachi Room, since those employees who found themselves invited into it could usually expect a pretty thorough grilling.

The *filet du jour* was none other than the Head Human

Resources Honcho. The bosses had brought him in to discuss various items he was perfectly prepared to address; and one particular item, which no amount of proper previous planning could have helped a fig, was now the next topic on the agenda.

"What's the status of that man we arranged the early retirement for? Moskowitz, wasn't it?" asked the CEO.

"Right," answered the HHRH. "Myron Moskowitz."

"He has, I take it, already succumbed to that rare, whatever-it-was he'd been diagnosed with?"

The HHRH opened a file folder and feigned searching diligently for something in it.

"As a matter of fact, no. Or, not as such, at any rate."

"What do you mean, 'not as such'? Either the man's deceased, or he isn't. Which is it?"

"Mr. Moskowitz appears to still be very much of this world, according to our records."

"How can that be?" the Executive Vice President wondered aloud and somewhat dramatically. "When you first brought this to our attention, his soul was on final countdown to launch. And that was how many months ago?"

The HHRH decided to treat this question as rhetorical, for the simple reason that he really didn't want to answer it.

"So, does this Mr. Moskowitz show any signs of passing into the great beyond anytime soon?"

"We, er, have no indication of that," said the HHRH, after pretending to glance at the file again.

"So, what you're saying is, this man may continue to defy death?"

"We cannot discount that possibility."

"Conceivably for many years to come?"

"One can never completely predict these things, but that, er, scenario should not be too hastily ruled out."

"And we're obliged to keep paying him at full salary for the rest of his life?"

"That *was* the arrangement, yes."

"Remind me," demanded the CEO, CEO-ishly, "How did we originally find out about this alleged insurance-fund-annihilating condition?"

"From our health plan administrators," replied the Head Human Resources Honcho, un-honchoically. The Hibachi Room had a way of un-honchoing a person.

"Could they have been mistaken?" posed the Executive Vice President, who had the uncanny ability to stumble onto a conclusion only slightly after everybody else did. "Maybe there was just a typo or something."

"Interesting you should mention that," said the HHRH. "I seem to recall Mr. Moskowitz making quite a point of asserting that very explanation."

"And what did you say when he did?"

"I reminded him that he was hardly qualified to contradict a legitimate medical diagnosis, whereas our health plan administrators were experts in these matters."

"Experts, eh? I don't suppose these so-called experts would be willing to take over paying this Moskowitz's salary if he persists in staying alive?"

"No, I can't imagine they'd be particularly receptive to that suggestion," the HHRH agreed.

"Then, we've got to get Myron Moskowitz back to

work. Retired, he's costing us a small fortune. If he was here, at least we'd be getting something productive for our money."

The assembled heads grunted agreement.

"But, we've officially retired him."

"Well then, officially *un*retire him. Just get him back to work."

"A reverse retirement?" the Head Human Resources Honcho pondered aloud. "I don't think that's ever been done before! Can't we just hire him on as a consultant?"

"What, and pay him his full salary *plus* some outrageous consulting fee? You do realize we're in business to make a profit, right?"

"I'll have to call Legal."

"So, call Legal. Call Moral and Ethical, too, for all I care. Just get it done. Oh, and while you're at it, find another insurance administrator. Preferably, one that isn't run by idiots."

The Head Human Resources Honcho could not see how a reverse retirement under these circumstances could possibly work. With any luck, though, the Legal Department would do what it did best and obscure the issue so deeply that, in the end, it wouldn't really matter.

Elsewhere, something resembling love was in the air. This did not affect the Moskowitzes, though Mike could be said to have indirectly been the cause.

In the course of their working together to rectify the great Myron Moskowitz debacle, Jackie and Kermit had discovered that spark from which such things as epic poems and romantic comedies are ignited. On Kermit's side, the attraction was obvious: Jackie was, as we've mentioned, kinda hot, *and* she could write code. Her reasons were a little less obvious, but love is like that sometimes.

This state of affairs was yet another source of vexation for Dan, who fancied that, as the leader, he should be the one who got the girl.

None of this has any bearing on our story, except insofar as it made Dan more determined than ever to put Mr. Myron Moskowitz back on the map again once and for all.

Chapter 16

If the train ride out seemed to have been something of a trial, the return one delivered all the joy of a sentence of death by lethal injection. Even Mike was forced to concede that this had been an astonishingly bad idea, which was especially harsh in light of the fact that there really hadn't been any other choice.

That, too, has little bearing on our story, except insofar as it made Mike more determined than ever to put himself back on the map again once and for all.

The journey was even harder for Christine. Well, most things were, really. The seemingly endless rail trip had proved all the more frustrating for her, however, since she had greeted the initial cries of *all aboard!* with a definite mission and had disembarked at the terminal back home without having put the slightest dent in accomplishing it.

The problem was an anatomical one, if Christine's mind could somehow be considered part of her body. That was a frequent culprit in most of her angst, but it had managed to perform way above and beyond on this particular occasion. For, in attempting to look at the problem from too many angles at once, Christine had inadvertently rendered herself incapable of focusing intelligently on any single one of them. This, interspersed with stubborn bouts of mental paralysis, had proved unremittingly aggravating. And it hardly needs mentioning that an aggravated Christine was decidedly *not* a Christine at its best.

Complicating the issue was a nagging doubt that there even *was* one. Christine had begun to believe that her conclusion about Mike seeing another woman might have been just a tiny bit premature. She could not fault herself for it, of course—all the signs clearly pointed in that direction. Sure, it was *possible*, but she could not have spent virtually her entire adult life living with a guy without having a pretty good idea of his *modus operandi*. Extra-curricular nooky did not figure prominently in her husband's.

It was not entirely out of the question that other women might find Mike attractive, she acknowledged. Hell, she herself had found him attractive, once. The new physique didn't hurt any, either. Where those muscles had come from, who only knew? But they added a little mystery to an otherwise-un-mysterious Moskowitz, and Christine found this development slightly tingle-inducing.

However, while a person may be able to change parts of his body—for the better, even—he could not change his basic nature. Christine had heard or read that more than once, so obviously it must be true. And romantic rendezvous of the clandestine kind were not in Mike's nature. They were something other people did.

Still, the signs...The apparent contradiction had left her feeling hopelessly stumped. Which, again, has very little

---

bearing on our story, except insofar as it made Christine more determined than ever to get to the bottom of things.

The Head Human Resources Honcho once again found himself seated inside a company conference room. This time, it was one much closer to his own corporate stratum than the Hibachi Room had been. That he was at the moment sharing it with the better part of the Legal Department, however, mitigated any additional comfort he may have otherwise derived by the distinction.

He had just finished recounting in painstaking detail the events leading up to the expedited retirement of Myron Moskowitz. This was his third time repeating the exact same narrative, an irritating requirement he experienced any time he had to get anyone from Legal involved in anything. The HHRH had come to regard lawyers themselves as being the single best reason for never, ever wanting to need one.

"Now, would you mind repeating that part—" began one of the junior attorneys.

"Yes," interrupted the Head Human Resources Honcho.

"Sorry?"

"I said 'yes.' As in, yes, I *would* mind repeating that part, or indeed any other part." The HHRH missed the days when youth and enthusiasm at least had the good sense to keep its mouth shut.

"But you don't—"

"No."

"But—"

"No. Does anyone who was paying attention any of the numerous times I went over all this have any suggestions?"

Hands began to gesticulate as a genesis of sounds began taking form within individual throats.

"*Intelligent* ones?"

Hands fell back on the table, or wherever else post-gesticulating hands come to a landing. The corresponding silence resonated throughout the room.

"Hello? Anybody?"

Throats were cleared. Could speech be far behind? The HHRH bided his time in silence, expectantly panning the other faces. These, in turn, expectantly panned for somewhere else to be. Eye contact became an increasingly rare commodity just then.

Finally, the head of the General Counsel cleared *its* throat, drawing everyone's attention onto himself. Surveying the audience much as an emperor might his subjects, he spoke: "Remind me, whose idea was this, originally?"

"Yours, I think. Or, if you didn't outright suggest it, you were an unabashed enthusiast. A veritable cheerleader, one might say."

The head of the Legal Department shifted in his chair uneasily.

"Were there any minutes taken during that particular meeting?" he asked.

"No, and that definitely *was* your idea."

The General Counsel sighed in relief.

"Well, then! Problem solved!"

Try as he might, the HHRH failed to make that connection.

"Okay, I give up. How do you figure?"

"Simple. If there is no record of the decision to impose involuntary retirement on this Moskowitz fellow, then who's to say it really happened?"

Lawyerly noggins nodded around the table like a display of excessively groomed bobble-head dolls. The only head that was shaking belonged to the Head Human Resources Honcho.

"Yes, well, while the meeting you're referring to may not have been documented, the retirement itself generated enough paperwork to cover The Great Wall. That's in China, by the way," he added, addressing the aside to the youngster who'd seen fit to speak earlier. "We covered our corporate backside with an exceptional degree of thoroughness."

"Hmmm, that's going to present a problem. You should *never* do that, you know."

"Do what?"

"Put anything in writing. First thing they teach you in law school."

"But, that's the *law*!"

"Now, it's best you leave determinations like that up to us. We're the ones who are most qualified at that sort of thing."

It was a very long meeting. When it ended, as even an eternity in Hell must eventually, the General Counsel had pledged to review every conceivable aspect of the matter, leaving no detail unexamined. This was exactly the out-come the Head Human Resources Honcho had been banking on, which was at least some consolation after all was said and done.

As the final curtain closed on this brutal test of his endurance, the HHRH wishfully pictured himself sub-merged up to the neck in a gurgling hot tub assisted by a bottle of single-malt Scotch. He decided he might even settle for a partially-warm bubble bath and blended Scotch, or even just the Scotch without the accompanying aquatics. He did not believe one should set one's expecta-tions unnecessarily high.

Chapter 17

"**M**yron, that wife of yours is driving me slightly crazy. Will you *please* tell her, already?"

"Only slightly crazy? And she's back to being 'that wife of mine' again, eh?"

"You are intentionally missing the point. That wife, *Christine,* is convinced you're up to no good. She thinks you might even have a girlfriend on the side. I told her that was ridiculous. Hookers, maybe. But a regular girlfriend? Uh, uh. I didn't raise you that way."

"You told my wife I was seeing prostitutes?"

"No, I only suggested *maybe.* No one regular, though. You're much too smart to bring all that extra aggravation on yourself."

"And this was your idea of being helpful?"

"It's what a mother's for. I don't think she believed me, though."

"Thank goodness for that, at least."

"All in a day's work. Now, you've got to do something for me. Get Chris—that wife of yours—*off my back*!"

Christine, having gotten nowhere with Celia, summoned that determined something only marathon runners and aggrieved wives possess. This something consists of, in equal measure, determination, sheer willfulness, and the kind of focus that put men on the moon and invented the concept of reality television. If neither of the one person she elected to ask was willing to help, she reasoned, she would just have to help herself.

She considered what her strategy ought to be for a full eight seconds before settling on the most blatantly obvious one: she would tail Mike everywhere he went and find out what he did once he got there. A search online uncovered a self-published paperback entitled *Surveillance Techniques for Nitwits*, which Christine duly purchased with the near-certainty that, by doing so, she was opening herself up to every paranoiac nutcase group's special mailing list. Then again, she reminded herself, with the volume of junk mail her husband received on a daily basis, she doubted anyone in any sort of official capacity who might take a business interest in things like paranoiac nutcase groups would ever notice that one little needle in an otherwise massive Moskowitz haystack.

Her first step was to secure a convincing disguise or three. She gave this exponentially more thought than she'd given the whole idea of forming a one-woman surveillance detail, partly because short of dyeing her hair, plucking her eyebrows, getting her nose done, dieting, and periodic Botox injections, Christine had never done even the slightest thing to try and alter her appearance. Also, it required accessorizing, which was a process she took very seriously, indeed.

This did not absolutely require that she go shopping. Chances were very much in favor of Mike not recognizing anything she already owned to wear, or for that matter his even being aware of it if she stood directly in front of him in nothing but her birthday suit, if his mind was on anything else. Still, one could never be too sure, so Christine began compiling a list of the things she thought she would need to effect convincing suburban camouflage.

According to *Surveillance Techniques for Nitwits*, altering one's appearance did not require anything especially complicated. The tiniest alteration in body shape or color was usually sufficient to throw off one's quarry. Christine, of course, wasn't buying that at all. In for a pound if she was in for a penny, there would be no half-measures taken on her watch.

Mike left the house the next morning in the usual way. He drove off in the direction of his former job, as much out of muscle memory as any actual sense of purpose. But today the car motored along entirely on auto-pilot. Mike's mind wasn't within a mile of the steering wheel.

His retirement routine had by now long outgrown its original novelty. Unless something didn't change drastically, and soon, Mike could see himself turning into one of those weird guys who hung around parks and office buildings talking to people who weren't really there. Not that this lifestyle was entirely devoid of good points, per se. One just needed to be prepared to stay in it for the long haul, and Mike's long-term view did not extend quite that far these days.

Among the things Mike Moskowitz neglected to notice as a result of his present distractedness was his rear-view mirror. One moderately attentive glance in it would have revealed a car looking very much like his wife's attempting to keep a discreet distance behind him. It had, in fact, been attempting to do this since the moment he'd first left the house.

Keeping a discreet distance behind a moving vehicle you do not want to notice you is not nearly as easy as it looks in the movies, or, for that matter, as the authors of certain self-published manuals on the subject would lead one to believe. Stay too far back, and you risk losing your subject. Too close, and you're practically guaranteed to be caught outright.

Christine was having a difficult time both finding and keeping that perfect distance, but so far her husband had shown no sign of being aware she was back there. She attributed this bit of good fortune more to spousal invisibility than to any amount of skill on her own part, but was grateful for it nevertheless.

And this was probably all going to be just a huge waste of time, anyway. Mike was obviously sailing a course directly to work, where he would undoubtedly remain until the proverbial whistle blew and he'd sail a course directly back home again.

Christine was pondering her apparent exercise in futility when she was suddenly jolted to attention. Rather than proceeding straight like he was supposed to, Mike's car made an unexpected right-hand turn into a strip mall parking lot, coming to a stop in front of a national chain coffee-based beverage emporium.

She pulled in behind him, narrowly avoiding being broadsided by a massive SUV that was in the process of backing out. Its driver honked his horn at her reprovingly (she assumed he was a him), panicking Christine that the commotion would cause Mike to turn around and thus blow her cover. But she need not have worried. The noise might as well have been happening the next town over as far as her husband was concerned.

She parked a short way down, effectively concealing herself within a row of cars which were mostly larger than her own. Mike, still sitting in his own car, could not be seen very clearly from this limited vantage point; but she would be able to spot him the moment he got out of it, at least if he had the good sense to keep moving forward. So far this had not happened yet, and enough time had elapsed to start gnawing at Christine's curiosity. Before she could decide what to do next, however, Mike came into view and could be observed abstractedly entering the coffee shop.

Surveillance Techniques for Nitwits describes the static watching post as the single biggest challenge to the practitioner of the stalking arts. According to the guide's author, static watching is either a necessary evil or a mixed blessing, depending on just how pessimistic the operator is feeling at any given time. It has the potential to be the most mind-numbing activity since, well, ever. Keeping one's attention sharp against attack from distractions, both real and invented by a restless brain straining at the chains of confinement, becomes a nearly superhuman effort for both the professional and the amateur alike. This is because one's head—and, for that matter, one's butt—feels keenly the desire to be doing absolutely anything else.

It is, however, while thus engaged that eventually whatever is going to happen, usually will. One is therefore encouraged to at least try and remain patient and hope like mad that events take their course sooner rather than later.

Unfortunately, Christine did not possess an overabundance of that virtue and was generally inclined to its exact opposite where her husband was concerned. So, after waiting far beyond what it should have taken for Mike to grab a cup of whatever to go, she began to get antsy. Studying her watch, she decided to give him five more minutes before going active.

Ignoring the admonition of *Surveillance Techniques for Nitwits* to stay focused on the target, Christine allowed her thoughts to drift onto nothing in particular until, when she next glanced down at her chronometered wrist, a full twenty minutes had gone by and Mike's car was no longer where she logically expected it to be.

Uttering a mild imprecation, Christine started her own car, turning the ignition and popping it into reverse almost simultaneously. Once her side window had cleared the tallest part of the vehicle next to her, she could see Mike's car pulling out of the parking lot at a leisurely speed. Christine uttered a slightly less-mild imprecation and frantically tore off after it.

From the exit, work was to the right. Mike turned left. Christine turned left, too, and was convinced now beyond a shadow of a doubt that she was right: something was definitely rotten in the state of Moskowitz.

Mike was...something. He was in a funk, at loose ends and unraveling all at once. As if to make matters worse, his brain felt as if someone had poured some sort of opaque, viscous liquid over it, muddling his cerebral functions annoyingly. He could not even remember leaving the house that morning, though he did have a vague recollection of Christine paying closer attention to him than was normal for her so early in the day.

He had found himself parked in front of his morning coffee haunt after being only dimly aware of having driven there, and had continued his morning in much the same vein. At the gym, Mike's exercise routine seemed even more mechanical than the equipment he'd been working out on. Lunch helped snap him out of it for a little while. But the dilemma over how to kill the next several hours snapped him right back into it again.

He wondered how most of the old people he knew managed to retire and stay so happy all the time. The fact that they weren't trying to keep it a secret probably didn't hurt, he thought. Then, none of them were married to Christine, either.

And speaking of Christine, there was something Christine-related nagging at the back of Mike's mind, but try as he could he could not put his finger on it. There was a slight hint of having spotted her back in the coffee shop parking lot, but that was impossible. What on Earth could

she have been doing there? No, it must have been someone
else. He forgot the matter, hoping that whatever image was
playing hide-and-seek within his brain would come to him
if he wasn't thinking too hard about it.

Mike then recalled with vivid, the-way-he-remem-
bered-it memory, the meeting in the Head Human Resources Honcho's office when he'd first learned of his
impending retirement. Once the initial shock had worn off,
it had seemed like the perfect arrangement: getting paid
for not working. Kind of like what the government did for
farmers to keep the price of things like fruits and vegeta-
bles from becoming too affordable. If he got bored, he had
reasoned at the time, he could always find another job, just
to keep his hand in, as it were.

Except that getting a job when one did not, technically,
exist, was pretty much an impossibility in this identi-
ty-obsessed day and age. Can't prove who you are? Then,
you need not apply. Off the radar? Sorry, Mr. Hiring
Manager can't see you now.

If only the HHRH would call and tell him this had all
been one big, terrible mistake.

Christine's mind was working. Overtime, that is to say.

"That's it!" she thought. "He's lost his job and is afraid
to tell me!"

Which theory did not explain the continued, di-
rect-deposit of her husband's regular paycheck.

"I know, he's taking a mental health day," she thought
next. But this, too, sounded impractical on a number of

levels, especially when you took into account her reckoning of the state of Mike's mental health.

Christine continued her tail until mid-afternoon, by
which time she was even more in the dark than she'd been
before the sun had first peaked its little yellow head over
the distant horizon that morning.

Celia had not heard from her Christine all day. She
wondered what was wrong, and if it was maybe because of
something *she,* Celia, had said or done. Daughters-in-law
could be so sensitive, sometimes.

Chapter 18

The Hibachi Room felt warm, even by Hibachi Room standards. The Head Human Resources Honcho noted this, as well as the extreme unlikelihood that the temperature would drop even slightly as long as he was confined to being there.

The HHRH had gambled that, once the Legal Department had been brought into the Moskowitz picture, irresolution would linger until the whole issue eventually joined the ranks of the out of sight, out of mind.

There is always a risk when one assumes their superiors have conveniently short memories. While this may quite often be the case, it is nearly impossible to predict with any degree of certainty when a higher-up will decide that something is worth paying a great deal of attention to; and apparently the Myron Moskowitz matter had, to the considerable misfortunate of the HHRH, proved to be just one of those somethings. As Desi might have said to Lucy, he had some serious 'splainin' to do.

"Has this Moskowitz business been resolved yet?" asked the CEO, who, as he usually did, already knew the answer.

"Um, no, not yet," was the already-known reply.

"Why not?"

"Well, sir, you see, I had been waiting for some guidance from the Legal Department, and, well, frankly, sir, they have not been especially helpful."

"I didn't tell the Legal Department to solve this," reminded the CEO. "I told *you* to solve this. Do you want me to put it in writing?"

The Head Human Resources Honcho did not want the CEO to put *anything* in writing.

"No, that won't be necessary," he said glumly. "I'll handle it."

"Please, if it wouldn't be too much trouble. Have you at least dumped that idiot insurance administrator you were using?"

"It's, um, in the works."

The CEO was becoming impatient, and impatient CEOs are generally not creatures to be on the wrong side of.

"What the hell does that mean?" he fairly erupted. "Either you canned them or you didn't! Pick one!"

"Changing benefits administrators is a complicated process. There are audits to be conducted, papers to file. These things take time. Not to mention all the potential legal issues."

"Ah, so it's the Legal Department's fault again, is it?"

Two more minutes of this and the Head Human Resources Honcho would be ready for basting.

It was a Big Meeting night, and Dan had not intended to go. In the end, unlimited free beer had won out over his self-respect. It usually did.

He was representing the Itinerant Life & Casualty Company cell on several matters, but the one that trumped them all was the one whose name he dared not speak. There had, two meetings past, been talk of banning Dan from ever coming back again if the words Myron and/or Moskowitz were heard emanating from his direction from that moment until the end of time. This, as far as he was concerned, would not have made the list of the harshest punishments he'd ever received. Not by a long shot. But being forcibly evicted would not have helped Mr. Moskowitz any, and above all Dan wanted to see the guy's life restored to whatever had once been considered normal for him.

He and his cellmates, or whatever you'd call them, had argued strategy late into the previous night regarding how to bring the issue up without Dan being summarily thrown out on his ear. In the end it was decided that Dan should approach a few of the key nuclei individually immediately following the main proceedings, after first handing each in turn a fresh beer. This had been Jackie's idea. Kermit had declared it completely brilliant just like the whipped puppy dog he was these days.

So this Dan duly did. He waited until the group's business had been thoroughly conducted, then set out to button-hole members of the head table one by one, a spare beer always at the ready. According to the plan, once he'd gotten them talking, Dan's job was to *keep* them talking, and on the only topic he really cared about. The first pair thus cornered recognized immediately what Dan was trying to do, and weren't falling for it. The third time, however, proved to be a charm. An indeterminately-aged techie geek from a local benefits administration company (which was presently in the process of losing one of its biggest clients, as it happened) had been the victim. Dan got him on a roll before the guy had caught even the faintest whiff of what he had just walked into.

"Have you tried the Bedouins?" said techie geek inquired.

"The who?" Dan replied, quite understandably.

"The Bedouins. You know who they are, don't you?" The techie geek was on the verge of thinking he was perhaps about to say something he shouldn't. Fortunately, he was only on the verge of thinking it.

"Um, I'm not sure. Remind me." Dan smiled encouragingly.

"They're a group of folks who are in the same boat as your Markowitz—"

"*Mos*kowitz."

"Moskowitz, then. They all fell off the radar one way or another, usually while one of us was trying to be helpful. Now they're like a secret society."

"Why are they called the Bedouins? Do they wander around like nomads or something?"

"No, nothing like that. They just think they're 'Bedouin' the rest of us. It's a joke, if you go in for that sort of thing. Which, frankly, I don't."

"And how does one get a hold of them?"

The saying-too-much thought began steadily creeping back into the techie geek's mind.

"Um, no offense or anything, but I've probably told you more than I really should have."

"Too late now. C'mon, out with it. How do I get in touch with these guys?"

The techie geek reluctantly relented.

"But you didn't hear that from me."

"Hear *what* from you?" Dan asked slyly.

"About the Bedouins, who their leader is, where to find them...that."

Not slyly enough though, apparently.

The Head Human Resources Honcho was sitting at his desk, his door closed, staring at his telephone. He had been staring at his telephone for nearly two hours, shifting occasionally as the need arose. The telephone, meanwhile, hadn't moved a muscle.

He would have much rather done what he was about to do via email. But the CEO's parting words—"and for God's sake, pick up the phone! I don't want you communicating something this important in an email!"—had pretty much killed that option outright.

Glancing at his computer longingly, he picked up the receiver, sighed and dialed Myron Moskowitz's home number.

It rang five times before going into voicemail. No, it wasn't even voicemail. It was one of those old-fashioned answering machines! In fact, it really *was* voicemail, only for some reason the HHRH experienced a glimmer of satisfaction in believing it wasn't. He hung up without leaving a message.

The Head Human Resources Honcho contemplated this, which was a bit of a feat considering how little there was in what had just transpired for him to think about. Having made the attempt once seemed to embolden him, however, so he tried again. And again and, dare we say it, again. No live person answered at any time. The HHRH left no messages in retaliation. For a brief moment he wondered if Mike had gotten another job somewhere else and wasn't sure whether or not this would be a good outcome for either one of them.

Having run out of things to do and the will to do them, Mike pulled into his driveway more than an hour earlier than was his usual custom. Christine's car was not in its place in the garage, which at least temporarily saved him from having to explain his own premature presence.

As he went through the ritual dumping of his pocket stuff on various surfaces throughout the house, Mike noticed the telephone light blinking, indicating people had called. Figuring none of them were for him, but then assuming that they probably weren't for Christine, either, he decided to check for messages.

There weren't any. But the caller I.D. showed the number of Mike's former employer, and showed it several times in close succession, to boot.

Mike's eyes opened wide. His hitherto depressed vital

signs sprang suddenly back to life, and with a vengeance. As far as he could work out on such short notice, there could only be two reasons for someone from work, or what used to be work, calling him. It was a classic good news/bad news scenario. On the bad news side, they had no doubt by now realized that he hadn't died the messy, horrendous and monetarily exorbitant death their experts had predicted, and they wanted their pension money back. The good news option would be that they had realized all of the above, and wanted *him* back. Of course, the answer might actually turn out to be some really inconvenient combination of the two, but it was best not to get carried away too hastily solely on the basis of a single familiar telephone number.

Mike was still in the land of endless possibilities when the telephone rang, snapping him back to a somewhat startled reality. At first, he could not remember exactly what one was supposed to do when that shrill alarm sounded. But suddenly the correct course of action dawned on him, and he grabbed the receiver a split second before it was too late.

His heart was racing, anticipating, as it was, that the voice on the other end of the line belonged to an official from his former company. It dropped precipitously, however, when the caller turned out to be only Dan.

"Mr. Moskowitz? Hi, it's Dan."

Mike quickly ran through the list of possible replies to this disappointing announcement, and concluded that he didn't like any of them.

"Hello? Mr. Moskowitz? "

"I'm here."

"Oh, um, good. Do you have a minute? I have some news."

To a man obsessed with having altogether more minutes than he knew what to do with, this was not an ideal question.

"*Good* news?"

Dan hesitated thoughtfully before answering.

"I'm not really sure."

Deja vu all over again, thought Mike.

"Well? Are you planning on sharing this news, or were you only calling to let me know of its existence?"

"No, no, this is definitely something you should know about. Probably."

Just then, Mike heard Christine's car pulling into the drive.

"All right. But now's not the best time. Can you meet me somewhere?"

Dan suggested their unknowingly mutual coffee hangout. Mike was surprised that, of all the coffee hangouts in all the towns in all the world, Dan would pick that one, but they arranged a rendezvous for later that evening.

When he hung up, Mike heard the universal voicemail beep, indicating there was a new message. It was from the Head Human Resources Honcho, urging Mike to phone him at his earliest convenience, and the earlier that convenience the better.

Christine walked in just then, shooting her husband a confused look. Mike shot her a confused look right back. If this had been a confused look contest, the judges would have been forced to declare it a draw.

Chapter 19

Mike and Dan arrived at their unbeknownst-to-them mutual coffee shop hangout at the same time. Then Dan led Mike to their unbeknownst-to-them mutual table at the back.

Neither felt particularly compelled to order anything, but both did anyway. For Dan, the smell of strong coffee triggered some sort of primal, Pavlovian desire in him to want some. Mike had ordered one, and when in aroma...

"Mr. Moskowitz, thanks for meeting me on such short notice."

"Seemed like the least I could do, considering it was my idea. So, I'm curious, how did you pick this place, of all places?"

"My friends and I come here all the time. It was the first place that came to mind."

"Ah, well, that explains it, then. Do you usually sit here?" Mike asked, gesturing toward the table.

"Whenever we can."

Just coincidence, Mike assured himself. Just some funny coincidence. No psychic connection, or anything weird like that.

"In fact, Mr. M., we're usually here discussing you."

Coincidence. Not psychic weirdness. Coincidence, coincidence, not psychic weirdness. Coincidence...

"Mr. Moskowitz?"

"You know, Dan, you might as well call me Mike. I mean, seeing as you know so much about me and everything."

"I know, but don't worry, Mr., er, Mike. I've forgotten most of it. I swear!"

"I'm sure you have. Come to think of it, you were probably right. 'Mister Moskowitz' is probably a much better idea."

Neither knew quite what to say after that. Finally, Dan began.

"Here's the thing, Mr. M. You remember what happened to you when we tried to remove that ridiculous diagnostic code?"

And they say there are no stupid questions.

"Vaguely," replied Mike, unwilling to believe he had just been asked that particular stupid question and, even more incredulously, by whom.

"Huh? Oh, I get it. Of course. I mean, you couldn't exactly forget something like that, right? Um, yeah. Anyway, apparently this sort of thing has happened before. Lots of times, as it turns out. In fact, you'd be amazed at just *how* many times something like, well, you, has happened."

Mike stared hard at his uncomfortable companion.

"You mean to tell me that you and your cohorts have screwed up other people like this? Frequently?"

"No, not me and my cohorts," Dan responded, somewhat defensively. "Other people and *their*, um, cohorts."

"And is this knowledge supposed to make me feel better?"

"No. Well, yes. Maybe. There's more. Some of the others, you know, in your, ah, situation, have banded together and formed a group."

"Like a rock group?"

It took Dan a second to remember what a rock group was.

"More like a social group. They call themselves the Bedouins."

"Move around a lot, do they?"

"No, they just think they're 'Bedouin the rest of us'."

It took Mike a second to remember what humor was.

"So there's a club. How, exactly, does that help me?"

"Well, I thought you might want to consider joining it."

"Why? Do you get discounts at restaurants and things? I mean, what would be the point?"

"These guys have been at this a lot longer. Maybe they've figured out how to navigate the grid when you're not officially on it anymore."

Okay, so maybe there *was* a point, after all.

"Sounds logical. Now how would I go about finding these Nomads?"

"Bedouins."

"Bedouins, if I felt inclined to?"

"You can't. They're invisible. Comes with being off the map."

Mike sighed impatiently. "So then, what are we doing here?" He rose to leave.

"Wait! You can't find them, but they can find *you*."

Mike sat back down. "And how do they propose to do that? I'm off the map, too, remember?"

"True, but you're not as far off the map as they are. If you'd like, I can get that particular ball rolling, so to speak."

Mike considered this. On the one hand, he was feeling a bit like Alice staring down into the rabbit hole. On the other hand, what did he have to lose?

Then he remembered his nearly desperate-sounding message from the Head Human Resources Honcho.

"Let me get back to you on that."

He left with his coffee-based beverage still untouched. Dan, not liking to see a perfectly good cup of overpriced java go to waste, made quick work of it. The result of which was he did not manage to fall asleep that night until an exceptionally boring staff meeting the following morning.

While Dan was dozing, Mike was dialing. He could not believe he was actually back at the same table he had vacated less than twelve hours earlier. But, and this was the current bane of his existence, he could think of nowhere else to be other than that stupid coffee shop.

The Head Human Resources Honcho was waiting for his call.

"Mr. Moskowitz! What a nice surprise!"

"Really? I had the distinct impression you were expecting this."

"Oh, I'm not surprised you called. Well, maybe I am, a little. Mainly, I'm just surprised you're still...how shall I put this...in any position to."

"Obviously, you haven't been keeping up with the obituaries. If you were, you would have realized I haven't been featured in any of them lately."

Once the pleasantries had been exchanged, Mike agreed to swing by the Head Human Resources Honcho's office.

"Well, here I am," Mike announced when he'd arrived and settled into the HHRH's guest chair. "Still above ground and lumbering along under my own steam, as they say."

"And pleased we are of that, I can assure you, Mr. Moskowitz. In fact, I would not be exaggerating if I told you that the CEO has taken a personal interest in the state of your health and well-being."

Mike considered inquiring into the state of the CEO's own health and well-being, but concluded that he didn't really care. He assumed the Head Human Resources Honcho had some ulterior motive for this unanticipated little *tète-a-tète* besides a keen interest in the general state of his health and well-being. Particularly since the Head Human Resources Honcho hadn't expected there to be any. Mike decided to play coy, and hoped that meant what he thought it did.

"So, was that it, then?" he asked, coyly.

"Well, no, ah, as a matter of fact, Mr. Moskowitz."

Mike remembered he had been deprecatingly Myron at their last encounter.

"You see, the CEO really *did* bring your name up recently," the HHRH continued, without a trace of blatant understatement. "It had somehow come to his attention that, despite what the so-called experts at our benefits administrator—*former* benefits administrator, I should say—lead us to believe, you weren't...that is, you hadn't...didn't...Well, that you are still, as it were, alive."

Mike could not tell yet whether the CEO had regarded this as a good thing or a bad thing, but it was always nice to be noticed by those higher up along the food chain.

"Was that a passing observation, or did he have an opinion on the subject?"

The HHRH smiled, sort of. It was more of a smirk, really.

"I'm glad you asked," he replied, again without a trace of blatant understatement. "He thought it was tragic the way such a valued, long-term employee was being denied the opportunity to make his rightful contribution as a member of the company's team. 'A darned shame,' I think he said. I'm sure he used the word tragedy at least twice. Seemed to genuinely miss having you around."

The Head Human Resources Honcho smiled again, this time allowing a few of his front teeth to peek out for the briefest instant. Contrary to Mike's belief, none of them ended in vein-piercing spikes.

"Is that right? And all this time I thought getting rid of me had been his idea."

"Yes, well, he now feels that decision might have been

arrived at somewhat hastily. Especially in light of the circumstances."

"What circumstances?"

"You still being here, for one thing. Not experiencing the coffers-depleting end you were supposed to. Er, expected to. *Predicted* to, I mean. By our benefits administrator. *Former* benefits administrator. Let me make that clear."

The light bulb suddenly flashed over Mike's head as to why he was there. Actually, it only started blinking, but things were beginning to make sense.

"In other words," he guessed, correctly, "it finally dawned on him that he was paying me for doing nothing, and under the terms of our agreement—his own, I might add—he is going to have to keep on paying me for continuing to do nothing for what will probably be an excruciatingly long time."

"I believe he may have mentioned something to that effect," the HHRH acknowledged, yet again without any visible trace of understatement.

"Presumably," Mike continued, "he finds this arrangement less than optimal?"

"One could say that, yes."

Mike tried to guess what might be coming next as quickly as he could without seriously straining anything. If the CEO was reconsidering this whole early retirement business, it could mean he'd be offered his old job back. And while that job might not have been anything to brag about, it had been his, and he'd lately been regarding it with the peculiar sense of longing one might feel for an absent appendage.

Then, there was the possibility the CEO was planning to renege on the original deal, with the threat of a protracted legal battle dangled menacingly overhead. Mike had never had much contact with the company's legal department, but he had no doubt they were perfectly capable of stalling the procedural taxi indefinitely, with the meter still running.

"Mr. Moskowitz?"

"Present."

"I've been told—asked, that is—to let you know on behalf of our senior management that the company misses you. In fact, they—we—miss you so much, we'd really appreciate it if you'd come back." The Head Human Resources Honcho felt instantly lighter, as if an enormous burden had just fallen like a heavy avalanche from his shoulders. Which, in a manner of speaking, one just had. Understatement and all.

Mike paused to ponder this. Here was exactly the outcome he had been hoping for since first listening to the HHRH's voicemail message the previous evening. He should be feeling ecstatic. He should be turning summersaults right about now. He should be blurting out, "When do I start?" at a volume totally incommensurate with the small, confined office space whose air hung saturated with anticipation. Instead, he said in his firmest voice:

"Forget it."

Christine, bewildered beyond her capacity for such things

by her husband's sudden, unexplained departure after dinner, had followed him again when he left the house the following morning. She noted the coffee stop, and was bracing herself for a repeat of the day before. But when Mike pulled into his company's parking lot and walked like a condemned man into the building's main entrance, she decided that whatever yesterday's aberration had been it was now over and everything had once again been restored to normal. She could deal with the ramifications of whatever *that* meant some other time.

"**W**hat do you mean, 'Forget it'?" asked an unhappy CEO. As previously noted, angry CEOs are things best steered well clear of.

"Those were his exact words," replied a differently-unhappy Head Human Resources Honcho. "Showed a definite lack of company spirit, if you ask me."

"Company spirit? This is about *money*, for crying out loud!"

"A lot of money," chimed the Executive Vice President, who had been invited mainly to take notes.

"I expect you to find a way to bring this Moskowitz back into the fold." Then, softening his tone a little, but only a little, the CEO added: "I may even be able to provide a little financial incentive if you can somehow manage to pull this off."

"Really?" asked a somewhat brightened HHRH. "What kind of financial incentive?"

"The continuation of your already over-inflated salary!

Now, get out, and don't come back without a Moskowitz!"

"**M**yron, I love you like you were my own son," said Celia maternally. "But explain to me. Please. What in the name of hell were you thinking?"

Mike sat at his mother's kitchen table with his head in his hands. His hair, an already endangered species, was in serious jeopardy of becoming even more so.

"Mom, if I could answer that question, I wouldn't have to."

Chapter 20

Still smarting from having thrust his foot so vigorously into his mouth, Mike arrived early for the rendezvous with Dan and his band of Bedouins. Or rather, *somebody's* band of Bedouins—Dan had disavowed any personal ownership of them.

Their meeting place was the same abandoned drive-in as last time. Mike wondered if the lot was available for weddings and bar-mitzvahs, or limited itself to clandestine loitering by gangs of geeks and weirdoes.

As before, he was the first to arrive. Just for old times' sake, he pulled into the same spot as last time, or at least he was fairly sure he did. One speaker post tended to look remarkably like every other one out there. No, on further consideration, he just knew he'd gotten it right. Mike had already begun thinking of that slot as his, which, in a strange, pathetic way sent his self-esteem spiraling hopelessly down onto the heavily crack-lined asphalt.

Dan pulled in shortly afterward and parked a few spaces away. Mike wasn't sure why, since the two men were practically comrades-in-arms by now. He performed a cursory under-arm sniff and, convinced that wasn't the reason, wasn't sure why all over again.

Dan did not appear to be in any hurry to join Mike, either. He sat in his car not doing anything, pretending to play with a cell phone only after becoming aware that Mike was staring at him.

Giving up on trying to figure out whom to call, text or email, Dan climbed out of his car and walked slowly over to Mike's, stopping first to make sure his doors were safely locked. Against whom or what was anybody's guess.

"Hi, Mr. M. I guess the Bedouins haven't arrived yet."

He can probably predict yesterday's weather, too, thought Mike. "Unless they got here ridiculously early and left already, no, I suppose they haven't."

Dan took the sarcasm for nervousness, instead of anything more personal. It was a sort of gift he had. "So, have you thought about what you're going to say?"

"Well, I figured I'd start off with something innocuous, like 'Nice to meet you.' But since they don't exist, I'm not sure that would be entirely appropriate."

"Kinda like a Zen riddle, huh?"

"Do you even know what that means?"

"Um, not exactly. But maybe the knowing is in the not-knowing, if you get my drift." Zen humor.

My life is in the hands of an idiot, Mike lamented with a twinge of silent woe.

The twinge did not have an opportunity to blossom into more full-blown woe, however, as the people who did not exist began funneling through the drive-in's entrance. There were, Mike noticed at once, rather a lot of them, and they were all on motorcycles.

Dan stiffened, realizing almost as soon as he had done so that his reaction was perhaps a little excessive and disconcertingly obvious. He tried to wiggle and dance his way out of potential embarrassment, succeeding only in drawing every Bedouin eye onto his frenetic, marionette form. He worried Mike might begin to suspect there was something seriously wrong with him, though he needn't have. His companion already considered him an idiot. Flopping around like one only seemed par for the course.

Mike took the scene unfolding in the drive-in's parking lot in stride. When you trust your life to a moron, he concluded, you deserved what you got. He was just working out a way to remove himself politely when one of the bikers pulled away from the pack and rode slowly over. Mike had a feeling the dramatic approach was supposed to look slightly menacing, like something out of a fifties movie. But since the guy wasn't exactly Marlon Brando behind the controls, the effect was more driver's test than *The Wild One*.

Within a theatrical eventually, Mike found himself facing a man of around his own age, dressed more like someone who lived in a bubble's idea of what a serious biker ought to look like, with a week's growth of salt-and-pepper beard on his face and a red bandana tied over his head. It was truly not a good look for him. To be fair, though, it would not have been a good look for any-body.

"Which of you is the guy?" he asked, in a voice pitched somewhat higher than might have reasonably been ex-pected under the circumstances.

Dan wasn't quite sure how to answer that. He extended a hand—or rather, an arm with a hand attached to it—which he quickly withdrew. He next attempted a pointing-like gesture, aimed approximately Mike-ward. All the while Dan's mouth kept making opening and closing motions, but no voice managed to find its way out. Sound seemed to be experiencing technical difficulties at the moment. Mike came to his rescue.

"I suppose you mean me," he said.

"Paco," the newcomer announced, extending a gloved hand.

"Mike," replied Mike, examining the gloved hand a moment before reaching out for it.

Neither man spoke next. Instead, each studied the other's face as if trying to recollect something. Finally, Mike broke the silence.

"You seem familiar."

"I was thinking the same thing about you."

"Not with the beard, though."

"It's pretty new."

Suddenly, Mike knew.

"Herman? Herman Rabinowitz?"

"Mike Moskowitz! Of course! I knew I knew you." Which he had since around the second grade.

"What's with this get-up?" Mike asked, waving his hand in the direction of said get-up. "And where did you come up with 'Paco'?"

His old schoolmate beamed.

"That's the beauty of being off the grid! You can to-tally reinvent yourself."

"Yeah, but you're about as un-Paco a Paco as ever drew breath."

"Exactly! That was the whole idea!"

Mike decided to postpone trying to figure out the line of reasoning behind that proposition until later. Or better yet, not at all.

"Come on, I'll introduce you to the gang."

Introductions were duly made, hands were duly shaken, and Paco, a.k.a., Herman Rabinowitz, proceeded to explain the Bedouins.

"It all started with me," he began proudly. "Some joker in Kazakhstan or Mongolia or some damn place like that got cute and stole my identity. You know, you really need to be careful about just how much personal information you share with internet porn sites. But that's a whole 'nother story.

"Anyway, whoever stole my identity did such a great job of it that, by the time the credit agencies and everyone else finished cleaning up the mess, they'd cleaned me up, too. Dumped the baby with the bath water, so to speak. You probably have a pretty good idea of exactly how things went from there."

Mike did, indeed.

The rest of the Bedouins had similar stories. Government lackeys around the country had somehow gotten it into their heads that they no longer existed and, despite all physical evidence to the contrary, utterly refused to be convinced otherwise. Or else a transposed number somewhere along the way had triggered a chain of other transposed numbers, until they were no longer recognizable anywhere numbers actually meant anything. Which, unfortunately, is everywhere nowadays.

"I can't believe there are so many of you," Mike observed.

"Heck, this is just the membership committee. We left the others at home."

Mike still couldn't believe it, until his gaze landed on Dan and it suddenly seemed a lot less implausible.

"And there's no record of you anywhere?"

"My college alumni office has even given up looking for me."

Q.E.D.

Mike and, he could hardly bring himself to say it, Paco, caught up on old times for a bit, sharing stories from their boyhood to the passive indifference of some of the more proximate Bedouins. After a time, or a couple of times, Mike addressed a question to anyone who might care to answer it:

"So, what's a guy fresh off the grid supposed to do?"

"Stop worrying," suggested one.

"Move around in total peace and freedom," suggested another, who did not know Christine.

"Get yourself a Harley!" declared a beaming Paco. "Oh, and by the way, how's that mother of yours?"

Convinced that I was switched at birth, probably, thought Mike. Or at least, hoping.

Later, on the phone with Celia, Mike mentioned running into the former Herman Rabinowitz.

"Remember Herman, Mom? He hung out at the house a lot when we were kids."

"Had to use the bathroom a lot? And he always seemed to have a cold, I think. Good manners, though."

"He had allergies. Yeah, that's him. He asked after you."

"If I was still alive, you mean?"

"No, he just sort of took that for granted. Asked me to send his regards."

"That was thoughtful of him. He was always such a polite boy."

You should only see him now, Mike mused.

He told his mother about the Bedouins while omitting most of the sillier details, which pretty much left out the bulk of them.

"It might not be a bad way to go. Travel the open road, no worries—"

"Myron, listen to me. Put your pride where the sun doesn't shine and go ask for your old job back. Beg, grovel if you have to. Plead temporary insanity. Anything! And quit futzing around with these Bed Linens."

"Bedouins."

"Myron!"

"All right, Mom, I'll think about it. Okay?"

"Enough with the thinking. Grovel, already!"

"Goodbye, Mother."

"Goodbye, dear."

Chapter 21

The Head Human Resources Honcho informed his assistant that he was leaving for a meeting outside the office and did not know whether he'd be back again. He did not add the word *ever*, though the thought had occurred to him.

He made quick time through the company parking lot to his car, then drove a short distance up the road to a small strip mall which, among other things, was home to a branch of a popular coffee establishment. He ordered an unnecessarily complicated, coffee-based beverage, found a seat at a table near the back, flipped open his laptop, and instantly looked just like everyone else in the place. Better dressed though, of course.

The CEO had laid his options out for him in language which left no room for interpretation. Option One: get Myron Moskowitz back to work. Option Two: there was no Option Two.

If only this Moskowitz character could have been even a bit more cooperative. If only the guy hadn't rejected the idea of coming back so completely out-of-hand, after it was presented to him practically with a bow. If only...well, let's face it: if only the bastard had been a good sport and kicked off like he was supposed to, none of this would make one iota of difference.

As he said that final *if* to himself, he realized it sounded mean, calloused, and excessively harsh. Good, he thought. If he could have come up with an even meaner, more calloused, and excessively harsher way to put it, he would have readily done so. But he couldn't and so, ultimately, he didn't.

It was just like the CEO to blame him, too. Granted, he wasn't entirely wrong there. Technically, the early retirement business had been someone else's brainchild, even if the HHRH had assumed a lion's share of the credit. A rather large lion, in fact, and one altogether accustomed to getting his own way. But the CEO was acting as if he'd only just heard about it, when the entire C-suite of executives had embraced the plan with the exuberance of a tailgate party at the time.

The Head Human Resources Honcho directed his next set of vituperative vibes to the company's now-former benefits administrator. How could they have believed that a sub-equatorial disease, declared officially extinct over a century ago, had miraculously found its way into the bloodstream of one of their erstwhile clients? What part of *extinct* did they fail to understand, for crying out loud? And why hadn't he listened when Moskowitz told him that the whole, stupid misunderstanding had been brought about by a simple, errant keystroke?

That last one the HHRH actually knew the answer to. He had, he recalled, been so euphoric over the unabashed adulation senior management had heaped upon his "solution" that the prospect of Myron Moskowitz's survival had no place cluttering up the scenario whatsoever. It was simply not invited to the dance.

And yet, it *had* been a possibility, and the winning one at that. Worse, his unnecessarily complicated, coffee-based beverage had gone cold, and he would now have to order another one. Good thing he still had a company credit card, he thought.

If he had any intention of keeping said company credit card, however, he was going to have to get Myron Moskowitz back to the bargaining table, and pronto. Unfortunately, the other man seemed to hold all the aces just then. But folding his own hand was not an option. The Head Human Resources Honcho was going to have to come up with one seriously spectacular bluff, or risk losing his immense personal stake in the game.

Being something of an amateur poker player, the HHRH knew that successful bluffing meant thoroughly understanding your opponent's strengths and weaknesses. Not knowing any of Myron Moskowitz's other than an uncannily robust state of physical health, he decided to find out everything else there could possibly be to know about the man. As soon as he got back to the office, the Head Human Resources Honcho concluded, he would engage the services of a good private detective.

By now his replacement beverage, too, had gone cold. Only this time, it didn't seem to matter quite so much.

Had the Head Human Resources Honcho pulled out of the strip mall parking lot a trifling thirty seconds later than he in fact did, he might have seen the object of his aggravation driving in. He might even have noticed Mike Moskowitz parking in the exact space he had just vacated, and equally possibly proceeding to the exact same coffee shop as well. He certainly would not have witnessed the man heading back to the exact same table. And, of course, would not have heard him disparaging the table's previous occupants for leaving a mess. The beverages thereupon were hardly touched, Mike observed as he relocated the cold remains of two overly-complicated, coffee-based beverages to another table. Some people are just lazy pigs, he declared to no one in particular.

There is only one thing worse than having other people making decisions over your destiny, and that is having to do all that destiny-decision-making yourself. It was bad enough having no control of events, but being alone in the driver's seat was creating a whole new world of headaches for an already achy-headed Myron Moskowitz.

A big part of the problem was the fact that, the more Mike thought about it, the more appealing the Bedouins' lifestyle seemed to be. He found too many good points to list without inadvertently counting at least a few of them twice. It would have been far easier to count the points against it, and so far Mike had not been able to come up with any.

Yet there was resistance gnawing at him from somewhere in the far recesses of his skull. Words like *responsibility* and *wrong* kept flashing on and off like some not-so-subliminal, subliminal message, *holding* him back from doing something *stupid* and *regrettable*. Guilt, for lack of anything better to call it. Guilt, moreover, that had been meticulously instilled and nurtured in him since the moment his nostrils first slipped free of the birth canal and sampled their introductory whiff of ambient air. Somewhere, once again, Celia nodded approvingly.

Then, there was Christine. Not a huge factor in his decision making, to be sure, but he still had to live with her. It was too much to ask that she might remain blissfully ignorant about his present state of affairs which, without knowing what was on his wife's mind, was a word surprisingly well-chosen to describe what Christine thought was really going on. She had not yet confronted him about it, though with Christine that could mean just about anything. Oh well. He would just have to drive off that bridge when he came to it.

Mike, of course, knew what he needed to do. He had known all along what he needed to do. Knowing how to do it, however, was something else entirely. On that subject, he lacked even the minutest clue. The decision was made, though: he would somehow have to get his old job back, pending the solution of one or two significant logistical problems.

Like throwing the opportunity back in his former employer's face, for instance. Celia had asked her son what he had been thinking at that very crucial moment, and he had had no answer for her. The instant before he'd blurted out "Forget it!" to the Head Human Resources Honcho, he recalled, he experienced a nearly intoxicating sense of power over the people who had once wielded so much power over *him*. The instant after, however, he had felt like a complete and total schmuck. It had been almost worth it to see the look on the HHRH's face, but that feeling passed away faster than hope after a general election. A quick-thinking "Just kidding!" would have probably salvaged the situation for everyone concerned. But at that moment Mike Moskowitz wasn't exactly quick and, as Celia correctly suspected, he obviously wasn't thinking.

The process of cogitating his way along the mental towpath thus far had consumed a pretty fair amount of time, and when Mike finally got around to sipping his own overly-complicated, coffee-based beverage, it had cooled beyond the acceptable limits of potability. Unlike the Head Human Resources Honcho, however, Mike did not possess a company credit card. So rather than forking out the cash for a replacement, he instead rose from his seat and headed frontward to the exit. His abandoned, barely-touched libation remained on the table precisely where he'd left it until the next patron came along and discovered it sitting there. Some people are just lazy pigs, the new arrival observed.

The Head Human Resources Honcho strode back into his department, to the annoyed surprise of his assistant.

"How did your meeting go?" she asked.

"What meeting?"

"The meeting outside the office that you didn't think you'd be back from. *That* meeting."

174

"What on Earth are you talking about? Look, hold my calls for the next hour or so. I don't want to be disturbed."

The risk of that happening was pretty minimal. The Head Human Resources Honcho was not someone people went out of their way to get in touch with. It came with the territory.

Secured in his office, the HHRH set about the task of investigating investigators. He soon discovered that private detectives, at least the local variety, were not big believers in company websites. Probably part of the low-profile thing, he thought. Or else they were just plain cheap. Either way, the world-wide web was proving uncharacteristically deficient for his purposes.

A memory stirred, causing him to walk over to an old, disused filing cabinet. The first two drawers he pulled out were both empty, but with drawer number three he struck pay dirt. There, unseen by human eyes for many years, was a yellow telephone book.

"I knew there was a reason I held on to this stupid thing!" the HHRH said to himself with more glee than any phone book in the history of directories ever generated before.

Fortunately, private investigation firms had not been quite as shy about advertising in this particular medium, and the Head Human Resources Honcho found a plethora of P.I.'s to peruse. He scrolled page by page the old-fashioned way, with his index finger landing just below the listing for the ClanDestiny Detective Agency. Their motto, *"We Leave No Stone Unturned,"* appealed to him for some reason. No, really. He picked up the receiver and punched in the number.

"ClanDestiny Detective Agency. This is Tammy. How may I help you?"

"I would like to engage the services of one of your operatives," said the HHRH.

"I beg your pardon?"

"I want to hire a detective."

"Oh! Very good, sir. You've come to the right place! May I get your name?"

"I thought you were detectives!" the Head Human Resources Honcho replied. He felt very clever.

I've never heard that one before, thought Tammy sarcastically. She waited silently, knowing that eventually the caller would feel like an idiot and speak first. This usually did not take very long.

The HHRH identified himself finally, and very professionally. He felt like an idiot.

"So, what exactly is the procedure for this? I've never hired a private investigator before."

Tammy told him. They arranged it that he would meet with one of their people the following afternoon at the location of his choice. The Head Human Resources Honcho chose the coffee shop.

Mike, upon making his own departure from that very same coffee shop, had driven past his old workplace a couple of times. *Several* times, actually, if one was keeping track. It had struck him as a moderately clever idea to try and figure out what lay behind his ex-employer's apparent eagerness to bring him back. If he knew that, he conjectured, he just might be able to figure out a way to re-broach the subject without security tossing him to the pavement.

The drive-bys were by way of remembering as much as he could about the place and the people there. It was amazing how much of a familiar environment one could forget in such a relatively short time. Mike hoped it was the sort of thing that happened to everybody. This was not one of those instances when he wanted to feel special.

Unfortunately for him, however, the concentration required to practice effective collision avoidance seriously impinged on that left over for effective recollecting. On his final pass Mike pulled into the company parking lot. The extent to which this seemed like a bad idea struck him more-or-less instantaneously. He turned the car around and pulled right back out again.

Trying to guess just how motivated the offer really was on his own was getting him nowhere.

"I need help," Mike thought to himself. "I need someone who can do a little discrete digging and find out why the company changed its mind, and just how serious they are about it. I need a professional."

Mike needed a private investigator.

Tammy looked quizzically at her boss.

"This can't be completely kosher."

"Why not?"

"I don't know. It just seems...unethical, somehow."

"There's nothing unethical about it at all. We have two clients. Each wants to know about the other. We're just in the unique position to obtain that information more or less, er, directly."

"Yeah, but wouldn't that be a conflict of interest?"

"For which one?"

"Good point."

"Exactly. We'll impress the hell out of both of them. Sherlock Holmes couldn't do any better. In fact," the ClanDestiny Detective Agency's owner rubbed his chin, "we'll even use the same person for both jobs. Cut out the middle-man, so to speak."

The detective he had in mind was named Jennifer. She looked like anything in the world except a private investigator, and, as a result, was quite staggeringly good at being one.

Chapter 22

Jennifer, star associate of the ClanDestiny Detective agency, found herself sitting in a coffee shop. She often found herself sitting in coffee shops since they were generally easy places to meet clients. They were everywhere, for one thing, and coffee shops offered the sort of privacy you can only find in crowds of highly disinterested people.

She was dressed in what could only be described as...clothes. There was nothing about them to suggest anything concerning their wearer, good or bad. This is not to imply that Jennifer did not look good in them. She had the unique ability to look good in anything from a little black dress to a large black plastic garbage bag, or even nothing at all. This last one being purely conjecture, naturally.

That she was sitting in this of all coffee shops was due to the unusual circumstance of having two new clients, each of whom had specifically requested it. That she was sitting at *the table* was just one of those freaky things that happen every once in a while.

Jennifer had scheduled her appointments back-to-back, allowing enough time in-between, in theory at least, to avoid the risk of Client One accidentally bumping into Client Two. Incidents like that were potentially unpleasant in the private detective business, and Jennifer was a firm believer in avoiding potential unpleasantness every chance she got.

The Head Human Resources Honcho was up first. On the phone he had asked Jennifer how he might recognize her. She'd suggested she would spot *him* long before that became necessary. True to her word, she picked the HHRH out within a microsecond of his crossing the shop's threshold. The Head Human Resources Honcho was considerably impressed by Jennifer's detective prowess, until it was pointed out that nobody wears a suit to a coffee shop. Nobody around these parts, anyway.

"Still, it was clever of you to know that." The Head Human Resources Honcho preferred to believe the observation wasn't too glaringly obvious, or that he wasn't either, for that matter. This was glaringly obvious to Jennifer, who could recognize a good time to change the subject when she saw one.

"All in the line of duty. So, what prompted you to hire a private detective?"

The HHRH thought carefully before responding. Partly, he wanted to explain himself without sounding like a total idiot. Mainly though, it was not in his nature to give a short, simple answer when he had a captive audience and didn't have to.

"Have you ever done something that seemed really brilliant at the time—and I'm talking Theory of Relativity brilliant—that, later on, turned out to be, er, not so brilliant after all?"

Must be good if he's mitigating before I even know what he's supposed to have done, Jennifer thought.

"Oh, I'm sure I have," she replied, just to be encouraging. "What was your brilliant idea?"

"It was like this: I work for a company that has its own health insurance plan. It's self-funded. We finance the plan ourselves."

Jennifer had already figured that out: the term *self-funded* being somewhat *self-explanatory*.

The Head Human Resources Honcho continued. "We contract out to a private benefits administration firm to manage our insurance plan. Anyway, this administrator gets access to all our employees' electronic medical records, at least those employees who are on the plan. Well, one day someone from the administrator calls me—and they almost never do that—and tells me that one of our employees has contracted a very serious disease. 'How serious?' I asked, and was told, 'As serious as it gets.' Which I took to mean, you know, pretty serious. Apparently, or as I can now safely say, allegedly, this disease was the stuff of epidemic-disaster movies, the symptoms far too revolting to discuss in polite company, and was one-hundred percent fatal. The really nasty kind of fatal, as if all the rest of it wasn't awful enough.

"I, being one of those concerned human resources professionals who is constantly looking out for his company's people, asked if it would be appropriate for me to send this employee—his name is Myron Moskowitz, by the way—a get-well card. That was when the plan administrator told me I'd be better off saving the card for myself, since Myron Moskowitz was about to bankrupt our entire insurance fund."

"And where do I come in?" Jennifer asked, hoping her client would get to the point sooner rather than later.

"Yes, well, to make a long story short..."

Jennifer sincerely hoped he had it in him.

"...it seemed as if the only effective solution would be to, er, hasten Mr. Moskowitz's departure from the company's employ before that could happen."

"And that's where your brilliant idea came in?"

"Exactly. You see, we couldn't just fire him. No real reason to, for one thing, and he'd still be able to continue on the insurance plan, which would defeat the whole purpose. It seemed pretty unlikely that he'd take one for the team and resign on his own, which he subsequently admitted to, by the way. So, the only option, as I saw it, was to retire him. Early. *Very* early. It was perfect, considering the guy was supposed to start singing in the heavenly choir before you could say Jack Robinson. Senior management loved the idea so much they took credit for it themselves."

"So, you forced this," Jennifer looked down at her notes, even though she knew perfectly well who they were talking about, "Myron Moskowitz into early retirement?"

"Um, yes. Of course, we didn't see it as being quite as severe as it sounds, you know, in hindsight. Oh, don't get me wrong, we paid him—*are* paying him—his full salary. But it got him off the insurance, which was the important thing."

"It would seem you'd solved the problem, then."

"Yes, well, we would have solved the problem if this man Moskowitz had departed this Earthly realm in the timely fashion he was supposed to. But so far he shows no signs of kicking the bucket anytime in the foreseeable future."

"Being uncooperative, is he?" Jennifer asked, trying hard not to make her indignation too transparent.

"Yes. No. It's not that we want him to die, per se. It's just that, you see, he's still getting his full pay but not contributing anything, you know, productivity-wise. And my CEO is not, er, entirely happy with the present arrangement."

"I'm guessing your insurance administrator is off the Christmas card list at this point."

"Ex-insurance administrator. And yes, I think that would be a safe assumption."

"I'm still not sure where a private eye fits in," Jennifer considered aloud. "How can I possibly help?"

"I have been ordered—strongly encouraged, that is—to find a way to get Myron Moskowitz back to work. The CEO is fairly adamant about it."

"Have you offered him his job back yet?"

"I have, and he turned me down. Mr. Moskowitz was fairly adamant about it, too."

"And I come in..."

"I need to find out everything there is to know about the man. What makes him tick, what his weaknesses are. His pressure points. I need to know what will get him back to the negotiating table. And I want you to find that out for me."

This was a switch. Jennifer had often been called in to help get people *out* of jobs. This was the first time she had ever been asked to help get somebody back into one.

"Right. Then let's go over the details, shall we?"

Jennifer had no trouble picking Mike out, either, when he staggered in. It was hard to miss the dazed-looking man who tottered up to the order counter as if on auto-pilot, appeared unable to return the attendant's greeting, then stumbled down to the other end to retrieve the beverage which was already waiting for him. Besides, the place had pretty much cleared out by the time he got there.

If Mike's timing seemed a little off—and let's face it, it did—it was because he had just observed the Head Human Resources Honcho standing in the parking lot. Fortunately Mike saw him first and had managed to take cover behind a convenient minivan before he could be seen by the other man in kind.

The experience had a touch of Macbeth about it. Here he was, preparing to plot and scheme against someone, and the object of the intrigue appears out of nowhere like an apparition. It raised alarums in the guilt receptors of Mike's brain and left him wobbly, slightly disoriented, and undeniably off his stride.

He made his way over to "the table," also apparently by auto-pilot, and was surprised to find a woman already seated there. A not unattractive woman, he noticed, which was when he noticed he was noticing things again. Things like women sitting at tables, for instance. Mike remembered he had come to meet a woman, here at this very coffee shop, and wondered if she could be it. Her.

"Jennifer?"

Jennifer nodded.

"Mr. Moskowitz, I presume?"

Mike thought the name sounded familiar enough that it could very well be his.

"Yes. Mike. Mike Moskowitz."

"Are you alright, Mr. Moskowitz? You look like you've seen a ghost."

The Head Human Resources Honcho a ghost? Or was that just wishful thinking?

"Um, yeah. Well, not exactly a ghost. It's not important. So, you're Jennifer?"

Jennifer might have dismissed her second new client of the day as an utter fruitcake if she had not already suffered through a meeting with new client number one first. In light of what Myron Moskowitz had experienced from *that* source, she was prepared to cut him a little slack. Maybe even a lot of slack. Jennifer was inclined to be generous.

"That's me, Mr. Moskowitz," Jennifer replied, extending her hand. "It's a pleasure to meet you."

Mike sincerely doubted it, but she seemed cordial enough. He extended his own hand in return and that first, awkward handshake was dispatched and over with quickly and with just the right amount of ceremony.

"So, Mr. Moskowitz, how can I help you?"

"Call me Mike," said Mike. "I'm afraid I have a rather long answer to a very short question. Are you up for it?"

"I'm paid by the day. Take all the time you need!" Jennifer gave her client a smile that could have done admirable duty for a wink, if it wanted to. It had the desired effect on Mike.

"All right, here goes. Stop me if we start running into overtime."

Mike relayed the highlights of his recent adventures in virtual Wonderland, beginning with his ill-fated visit to Dr. Katz, and ending with his current status as a premature pensioner. The Head Human Resources Honcho figured prominently in the role of Mike's arch-nemesis. The Fu-Manchu mustache was more implied than added.

"Okay, let me get this straight: you have all the free time in the world, you're still getting your full salary, and you're healthy as a horse. So far, I'm not seeing any downside, here."

"Yeah, I know. It sounds ideal. But it isn't, trust me. As far as every computer in the world is concerned, I don't exist anymore. I can't even order a pizza without paying for it first. In person, and in cash. And the free time! I'm on the verge of losing my mind trying to figure out what to do with it all! No, I need to get back to work. I need to get back on the grid, and the two things are, unfortunately, inextricably linked."

"Have you talked to your old employer about getting your job back? I mean, you're obviously not a threat to their insurance, and since they're already paying you, anyway..."

Mike's palm came up to his forehead striking it audibly, his pinky nearly poking him in the eye.

"Sore subject?"

"Yes, I spoke with them about it. The Head Human Resources Honcho called and asked me to meet with him, and we discussed my coming back to work."

"And?"

"And I told him no dice. I was fairly adamant about it, in fact."

"Why did you say 'no'? Were they offering you a pay cut or something?"

"No, and I probably could have talked them into a raise, if I'd wanted. But there was something about the way the Head Human Resources Honcho explained *why* they wanted me back that just didn't sit right. I can't even describe it, really."

You don't need to, Jennifer thought. I've met the guy.

"Well, again, Mr. Moskowitz..."

"Mike."

"Mike. How can I help you?"

"I need to find out everything I can about the Head Human Resources Honcho, find out what makes him tick. Things I can use to get him back to the negotiating table. I need dirt, and I'd like you to dig it up for me."

Like taking candy from a baby, Jennifer mused, and not a particularly bright one at that. ClanDestiny should get assignments like these all the time.

"Right. Then let's go over the details, shall we?"

Chapter 23

Jennifer had her assignments. The Head Human Resources Honcho felt that, with her on the case, he could safely avoid thinking about Myron Moskowitz for at least a day or two, and thus preserve what remained of his sanity. Mike, for similar reasons, felt that he could safely avoid thinking about the Head Human Resources Honcho for a day or two, too. He was not quite as sanguine about the sanity part, however.

That is, he *should* have been able to keep the HHRH out of sight and out of mind. But one of the downsides of a mind that has been under-stimulated for too long at any one stretch is its annoying tendency to grasp onto the first thing that crosses its path, and cling to it desperately until something more interesting strolls by. Usually, though, it's too busy falling all over that first thing to notice the next synaptic pedestrian when it ambles along.

And then there was Jennifer. She did not look like any detective Mike had ever seen before. Granted, his experience of the profession consisted mostly of actors in movies and TV, but that included all those reality cop shows, and she resembled those detectives least of all.

Still, Jennifer had asked him a lot of remarkably precise questions and seemed astonishingly well-informed about a company she was only just hearing about for the first time. So much so, Mike thought, it was almost as if she'd been talking to someone who worked there.

Jennifer had been flatteringly attentive to Mike's description of the events leading up to their meeting. That a split-second gap in concentration could result in such a massive misadventure for her client was, she found, sadly fascinating. And now all evidence of the poor guy had been wiped out entirely, conceivably until the end of time itself. Jennifer made a mental note to collect the ClanDestiny Detective Agency's fee up front, and in cash.

The forces of good intention had not entirely thrown in the towel. Dan was itching to regain a bit of the face he'd lost following his humiliating performance on Bedouin's Day. And if any additional incentive was needed, Kermit and Jackie had lately appeared to be on the outs with one another. A victory now could come in handy along multiple fronts.

Dan was certain he'd figured out how you solved a problem like Myron Moskowitz. All it would take was some legitimate entity creating a halfway-decent-sized computer file on the subject in question. Once that file existed, Dan felt confident that he could copy it onto every single database worth being stored in with just a few well-placed keystrokes. Well, a *lot* of well-placed keystrokes, as it happened. But it could be done, and that was the mainframe. Thing. The main thing.

There were only two problems, as he saw it. The first was finding a legitimate entity that wanted a half-way-decent-sized computer file on what was for the moment a mere phantom Myron Moskowitz. The second problem was one he had probably created himself, when he'd introduced Mike to the Bedouins. To wit: Mr. M. might decide to stay off the grid permanently. Which would be fine for him, but lousy as far as Dan's chances of finally hooking up with Jackie went.

"**Y**ou hired a shamus?" asked Celia, with almost prurient interest.

"A what?" asked Mike, thinking that, whatever that was, it sounded Jewish.

"A shamus. A peeper. A dick."

That didn't sound Jewish.

"I hired a private investigator, Mother."

"Cool!" she exclaimed very un-Celia-ly. "What did he look like? Do they really wear trench coats, even in the summer?"

Mike described Jennifer to his disappointed mother.

"Doesn't sound like any P.I. I've ever heard of."

Mike didn't want to ask, but did anyway. "Have you heard of many P.I.s, Mom?"

"Plenty, I'll have you know."

"Where?"

"On the television," she replied, as if he should already have known that. Correctly, as it happened.

Jennifer had stuck around after Mike left the coffee shop, digesting her two newest clients. She was aided in this by a free large beverage, courtesy of the recent college grad manning the counter. Based on the recent traffic at her table he figured she was interviewing people for some kind of job. If it was better than the one he had, which was pretty much a given, he wanted to get on her good side.

Her own job was almost too easy. Again, it was like taking candy from a baby, and not a particularly clever one. If either of her clients had been completely upfront with the other from the beginning, Mr. Moskowitz would now be happily back at work and the Head Human Resources Honcho would be happily back doing whatever Head Human Resources Honchos do. Not even a skilled investigator like Jennifer could have gotten to the bottom of exactly what that entailed.

She made a few inquiries after meeting both men, mostly just to justify charging them the ClanDestiny Detective Agency's standard fee, and she'd completed them in about the time it would take to lick a postage stamp back in the days when you had to do that in order to get them to stick to the envelope. For most private detectives this would have been enough. But Jennifer was a private detective with a conscience. She needed to feel she was truly earning her money. So she decided to go undercover and check the company out first-hand.

She arrived there the next morning armed with the most ubiquitous office tool in corporate America: a coffee mug. This one bore an inverted smiley face with the legend *I hate mornings* in distressed lettering underneath, and looked like it had seen more than its fair share of them. Jennifer had a special place in her heart for that mug. It had helped open more doors than a master key.

She made her way first to the copy room, which she found by following the smell of warm ink and machinery. She waited until a copier was available and photocopied a few random documents she had picked up off of somebody's desk on her way in. Jennifer returned the originals, hopefully to the right desk, smiling and wishing good morning to the few people who appeared to notice her. One or two even smiled and wished her a good morning back before completely forgetting she was there.

She next strode purposefully over to a small cubicle farm, more of a cubicle croft, really, and zeroed in on the sole male inhabitant. The man was middle-aged and separated only by thin partitions from women a couple of generations down who seemed completely oblivious to him. Jennifer thought he looked lonely. In reality, he had merely given up hope.

She approached her target almost deferentially.

"Excuse me? I'm really sorry to bother you. You look like you're so busy. But my fax machine doesn't seem to want to work this morning. Would you mind terribly if I used yours for a moment?"

Jennifer was gambling that the company still faxed things the old-fashioned way and not from people's personal computers. It was a pretty safe assumption from the look of things so far, and she was not a detective for nothing.

The man looked up at Jennifer and immediately felt that spark of simpatico that adults at a Chuck E. Cheese's all share with each other.

"Please, help yourself," he answered, smiling. He had not smiled at his desk in, well, probably ever.

"Thanks. I'm Jennifer."

"Howard."

"Hi, Howard. I really appreciate this."

"If you're nice enough, I might even let you use my stapler."

"Be careful what you offer!" Jennifer said, waving her finger in mock admonishment. "I may decide to take you up on it!"

Howard smiled at his desk for the second time in, well, probably ever.

"It would be nice to have somebody test my largesse instead of just my patience, for a change," he replied, wondering where on Earth the word 'largesse' had spontaneously materialized from.

It was refreshing, Howard thought, to have a fellow employee—and, let's admit it, a female one, at that—who did not look and act like some developmentally recessive, superannuated teenager in a reality show. One of those series with too many beaches, too much alcohol, and not nearly enough common sense. A—he groped for the right word here—professional. No, that wasn't it. A grown-up! Yes, a grown-up. One who wasn't afraid to wear her adulthood on her immaculately-pressed sleeve. Howard felt sure that Jennifer was the sort of person another person could put their trust in.

He was, therefore, not a little disappointed when she failed to show up a few days later, then failed to show up again any time after that. Howard's cubicle-farm mates teased him relentlessly about his missing girlfriend, until what eventually became known in company lore as: *The Incident.*

Jennifer, having gathered enough first-hand information about the company to be seriously puzzled by Mr. Moskowitz's enthusiasm to go back to it, was now ready to deliver her findings. She decided to put off doing so, however, for one more day. Both Mike and the HHRH would probably appreciate having an extra twenty-four hours of vacation from one another, and she always endeavored to make her clients as happy as the law allowed.

"You mean, just *tell* him? Everything? Just like that?" asked an incredulous Head Human Resources Honcho from the same chair at the same table in the same coffee emporium. The store's owners were, at that very moment, discussing the radical business idea of giving the coffee away for free and installing parking meters at each of the tables.

"Based on my investigation, that would be the quickest and easiest solution. An 'I'm sorry' would, in all likelihood, completely seal the deal," answered Jennifer.

"An admission *and* an apology? Both? At the same

time? It's never been done before. There's no precedent!"

"Like they say, there's no time like the precedent. You'd get Mr. Moskowitz back, the CEO would get off of *your* back, and you could spend your time more productively doing...well, you know...whatever it is you, um, do."

"Hmm, I'll have to think about that. In the meantime, did you get the 'what makes him tick' stuff I asked you for?"

"It's all in my report. He's not a very complicated person," Jennifer said. Boring even, she could have added. "I don't know how that plays as far as your poker scenario goes. But, as I've said, you could probably save yourself a lot of time and grief just by laying your cards on the table. To continue the metaphor."

The Head Human Resources Honcho smiled somewhat condescendingly. Like they do. "Young lady, you obviously have no experience working in a company like mine."

"You might be surprised," Jennifer replied, with a knowing wink.

"No, on second thought, you just might, at that."

Her meeting with Mike Moskowitz, once again at the same table at the same coffee shop, seemed less like business and more like a conversation with an old friend. An imaginary one, Jennifer mused, since officially there was no such thing as a Mike Moskowitz.

"Look, they want you back. That Head Human Resources guy is under a lot of pressure to make that happen.

You want to go back. No, you *need* to go back. If you're left to your own devices for too much longer you'll go completely over the edge. Heck, you're part way there already! So, does it really matter what their motivations are?"

Jennifer had already brought Mike up to speed on the state of things with his former employer.

"There's always the Bedouins."

"Yeah, right. Somehow, I just don't see you tooling along the open road on a motorcycle. Frankly, I can't even picture you *on* a motorcycle. Especially with that Paco character playing Leader of the Pack. You should just go get yourself a tattoo and call it a day."

Jennifer had a point. He couldn't see himself on a motorcycle, either, and without that, the rest was pretty much a non-starter.

"So, you think I should just call the guy up and admit I was wrong?"

"That is, of course, entirely up to you. But yes, as long as you're asking. I do."

"And I suppose you think I should apologize for turning the offer down flat the last time?"

"Again, up to you. But that probably wouldn't hurt."

"An admission *and* an apology? At the same time?"

Jennifer experienced a strange sense of *deja-vu* as she glanced across at her client. And while smacking him up-side the head with the flat part of a shovel would likely come off as excessive, grabbing Mike by the shoulders and shaking vigorously was still very much on the table.

Instead, though, she appealed to what was left of his

reason.

"Apologize or not. But he really needs for this to happen. Which means that, if you help get him out of this mess, he'll probably owe you one. I'm sure a smart guy like you could figure out a way to use that to your advantage."

"Jennifer, Jennifer. You obviously have no idea how things work in a company like that."

"No," she sighed, crossing her arms resignedly in front of her. "I guess I don't."

When Mike got up to leave, he turned absently toward the exit and nearly collided with a pole he hadn't noticed before. Atop it was what appeared to be a parking meter. He looked around and noticed there was one next to every surface a person could conceivably set a beverage on. He pointed them out to Jennifer.

"It was bad enough when they only got you coming and going," he said.

Chapter 24

The phone rang. Mike answered it. Then he picked up the receiver.

"Mr. M.? Dan here."

Mike had not spoken with Dan since their meeting with the Bedouins. He'd assumed the two things were somehow connected.

"Hello, Dan. How've you been?"

"Um, fine, thanks, Mr. M. Oh, um, and how've you been?"

Mike guessed from the number of *ums* that Dan had something important on his mind.

"Oh, fair to middling, I suppose."

Dan had never heard that particular expression before, and wasn't quite sure if it was good or not. The *fair* part sounded relatively positive, though, so he decided that it probably was at least okay.

"Um, that's good," he hoped. "Actually, I'm relieved to find you at home."

"As opposed to where? Mt. Everest? The Great Barrier Reef?"

"I don't know. Halfway to the coast with the Bedouins

or someplace."

"Oh, are they headed to the coast? Is there still time, or have they left already?"

"I was just...figure of speech."

"No, I haven't gone off playing *Easy Rider* with the Bedouins. Not yet, anyway. It was nice seeing Herman again, but that's as far as it went."

"Who?"

"Herm...Paco. You remember Paco?"

Dan remembered Paco, and with any luck, better than Paco remembered *him*.

"Yeah, I remember," he said, without apparent enthusiasm.

Mike recalled that Dan had been seriously off his game on that occasion. This was saying something, since, in Mike's experience, Dan *on* his game was nothing to write home about.

"Yeah, well, I'm sure Herm—*Paco*—has forgotten all about both of us by now," Mike said, without actually believing it. Dan's silence suggested that he didn't, either.

"So, Dan. Did you just call because you missed me? Or have you finally figured a way out of my personal little debacle?"

"I've figured a way out," Dan replied, regaining a modicum of his former self-esteem.

Now it was Mike's turn to be silent.

"Mr. M.?"

"What? Oh, I'm still here. You've...you say you've solved it?"

"I've figured out *how* to solve it. Whether that actually

happens or not is going to depend in large part on you."

There was no evidence of any further *ums* on the immediate conversational horizon.

Mike did not hesitate.

"What's left for me to do? I've already tried everything under the sun at least once, and nothing's worked. Even suicide would probably be redundant at this stage of the game. What else is there?"

Dan paused pregnantly, which was not at all the same as merely hanging on the line not saying anything. He allowed his answer to gestate to full-term before speaking.

"You have to get a job."

This revelation failed to justify such an especially prolonged gestation period.

"A job? Where am I supposed to get a job, when..." the answer suddenly dawned on him. "And anyway, even if I *could* get a job, how is that supposed to change anything?"

"By itself, not at all," said Dan. "But it would start a chain reaction of events which, if handled correctly, would return you to the realm of the virtual living."

Dan explained in a general way what he had in mind, without becoming too technical about it. This was in some small part due to his belief that Mike wouldn't be interested in the details, and in even larger part to the fear that he would, and would be curious to know why this new approach hadn't occurred to him a great deal sooner.

"What happens after that," he added, "I can't help you with."

Mike enjoyed a mildly distorted smile at the irony. He could finally reclaim his identity, but only on the condition that he was willing to give it right back up again to some soulless corporation. He shared this thought with Dan.

"Yeah, I suppose that's what it comes down to. But look on the bright side."

"What's that?"

"After all this time, you probably won't miss it."

Dan had a point.

"Right. So, what do you need me to do?"

Unbeknownst to Mike, his end of the conversation had attracted an audience. Christine, who had been hovering unrelatedly nearby, just happened to overhear that part of her husband's minor outburst in which the words *Where am I supposed to get a job?* had fairly exploded from his lips. This had naturally gotten her complete and undivided attention.

Without absolutely meaning to, Christine had continued to listen. If it seemed that she'd somehow maneuvered herself into better hearing range, this was accomplished only absently. Christine was not the sort of wife who would never intentionally eavesdrop on her husband. No, seriously.

As she gathered up more of the one-sided conversation, gears began to turn. Light bulbs started going off. Klaxons sounded. Okay, there weren't any klaxons. But things quickly started coming into what passed for focus for her.

If Mike needed a job, her more analytical side told her, that probably meant he did not currently have one. And if he did not currently have one, she further reasoned, then it was equally probable that he had not had one for a quite a while now. This scenario, Christine concluded, would go a long way toward explaining at least some of the odd behavior she had previously credited to a garden-variety mid-life crisis, one she hoped her husband would simply grow out of eventually.

But if Mike didn't have a job, where was all the money coming from? And what had he been doing every day?

It was time to invite Celia over for dinner again.

"I've invited your mother over for dinner tonight," Christine informed her surprised spouse.

Mike greeted this announcement with the wariness it deserved.

"You did, huh? What's the occasion?"

"No occasion. I just thought it would be nice to have her here."

Which was where Christine made her mistake. If she had even *tried* to come up with something (anything!) with just the slightest ring of plausibility to it, Mike would have easily given her the benefit of the doubt. But now he had absolutely no doubt: his wife was up to something.

The revelation came entirely out of left field, as far as Mike could tell. Christine had been acting more-or-less normally for quite some time now, having determined that her husband was guilty of nothing more sinister than middle age. Inviting Celia, however, was a clear sign that a ripple had occurred somewhere in the status quo. Not a happy sign, either. More *Danger!* than, say, *Keep off the Grass*, or something equally less likely to ruin his day. Or week, or year.

On second thought, *Keep off the Grass* might be good advice as far as where and how to tread through what Mike was certain would be another impending Moskowitz minefield.

Fueling Mike's anxiety was the fact that he had not seen or spoken with his mother for the better part of two weeks. This was probably a record, and even though it was a purely unintentional one, he was sure Celia would fail to appreciate the distinction. The woman could take acts of God personally, even ones happening on other continents. She was unlikely to let such an obvious example of filial neglect slip under her affront-radar. Mike had more en-joyed than lamented the respite up 'til now, but he found himself quickly making up for lost lamentation time.

Uncharacteristically, Christine had taken it upon her-self to cook for the occasion, prompting her husband to make a quick trip to the basement to check for pods. She was even whistling while she worked. Well, more of a humming, really, or something between the two. Listening to it made Mike feel rather like an atheist in a foxhole.

Christine outdid herself in the kitchen. Granted, the bar was not an especially high one where matters culinary were concerned; nevertheless, the dinner she prepared was truly magnificent. Mike took some comfort in knowing that, as long as he was a condemned man, he would at least get to enjoy an exceptionally hearty last meal. Even Celia was impressed, and wondered to herself what else her daughter-in-law might have been holding back on all these years.

Christine had not stopped in the kitchen, either. The table was set with the closest thing to fine china the couple owned, and which Mike had not seen in the same company as food in well over a decade. She had even placed a floral centerpiece, the doing of which had caused her no small frustration. It could not be high enough for her husband to hide behind; too short and it risked looking like a boutonniere depository. Getting that stem length just right had cost her a great deal of patience and left a heap of unhappy flowers behind for the trash man.

The presentation of the meal itself was a veritable work of art, too. Performance art, even, if the level of fussing Christine made over Celia was anything to go by. The senior Mrs. Moskowitz was curious to know if her son had been down to his basement lately, and if he'd observed any large, pod-like things that hadn't already been there before.

After making sure everyone and everything was as they were supposed to be, Christine decided it was time to kick off the dinnertime conversation.

"So, honey, how's your job search going?"

Not used to being called *honey,* and especially by his wife, Mike assumed she had been directing the question to Celia.

"Mom? Have you been looking for a job?"

Mrs. Moskowitz senior had, as predicted, not failed to notice Mike's recent inattention streak, and was, therefore, not inclined to let an opportunity to rub his nose in it slip through her doll-sized fingers.

"A lot you care. A *real* son wouldn't have to ask. He'd know, already."

Mike was prepared for this, to a point.

"What do you mean, a *real son*? I don't talk to you for a few days and now I'm some sort of ersatz offspring?"

"'A few days,' he says. It's been nearly a month, and nothing. You don't call, you don't write..."

"I *never* write. And it's only been two weeks. It wasn't personal. I've just been very busy."

"Picking up a telephone isn't exactly what you'd call a commitment, Myron. Excuses from you, I don't need. And don't think you're gonna make it up to me just because you invited me to dinner once."

"I didn't invite you to dinner. Christine did."

"Aha! So you admit it! It wouldn't even have occurred to you to invite me over yourself!"

Christine followed this game of verbal ping-pong with mild disbelief and not-so-mild consternation. She'd had a plan and nobody seemed to be following it. It was time to get things, dinner included, back on the right course.

"Celia, I mean, Mother," she said, "Regardless of who actually invited you, we're both very happy to have you here. Now, Mike—"

"It's no use covering for that husband of yours, dear," Celia replied. "He doesn't deserve you."

Christine opened her mouth to try and redirect the conversation back to that husband of hers, but said husband had opened his first.

"Look, Mom, I'm sorry, okay? I didn't call you. I

should have. I was wrong. I promise not to do it again. There, satisfied?"

Apparently, Celia was not.

"Something could have happened to me, for all you cared. And besides, I just like to hear from my son occasionally. I can't help it. I'm a mother."

"You certainly are," mumbled Mike under his breath.

"Speak up, Myron. You're mumbling."

"I said yes, you are most definitely a mother."

"Of course I'm a mother. I just said that, didn't I?"

Christine tried in vain to get a word of her own in, but between Celia and Mike it was as if she wasn't even there.

Nobody touched their food. Things that were hot became cold, and vice-versa, though Christine was not around to notice. By then she had retreated to the kitchen and was tugging at her hair with a great deal more vigor than was probably healthy for it.

Chapter 25

"In this corner, wearing corporate pin-stripe trunks and weighing in at one hundred and eighty-seven-and-a-half pounds, the Head Human Resources Honcho! And in *this* corner, tipping the scales at a nearly svelte one-hundred-and-seventy-five, Mr. Myron Moskowitz!

"Now gentlemen, if you'll kindly step to the center of the ring and touch gloves...Gentlemen? Gentlemen?"

The Executive Vice President arrived unannounced and unexpected at the Head Human Resources Honcho's door. It was obvious immediately that this was not intended to be a social call.

The HHRH found the other man's presence merely annoying. Unlike the CEO, the EVP was more pretender than king. This did not mean that he did not have some serious weight behind him. It was just that rebukes, threats, and all-out tirades were not nearly as scary coming from a mere intermediary as they were when the CEO handled those little niceties personally.

"I suppose you know why I'm here," was how the

Executive Vice President opened the conversation.

"Well, let's see. It's probably not a policy issue, since you guys never seem to worry very much about those sorts of things. And it's probably not about how much vacation time you have left. You haven't used any since the Bush Administration. The first one, if I'm not mistaken. Oh, wait. I know! The CEO sent you on an errand! That's it, isn't it?"

The EVP realized he was being insulted, only not before he had already started to speak.

"Yes. I mean, no," he corrected himself, somewhat doubtfully. "I have personally taken on the responsibility for this Moskowitz issue, and will be dealing with you as regards the situation directly."

"I'm sure your initiative will be reflected favorably in your next review," replied the HHRH dryly. Or ironically. Knowing the HHRH, it could have been either.

"So, er, where are we, Moskowitz-wise?"

"Same place we were yesterday. And the day before that, and the several preceding, when the CEO last asked me."

"Well, I'm not the CEO."

You can say that again, the Head Human Resources Honcho thought, hoping there was no such thing as telepathy.

"As I say, I'm not the CEO. I need to be brought up to speed as completely as possible."

The Head Human Resources Honcho brought the Executive Vice President up to speed. It was over quickly.

The EVP tried to think up at least a few intelligent

questions. That was over quickly, too.

"So, um, that's it, then?"

"That's it."

"Not much, is it? Since the last time, I mean."

"No," the HHRH conceded. "It's not much."

"The CE...we...I...expect this to be resolved by the end of next week. Otherwise, the CE...we...I...will be making other arrangements."

"What other arrangements?"

"Just...other arrangements. I would strongly advise you not to fail."

Even coming from the Executive Vice President, this was not advice to be regarded lightly.

Dan had explained to Mike in a vague way how his plan was supposed to work. Mike wasn't completely sure at the time whether the vagueness was for his sake or because Dan himself still faced some serious gaps in the detail department. But what Mike took away from the conversation was this: his new employment information, if indeed there was to be any, had to be entered into some government database at the exact same instant as a whole bunch of other Moskowitz-specific information was entered into a whole bunch of other databases.

According to Dan, this massive Moskowitz bombardment would confuse the system's defenses long enough to allow at least a few bits and bytes to slip through. After that, there'd be a lot of typing on somebody's part, but Mike would be his own cyber-person once again.

This, of course, took rather a lot for granted. There was that getting a job part, for starters. Then, there was that whole business of simultaneous mouse-clicking to contend with. But it was either that or join the Bedouins, and, as previously noted, Mike was not exactly inspired about his prospects for learning how to ride a motorcycle at this stage of his life.

Well, he reasoned, every minute he put off calling the Head Human Resources Honcho was merely another minute of postponing the inevitable. Granted, Mike could probably continue postponing the inevitable indefinitely, if he tried hard enough. But ultimately, being inevitable, he would have to get around to it sooner or later. No time like the present, he told himself, without really believing it for a second.

Of course, it wasn't officially putting it off if he was still actively working on a strategy, he rationalized. And since he had so far not succeeded in working one out on his own by now, perhaps it was time to call in the experts.

But *which* experts? There was Celia, though she was still a little miffed at him and would probably only recommend the direct approach. That is, if she could stay on-topic long enough to even get that far, which he had serious doubts about.

There *was* one person intimately enough acquainted with every gory detail of the situation to qualify as an expert. That person was Jennifer, the private eye Mike had hired the first time he'd tried to postpone the inevitable by working on a strategy.

He called and arranged a meeting.

To have simply forgotten about Christine, especially after her latest dinner ambush debacle, would have been tempting. Fate. Tempting fate. This, of course is precisely what Mike did, not thinking about Christine being for him something on the order of breathing.

This was not a course Darwin would have remarked favorably upon, survival-of-the-fittest-wise. Christine was not one of nature's minor adversities simply to be written off willy-nilly without the fear of certain unpleasant repercussions to the species. And, she was a lot harder to shake than a score of lesser adversities all lumped together. She pretty much had to be, living with a guy who could ignore anything, and her in particular, as though he had a Ph.D. in it.

She was back at square one, and she really, *really* hated square one.

Drawing from her wide knowledge of reality television, Christine narrowed the scope of the Mike problem down to one of two things: out of work or other woman. Or man. No, definitely woman. It was even possible that her husband was both out of work and keeping a mistress. On TV, folks with no visible means of support carried on all the time. Love being free, after all.

It was time to break out that book on surveillance techniques once again.

The Head Human Resources Honcho, too, had hit upon the idea of postponing the inevitable with another strategy session with Jennifer. When he asked, however, she offered only a very polite no-way-in-hell.

The following day began the weekend, a fact Mike might not have known if Jennifer hadn't explained why she would be unavailable to meet with him then. Apparently, even private investigators feel entitled to their Saturdays.

Weekends had become one of the greater strains on Mike's existence ever since he'd begun spending the rest of the week in exactly the same fashion. He had quickly, all *too* quickly, run out of places to go, things to do and movies to sleep through for weekends to hold any appeal for him. And Christine's never-ending suggestions had a funny way of somehow making this particular weekend exponentially less so.

Christine was being especially helpful in the suggestion department this morning, which was having a strangely opposite effect on her husband. Or perhaps not so strangely, after all. She was being *so* helpful, in fact, that it was overriding Mike's ability to completely shut her out. If this kept up, before too much longer he was more than likely to find himself agreeing to spend the day with her.

Before too much longer, Mike found himself agreeing to spend the day with his wife. But there was no way, he insisted, that he was letting himself be talked into two entire days of together time.

Since the best laid plans of mice and men often gang agley, as ol' Robbie Burns might have put it, Mike and Christine spent the entire weekend doing things together. On the whole, it really wasn't all that bad from anybody's perspective.

Monday came along right on schedule, signaling the beginning of the end of Mike's repertoire of delaying tactics. Well, almost. He still had one left in consulting with Jennifer, so technically you could say he was at postponement-minus-one and counting. But then, who was counting?

He left the house in the usual way and headed over to the agreed-upon Jennifer rendezvous point. Mike sincerely hoped the detective would have something new for him. Something he hadn't already thought of would be extremely refreshing right about now, even if it wasn't anything he especially wanted to hear. Mike was not overly optimistic about either prospect.

Right behind him, with a more masterly stealth than she'd demonstrated the last time, trailed Christine.

Purely out of habit, Mike had arranged to meet Jennifer at the usual coffee shop. He found her already entrenched at his usual table, which by now had become her usual table, too.

"I really appreciate your doing this," Mike said, by way of hello.

"No worries. I don't know how much help I'm going to be, though."

"You never can tell. Besides, my next shot is for all the marbles. It couldn't hurt to cover each of the bases one last time, right?"

"One final bit of procrastination, you mean?"

"In a nutshell."

The two sat drinking their expensive coffee-based beverages and rehashed the highlights of their previous conversation. To an outside observer, they appeared to be having a great deal of fun doing it.

At least, that's how it looked to one outside observer. Christine had been watching her husband from a vantage point just outside the door. Then, slipping in as soon as she saw Mike heading away from the counter, she quietly purchased her own expensive coffee-based beverage and plopped herself down at a small table strategically located within a hair's breadth of the exit.

She didn't know whether to be pleased or shocked at what she was witnessing. On the one hand, her husband was clearly involved with another woman, which effectively settled that question. On the other hand, her husband was clearly involved with another woman which, despite all the damning evidence, she still considered too incredible to ever possibly be true.

Christine observed the pair scientifically. They were talking animatedly and were obviously well-acquainted with each other. But to her eyes this hardly looked like your garden-variety guilty liaison. Not her idea of one, at any rate. And if this was some sort of romantic rendezvous, they'd have been hard-pressed to have picked a lamer spot for it.

Jennifer listened with caring interest as Mike related his interpretation of Dan's simultaneous-data-entry theory—or hypothesis. Mike had never been altogether clear on the difference.

"So, not only do I have to get my old job back, or any other job, though let's face it, there *is* no other job, I have to be 'activated' by the company at the exact instant that I'm being 'activated' in, like, six thousand other places." Mike slumped as he sighed. "The whole thing is completely overwhelming."

"No, it's not. Just take it a step at a time. Call the Human Resources guy and make an appointment. Then, in your nicest voice, ask for your job back. Eat a little crow, if you have to. It might make him more inclined to go along with that whole re-activation business."

"Yeah, but—"

"No more buts, cowboy. Time to pony-up!" Jennifer leaned into Mike as she said this and tenderly placed her hand on his arm.

Not coincidentally, Christine chose that particular instant to throw up her own hands, accidentally sending her expensive coffee-based beverage flying out the door and half-way across the parking lot. She followed the running liquid onto the sidewalk, hot on its highly-caffeinated heels.

Chapter 26

Christine sat in her car and...sat. Real-reality had just collided head-on with her own, personal version of reality, creating a vortex in her brain and seriously messing with the order of the universe as Christine had imagined it.

She could never in a million years have pictured Mike pursuing another woman. This was partly due to her version of reality again, specifically as it related to her perception of herself as a woman and a wife. But it was also partly due to knowing her husband so extremely well. He just didn't have the chase in him anymore. He'd hardly had it in him ever, for that matter. Christine remembered practically having to hit him over the head with a club and drag him back to her cave by his hair back when they'd first begun dating and Mike still had hair to speak of.

The only possible explanation, as Christine saw it, was that this young, attractive, and obviously deranged female was pursuing *him*. This, too, did not make any sense, when you stopped to consider that the *him* in this case referred to her own Myron Moskowitz. A nice enough guy, as far as it goes. Hell, he was even fun to be with occasionally. Hardly, however, the stuff to inspire bevies of hot chicks to line up and take a number.

As Christine continued staring blankly at her steering column, Mike and Jennifer appeared out on the pavement, after first carefully sidestepping the remains of an expensive coffee-based beverage casualty which had formed a puddle near the door. They stood facing each other, laughing in a shaking-Santa sort of way. Then, to Christine's absolute astonishment, the two shook hands. The young woman turned off in the direction of a non-descript, light gray car that was parked nearby. Mike headed back into the coffee shop, this time without regard to the minor lake of coffee-based beverage pooled in his path.

Christine remained in the car. She figured her husband was bound to come out again sometime. And maybe, when he ultimately did, she might feel at least slightly less confused than she was feeling at the moment.

Mike did come out again, eventually. He found that he could only justify *not* coming out again for so long, the interval determined by the amount of time it took to slowly nurse yet another expensive, coffee-based beverage. *Really* slowly. The final sip came and went entirely too soon, as far as he was concerned. But he could hardly fail to recognize zero-hour when it was right under his nose, and it was hovering annoyingly in-between lip and nostril right now.

He took out his cell phone and stared at it for a minute. He then stared at it for a second minute, and was seriously contemplating staring for a third minute when his thumb took the initiative and punched in a number. It punched in still more numbers, until the full complement required to complete a local call appeared on the tiny screen. His thumb next pushed *Talk* and shortly thereafter was rewarded with a dial tone.

When a receptionist answered, Mike asked to be connected to the Head Human Resources Honcho. Actually, he requested the HHRH by name, this being the more professional way to do that sort of thing. The call was transferred instead to the department secretary, or assistant, as they are calling themselves these days, who informed Mike that the object of his inquiry was presently unavailable. After declining several offers to leave a message with the assistant, Mike was grudgingly forwarded to the Head Human Resources Honcho's personal voicemail.

The Head Human Resources Honcho would have much preferred to have been presently available to what he was presently unavailable doing instead. By at least a power of ten, and, if he was being honest, probably even two of them. What he was otherwise occupied with at that moment was smoldering quietly while the Executive Vice President painfully pontificated on the painfully obvious.

"Your deadline is nearly up," the EVP fairly mused, which pretty much summed the situation up in a nutshell.

"Thank you for mentioning it," the HHRH replied. "I might have forgotten, otherwise."

It took the Executive Vice President a second or two to realize he had just been on the receiving end of the other man's sarcasm.

"I'm glad you still have your sense of humor. That will at least leave you with something."

It took the Head Human Resources Honcho no time at all to realize he'd just been out-sarcasmed.

"I still have a good feeling about this," he lied. After all, there could always be an eleventh-hour miracle. And a Tooth Fairy, and Santa Claus...

"If you're thinking about an eleventh-hour miracle," said the EVP, interrupting the HHRH's thoughts, "I would remind you that the eleventh hour is already well past its sell-by date."

"Then I probably shouldn't be wasting my time hanging around here, engaging in idle chit-chat."

The Head Human Resources Honcho stood up and double-timed it out the door and back to his office. He eschewed the customary exchange of pleasantries with his assistant and, closing his own door behind him, leaned limply against his desk. He didn't even make it all the way to his chair.

Out of the corner of his eye he noticed that the red message light on his telephone was blinking. This was unusual, since his assistant was, as a rule, particularly mercenary about intercepting his calls. Whether exceptionally dedicated or just exceptionally nosy, it was rare for anyone not in a position to fire her to make it all the way into voicemail.

After listening to his message and determining conclusively that the Mike Moskowitz on the recording and the Myron Moskowitz at the root of all his current difficulties were one and the same Moskowitz, the Head Human Resources Honcho stood bolt upright. He played the message again, and just to make sure he wasn't imagining things, allowed himself one final encore before completing the remaining distance to his swivel chair. He sat, rose, then sat again and, with trembling fingers, dialed the number that kept reciting itself over and over in his mind.

Mike answered on the second ring. Thirty seconds later, he and the Head Human Resources Honcho had an appointment to meet the next day for coffee.

Mike hit the *Stop* button on his cell phone with a sensation approximating relief. This part had gone surprisingly well; the HHRH hadn't sounded like the fatuous, officious jerk-o-crat he had seemed in all their previous conversations. If anything, the man sounded more like an anxious, prospective suitor than the all-powerful Oz he typically made himself out to be.

Mike had been driving when the Head Human Resources Honcho's call came through and the whole conversation was over too quickly to pull over and park for it. This worked out well for Christine a few cars behind, who might have lost him if he'd made any sudden detours.

She had, however, noticed Mike in the posture of someone holding a cell phone to his head, which caused her to wonder whom he might have been talking to. That young woman, again? But he had just spent a good chunk of the morning with her. Was there yet *another* young woman out there somewhere? Had Mike suddenly become some sort of chick magnet?

Maybe there was more to her husband than she gave him credit for. Though for the life of her, Christine hadn't the slightest idea what it could possibly be.

When Mike pulled into the parking lot of a large fitness center, Christine kept on driving. It was obvious that he was not going to work, so she had, she was satisfied, successfully sussed that one. The other woman—women?—business was a bit trickier. There still may or may not be something fishy going on in the surplus-female department, but Christine was surprisingly unconcerned about that possibility. If anything, she was just curious about what the attraction was. She was going to have to give this particular mystery a little quality time with her little gray cells.

For his part, Mike enjoyed a leisurely workout completely oblivious to the machinations taking place in his wife's mind. In other words, it was back to business as usual as far as he was concerned.

The Head Human Resources Honcho, for *his* part, continued holding onto the telephone receiver long after Mike had ended things on his end, as if putting the receiver down might break some kind of spell. When he finally did set it back in its cradle, he sank deeply into his plush executive swivel chair and remained there in perfect stillness, as if the act of moving might break some kind of spell as well.

As the reality of what had just transpired gradually became inescapable and the spell momentarily appeared jinx-proof, the HHRH began to smile. This started as a slow loosening of the tension originating at the corners of his mouth, and was followed closely by a relaxing of the vice-like pressure his upper and lower lips had hitherto been exerting upon one another. The edges of his jaw spread out next, causing a barely discernible drop of his chin and allowing his cheeks to rise ever-so-slightly. Momentum carried all the relevant parts into an upwardly curved position, culminating in a grin the Cheshire Cat would have felt proud to display.

The smile, as these things sometimes do, begat a laugh. This also developed in phases. From a truncated, swallowed-burp-like sound to the chug of a hesitant seven-fifty cc motorcycle, culminating in the sort of hysterical outburst that makes people in authority extremely nervous. His assistant, unable to avoid hearing it, decided that now might be an excellent time to consider going to lunch.

Once the laugh had run its course, the Head Human Resources Honcho briefly entertained engaging the Executive Vice President in a further discussion of eleventh-hour miracles. But since his prospective chickens were not, as yet, officially hatched, it seemed more prudent to save that conversation until the absolute-last minute. With any luck, it would prove to be a showstopper.

Chapter 27

Celia weighed in.

"It'll never work," she assured her son.

"Thanks for that vote of parental encouragement. Why are you so sure it won't work?"

"It's way too complicated. That's why."

"Complicated things work, sometimes."

"Myron, the whole idea is cockamamie. I'm only suggesting that maybe you should try something else instead."

"Mother, there *is* nothing else instead. If this doesn't work, I'll probably have to take up riding motorcycles with Herman Rabinowitz."

"I remember Herman. He was a nice boy. What'd you say he was up to these days?"

"He calls himself 'Paco' now, and...it's a long story. Look, I've got to give this a shot. So will you wish me luck, at least?"

"All right, so good luck already. What does Christine think about all this?"

Myron, er, Mike, looked down without answering.

"You're kidding! Don't tell me she still doesn't know?"

"We...haven't had that conversation yet, no."

"Haven't...What do the two of you talk about? The weather?"

"And the news, sometimes. You know, current events, that kind of thing."

"Explains a lot."

"What does *that* mean?"

"Nothing. So when is this miracle of perfect timing supposed to take place?"

"I'm meeting with the head of human resources tomorrow morning, and if that goes well...well, hopefully soon after that."

"I see. Myron, I know I'm only your mother, but may I make a suggestion?"

"Go ahead. You will anyway."

"I'm a mother. That's my prerogative."

"Then please, Mother. What's your suggestion?"

"Get your job back first. *Then* run that *fakakta* scheme by them. It's important you should do it in the right order."

Mike couldn't really argue with that.

"Good advice, Mother. That's what I'll do."

"Job...*fakakta* scheme. Job...*fakakta*. Remember that."

"I think I've got it."

"I'm glad, Myron. And in case of something, there are worse things you could do than hang around with Herman Rabinowitz."

He couldn't really argue with that, either.

Christine had spent the time between breaking off surveillance and figuring out what to do for dinner in serious contemplation of her matrimonial housemate. It seemed entirely possible there were aspects of Mike she had lately overlooked. As she considered that, it occurred to her just how that little oversight might have slipped by her.

They say that familiarity breeds contempt, but this is only half true. After contempt it breeds pretending the familiar object isn't really there, and then it is only a matter of time before he (since we're talking about Mike, after all) becomes downright invisible. The large pile of extra laundry notwithstanding.

And Mike had, for all intents and purposes, become invisible. Or invisible-ish, anyway. More translucent than transparent, perhaps. But if one was being honest, which Christine honestly was at the moment, she had developed the habit of looking *through* him rather than *at* him lately. Well, a bit longer than lately, if she was still being honest, which she still honestly was. It was, Christine had to admit, much harder to notice things when your mind kept making them disappear.

So from now on she would have to start paying closer attention. That meant spending more time with Mike in his natural *milieu*, and, frankly, she wasn't even sure what that was anymore. That coffee shop seemed to be prime Mike real estate these days. Perhaps she would become a regular there, too. Christine hoped there were other featured haunts in the Mike milieu as well, since she really didn't enjoy coffee-based beverages all that much.

The Head Human Resources Honcho intended to meet the Moskowitz fully armed with the weapons of his trade. These largely consisted of forms, reams and reams of them. There were long forms and short forms, government forms and company forms, and forms whose purpose the HHRH had long ago lost sight of. What this last group of forms did that all the others didn't he had no idea. Taken together, there were enough individual documents to populate a planet with, in a strictly *pro-forma* sense.

Signing people up was one of those administrative functions he had happily delegated decades ago, but he still reserved the processing of new VIPs for himself. Fortunately, the company had not hired a new VIP since he'd originally delegated the signing-up work, so he had successfully avoided having to perform this tedious duty ever since.

Myron Moskowitz, however, distinctly fell into the VIP category. For altogether stupid reasons, getting the man on board, or rather, *back* on board, had become the single most important objective in the Head Human Resources Honcho's professional existence. His personal one, too, since he was in no position to join the ranks of the unemployably unemployed at this particular stage of it.

He did not know if Mike would be prepared to sign on the dotted line, any of them, when the two men met. But he was willing to let his new-found hope run quite zealously amok until further notice.

Dan had been busy behind the scenes lining up the various

and sundry people and machinery that would be called for if his plan was ever going to get off the ground.

This was much more complicated than it seemed, which, let's face it, was already seriously complicated. He had first broached the subject at the next monthly meeting of the nuclei, and found their support and encouragement to be completely underwhelming.

"I thought we'd resolved that one, like, two presidential elections ago," had been the official consensus. When Dan suggested that *resolving* and *ignoring until it goes away* were not, in fact, the same thing, he was informed in no uncertain terms that, where Myron Moskowitz was concerned, yes, in fact, they were.

Fortunately, while that may have been the official consensus, it did not happen to be the exclusive one. There were still a few nuclei who, whether out of humanitarian impulses or just unable to resist a totally insane challenge, offered their cells in aid of the Moskowitz cause. They agreed to meet later that evening at a coffee shop Dan knew about and which, by now, everyone else does, too.

Dan phoned Kermit to bring him and, by extension, the rest of the cell, up to speed.

"Yeah, well, we may have a problem," said Kermit.

Now what? thought Dan.

"Now what?" he said.

"There seems to be some, uh, *disagreement* about whether the technical pathway you mapped out is going to work. Isn't that right, Jackie?"

Jackie did not reply in a way Dan could have heard.

"What did Jackie say?"

"Nothing. She's not talking to me, unless you count flipping me the middle finger as a form of sign language."

Things may be looking up on the old personal front, Dan told himself.

"I've gone through it a hundred times. You guys have, too, and everybody agreed it was perfect. So, what's changed?"

"Most of us still think it's perfect. Practically all of us. We're nearly unanimous in our agreement. Virtually..."

"Shut up, Kermit! Give me the phone," came a voice which was distinctly female and distinctly very ticked off.

"Hello, Dan? It's Jackie."

No? Really?

"Hi, Jackie. Sounds like I've missed something by not being there."

"You've missed something, all right!" she replied, using her outdoor voice. She toned things down considerably when she next spoke.

"You missed something. We all missed something, since none of the rest of us caught it, either. It's the logistics, actually, not the technical pathway. If Kermit wasn't such a total fathead he'd..."

"Um, Jackie, let's stick to the topic for a minute. What about the logistics?"

"There's a flaw in it that you, we, haven't accounted for. It could screw up everything."

Jackie proceeded to describe the potential fly in the ointment as Dan listened, first with a huge smile, then with a huge non-smile, and then with mild catatonia. His brain was still functioning, more-or-less, and he responded to the news with the only thing he could think of at that moment.

"We'll just have to drive off that bridge when we come to it."

The problem, as Jackie had correctly identified it, was the government. More specifically, it had to do with the time delay between data being entered into the government's computers and that same data being permanently posted within the system. Dan had known there would be a delay. There always was. What he hadn't known, however, was that the length of the delay was different for every governmental agency. Which meant that, while an infinite number of *ENTER* buttons could, theoretically at least, all be pushed at the exact same instant, the actual entries could be minutes, hours or even days apart. This would, of course, throw the simultaneous requirement of Dan's plan completely out the window, placing the whole operation in serious jeopardy.

Or, as Dan himself put it: "I'm doomed!"

Mike breezed through his workout, causing several of the fitness center's other patrons to complain of a draft. He had found it increasingly hard to concentrate on what he was doing, which made a normally long and exhaustive exercise routine fly by swiftly and effortlessly. He hardly even needed a shower afterward, but he had already finished taking one before he'd realized it.

Mike wasn't sure whether tomorrow's meeting was more terrifyingly-exciting or excitingly-terrifying, but he knew that both excitement and terror figured prominently, whatever the proportion. He also knew that coming out of it without his old job back—or without *anybody's* old job back, he wasn't going to be picky—would be unthinkable. And after months without anything more stressful to deal with than boredom and being Celia Moskowitz's son, the real pressure of real pressure was posing a real shock to his pathetically out of shape system.

Preparation, Mike thought. That was the key. The better prepared he was, the less likely he would be to say or do something unsalvageably stupid. Even salvageably stupid could probably be prevented if he was properly prepared.

Mike stopped off at a nearby drug store and picked up a medium-sized, college-lined spiral notebook, and three pens. He did not need three pens; one would have been more than sufficient for his purposes. But since it is virtually impossible to buy only one of anything anymore, the pen-purchasing customer's choices these days were pretty much limited to quantities of either three or ten, and Mike did not have ten pens' worth of writing left in him between now and the hour of his ultimate mortal breath.

His next port of call was the friendly neighborhood public library. This was a bit of a risk, as far as being seen by someone either he or Christine knew. But he took it on faith that his wife would not suddenly decide to make an appearance, especially after what happened last time with the Cossacks posing as librarians there. She had avoided the place like a tuberculosis ward for years. Mike saw no reason why she should reverse that trend any time within the next few hours. As for anyone else…well, at this point, who really gave a rat's patootie? Bring 'em on. He *did* choose a table out of sight of the main entrance, however, just to be on the safe side.

Opening his newly-acquired, medium-sized, college-ruled spiral notebook on the surface in front of him and extracting one-third of his newly-acquired pens, Mike began the process of not writing anything. This is, of course, the first step in the process of writing something, in the manner of taking aim before pulling the trigger. The imminent scribe lines his thoughts up along the line of the stylus, steadies his grip and, in Mike's case, continues holding that attitude until purposefully dropping his pen.

He looked around and observed no one apparently observing him back. Picking the pen back up, he began jotting down whatever thoughts popped into his head, in whatever order they happened to pop there.

Get job back.

This took its rightful place at the top of the page.

Make HHRH want me to get my job back.

So far, so good.

Don't say anything stupid.

He was clearly on the right track.

Only say things that are the opposite of stupid.

Still on the right track, more-or-less.

Say smart things.

Sometimes a list can become its own worst enemy.

After slightly less than two hours of scrivenly toil,

J. Bresler

Mike had produced a script he believed he could follow with minimal risk of misadventure. He had covered all the bases his mind was willing to conceive, such as asking for his job back, giving great reasons for them giving him his job back, and expressing the proper amount of gratitude for getting his job back. He even worked in some contingencies for having to justify the proposition if it became necessary, overcoming any objections the Head Human Resources Honcho might throw at him, as well as how to grovel appropriately if push came to fall down on your knees and beg 'til the cows come home.

Mike headed home with the happy delusion that he might, very possibly, pull this off.

The Head Human Resources Honcho did not want to blow it, either. Failure was not an option he was at all eager to contemplate by any stretch of the imagination, and the HHRH had a pretty vivid imagination.

Preparation, he thought. That's the key! The better prepared he was, the less likely he would be to find himself middle-aged and unemployed. Late-middle-aged, if acknowledging that fact could in any way be conceived as liberating. He decided it would probably be a good idea to script out his pitch to Mr. Moskowitz, including the "Mister" part. Make the man feel important, at least until he was safely back on board and could be treated just like any other pedestrian cog in the corporate machinery.

Being able to offer him a raise and promotion, even a token one, would have added an extra arrow to his recruitment quiver, in the event a little negotiating was called for. But the Executive Vice President had put an emphatic kibosh on that idea, either out of pure spite or simply to save those options for himself to fall back on as a last resort. The HHRH, however, had his money on pure spite. The EVP could be a real buzzkill that way.

He produced a letter-sized legal pad from his topmost desk drawer, and set not one but two pens on top of it. The Human Resources Department went through ten-packs like the Myron Moskowitzes of this world went through oxygen. Mostly this was because practically everybody who ever set foot in the office tended to walk out of there with one.

The Head Human Resources Honcho found this strange, considering that, outside his department, hardly anybody ever wrote anything down on paper anymore.

His efforts took a scant half-hour, since his options in the potential misadventure arena were considerably fewer than Mike's. He supposed he had the Executive Vice President to thank for that, though he somehow failed to fully appreciate the favor just then. The HHRH's arsenal consisted of the offer, a few words about the value of Mr. Moskowitz *accepting* the offer, some vacant platitudes he'd probably attribute to various executives higher up on the organizational chart, and that was about it. Not a lot of wiggle-room, foot-in-mouth-wise, unless maybe he over-did it on the vacant platitudes, which would be easy enough to avoid. The HHRH had never been much of a lavish platitude sort of guy.

After that, however, it was up to fate, or luck, or, more

plausibly, Moskowitz himself.

At dinner that evening, Christine found her husband acting unusually preoccupied.

"A penny for your thoughts," she might as well have said to herself. "I said, a penny for your thoughts!" This time leaving no doubt whose thoughts she was bidding so cheaply for.

"Hmm?" Mike replied to no one in particular.

"Mike, look at me."

He obeyed mechanically.

"You're in another world this evening. Anything wrong?"

"Huh? Oh, no. Fine. Fine." He returned to his previous activity, which did not involve looking at his wife.

"*Something's* on your mind tonight."

"I'm just thinking. I do that, sometimes." He looked back up at Christine, and immediately wished that he hadn't. Not that he had any reason for wishing it. He just did.

"Are you worried about something?" Christine asked, nowhere near ready to give up yet.

Mike had to think about that for a minute. He decided that no, after all, he really wasn't. Looking up at Christine again, this time bearing a triumphant smile, he answered "Nope. Everything's coming up roses."

Christine gave up.

Chapter 28

Try as he might, Dan could not force himself to concentrate on anything he was doing at work. Fortunately, in his job with the Itinerant Life & Casualty Company this was not an occupational requirement.

He had just spent a sleepless twenty-four hours frantically researching how long it would take each of the various agencies his plan depended on to put newly-entered data on-line. It had been like eating spaghetti: no matter how much you thought you'd put away, you still seemed to have the same amount of the stuff left sitting on the plate that you originally started with. There were, in other words, a hell of a lot of them.

Eventually he'd cleaned his plate, and that was when the real fun began. Dan now needed to put all the information he had gathered into some sort of intelligible order. For this he could have really benefited from one of those sophisticated logistical programs like the ones shipping companies used. Unfortunately, like most things, there was never a convenient shipping company around when you needed one. Like now, for instance.

Kermit had attempted to hack into a major, international transportation company's server, only to have been out-hacked by the company's own computer security. If Jackie hadn't yanked the power supply out of his laptop when she did, Kermit would have found himself facing some serious Federal time by now. Still, it would be safe to say that, for a second or two there, Jackie considered that prospect rather favorably before finally pulling the plug.

"Are there any of these you think might be, I dunno, more important than the rest of them?" Dan had asked the group, but addressing himself to Jackie.

"This was all your idea," replied Kermit, who, frankly, was not taking all the Dan-and-Jackie eye contact he'd been noticing lately very well.

Unfortunately, Dan *did* know. They were all the same. This was an equal-opportunity conundrum.

"Look on the bright side," someone had suggested. "Maybe this Moskowitz guy won't get his job back, and you'll have been worrying over nothing."

Which was when Dan knew for certain that the show would go on.

Back in his Itinerant Life & Casualty Company cubicle, Dan's pocket buzzed and vibrated. He was vaguely aware of some change in his immediate ionosphere, but his sleep-deprived and troubled brain was so detached from the world around him that it failed to connect these phenomena with anything personal. When his desk phone rang, however, a voice, somewhere in some remote part of that same brain, told him he was in some way expected to do something by way of responding to it.

There was a brief but anxious interval while Dan determined that this shockingly loud disruption was not the result of a tornado warning or, indeed, any other cause for retreating to relative safety underneath his desk. By the time he could successfully name that tune, though, it had stopped.

The faint buzzing and vibrating in his pocket resumed once again, and this time Dan had no difficulty placing the source. Well, almost no difficulty. After rummaging around for his cell phone, he found two new text messages from Jackie, the first expressing concern for his well-being, and the second suggesting they get together after work. If Dan had had the energy, he would have given an air high-five, or at the very least, smiled.

On a tired hunch, Dan did a search of all the programs loaded onto his laptop and discovered some unused financial software, which had either been loaded as part of the original package or added later in yet another waste of corporate resources. Probably the latter, Dan guessed. He opened it and found what he had hoped would be there: an accounting program with a spreadsheet function. He got straight to work filling in the blanks; there were, as already alluded to, an awful lot of them. His rendezvous with Jackie would have to wait.

Mike showed up for his date with destiny somewhat early. *Really* early, as a matter of fact. He had not wanted to be late for such an important occasion and had managed to overcompensate for it accordingly. He considered going inside and getting a head start on the caffeine consumption, but feared that he would probably overcompensate there, too. And the last thing he wanted was to be bouncing off the walls by the time the Head Human Resources Honcho arrived. Or worse, find himself in ferocious need of a pee at a critical place in the discussion.

While he was no stranger to killing time, Mike's expertise in this field was more along the lines of the open-ended variety. This situation was awkward, or at least the amount of time needing to be killed was. There was too much of it to do nothing and not enough to do much of anything. A book or magazine would have come in really handy right about now, but by the time he'd found a store, picked something out and driven back, there would be no opportunity read any of it. Mike took out his cell phone to aimlessly surf the internet in the interim, and, looking at it, remembered the device was old enough to have come with a rotary dial. No internet. Inter-not.

He exited the car and took a walk around the block, to the extent that one could effectively do a lap around a strip mall. There was still more time left over than he could ignore comfortably, however, so Mike surrendered and made his way inside the coffee emporium.

By habit, he gravitated toward his table, only to find it already occupied. He did a visual three-sixty in search of a suitable alternative when he heard someone calling his name.

"Mr. Moskowitz!" came a cry from somewhere in the back.

Mike followed the sound and recognized the Head Human Resources Honcho waving and looking around with obvious self-consciousness. He gave a short wave back, raised his index finger in the universal sign for "one minute," and turned toward the service counter.

Glancing skyward at the menu of coffee-based beverages, Mike found himself unable to read anything. He knew he was looking at the menu, and that there were words up there. He could make out the letters. But stare as he did, none of them combined in any sensible way for him.

Now, admittedly, the names of the coffee-based beverages on offer were mostly made up and silly-sounding. Still, they were comprised of the usual complement of vowels and consonants, and in the correct proportion to be pronounceable by the average reader of English. Or even American, for that matter. Yet despite his many years of familiarity with the language, Mike could not focus his attention enough to make heads or tails out of any of them. Fortunately, at that moment he was saved by one of the servers.

"Good morning, Mr. M! Your usual?"

Mike just nodded, slowly. Sometimes it paid to be a regular.

Mr. M. and his usual walked cautiously over to their table, while the HHRH watched with the anticipation of a spectator at a tennis match. Mike's eventual arrival was only slightly less anticlimactic than the average net serve.

The two men sat facing each other, not sure whose turn it was. The Head Human Resources Honcho held one of those unwavering public relations smiles gone ever-so-slightly out of kilter. Mike's expression fell somewhere between a nervous grin and that thing undertakers do. Finally, Mike got the party started.

"Thank you for agreeing to meet me," he said. So far, so good.

"Oh, my pleasure!" replied the Head Human Resources Honcho. "I should probably be thanking *you*!"

The conversation had opened to a draw. Service, Mike.

"So, um, as I say, it was nice of you to go out of your way like this."

"I was more than happy to."

Had this been a real tennis match, the fans would have all started reaching for their smart phones right about now.

"Right. Well, thank you for saying so. Anyway, as I mentioned on the telephone the other day, it's hard to leave a company as wonderful as ours—well, yours now, I guess. . . And not miss the, er, company."

"You miss the company?"

"Oh, yes. Very much!"

"The company, or the *company*?"

Mike wasn't sure which was which, so he played a safe shot.

"Both."

The HHRH was visibly relieved.

"Yes, well, and Mr. Moskowitz, the company misses you too, I assure you."

"The company, or the *company*?" Mike blurted out before he could stop himself.

The Head Human Resources Honcho knew how to play a safe shot, too.

"Oh, both, of course," he said, nodding like a bobble

doll.

The score was holding firm at love-love. It was time for somebody to break volley.

"Right. So. This early retirement thing you had me try...You know, when you first suggested it I thought, wow! Really great opportunity! All that free time and no loss in pay...I mean, what was there not to like, right?"

Mike made eye contact with the HHRH, his gaze imploring; the HHRH's like a deer's caught in headlights. Mike went on:

"Yes. Well, you see, I've tried it for a while now. As you know, of course," he added, acknowledging the obvious, "and, frankly, I just don't really think it's for me. Not yet, anyway. Maybe, you know, down the road a ways. A *long* ways. Do you know what I mean?"

The Head Human Resources Honcho just nodded again, slowly, rhythmically and mechanically. This time he kept it up long after it was technically necessary for him to, and long after it would have been appropriate for him to say something in response.

Mike had braced himself after asking that last question, and was still bracing himself. All that bracing was proving to be a strain, and he was just on the verge of beginning to vibrate when the HHRH finally elected to open his mouth.

"Ah, Mr. Moskowitz," he managed, in his best reassuring, human resources voice. "These things go like that sometimes. We strive to do the best for our employees, trying new things, *experimental* things, and unfortunately they cannot all work out as we hope they will. Of course, we would prefer to be right all the time, ha, ha...but we're only human. Not to imply that *you* are human, I mean, flawed in any way, that is..."

Mike loosened the brace. He immediately noticed a powerful urge to use the restroom that hadn't been there a moment earlier.

"So you're saying that this was an experiment," he volunteered, "for my benefit, which did not turn out as well as, well, certain *other* experiments might have, if there'd been any."

"Exactly, Mr. Moskowitz!" exclaimed a relieved Head Human Resources Honcho.

Mike nodded. It seemed like the right thing to do.

"That makes perfect sense," he lied. "So, we can just chalk this, um, experiment, up to experience, then?"

"One for the books, Mr. Moskowitz. One for the books."

Mike still needed to use the restroom, but the match had reached a critical stage. The Head Human Resources Honcho had developed a similar urge, and chose now to mention it. Mike chose now to mention it, too. What followed sounded like what you'd get if you combined:

> "Mr. Moskowitz, will you please excuse me a moment? I'd like to make a quick visit to the restroom."

and:

> "Excuse me, but I *really* need to run to the restroom, if you don't mind."

This was followed by choruses of: "Oh, please, go right ahead," and a refrain of two guys urging each other to go first. The Head Human Resources Honcho won. Or lost, depending on how you look at it.

"No, no, Mr. Moskowitz, I insist. I can wait. Really."

Mike knew when to take *yes* for an answer.

Pit-stops duly taken, Mike and the HHRH returned to the business at hand.

"I'd like to come back to work."

"We'd like you to come back to work."

And with little additional fanfare, the deal was sealed. Mike held off on any reference to the Dan complication. There were still a few days left before his reinstatement became official; and, as he'd been doing so often lately, he decided he could drive off that particular bridge when he got there.

Deep within the bowels of the Itinerant Life & Casualty Company's corporate headquarters slumped one tired little teddy bear. *Ursus exhausticus,* Dan might have quipped, if quipping did not require substantially more energy than he had left in him.

Within the devastating fatigue, however, there existed a feeling of calm contentment. For, against all odds, Dan had successfully calculated a perfect batting order for all that data entry. The near certainty of its never coming off did not diminish the sense of accomplishment a jot.

He had not strained his brain cells so hard since cramming for his last set of finals in college. Back then, all he needed to do was commit a bunch of relatively unimportant facts to short-term memory for a few hours. This, on the other hand, had been like one of those interminable word problems that keep going on and on without ever getting to a question. Relying on an outdated accounting program to do it with hadn't helped, either.

Dan noticed the familiar buzzing in his front pocket. He correctly identified the source as his cell phone, and that was as far as consciousness would allow him to go.

Chapter 29

The Hibachi Room had an airy, cheerful quality to it that the Head Human Resources Honcho had never experienced before. The long conference table, surrounded as it was by its matching swivel chairs, possessed an almost poetic symmetry: ordered, but not obsessively so. The wall-length bank of windows (had he known the room had windows?) framed a cerulean sky accented here and there by an occasional gray or white cloud. The image recalled a painting the HHRH had once seen in a museum somewhere many years ago. A Monet, perhaps, or maybe a Manet. He could never remember which was which and wasn't sure it really mattered all that much anyway, in the grand scheme of things.

As it happened, the patches of gray or white cloud probably outnumbered the patches of cerulean sky by a pretty wide margin, but you could not tell that to the Head Human Resources Honcho this morning. God was in his heaven, *he* was in the Hibachi Room, and all was right with the world.

That he was in the Hibachi Room at all was due to his having been summoned there by the Executive Vice

President's secretary. The twerp himself either couldn't be bothered or wouldn't demean himself enough to pick up the phone and do his own dirty work.

Well, no skin off the Head Human Resources Honcho's nose. Besides, for the first time in memory the HHRH found himself enthusiastically embracing the opportunity of a meeting with senior management. So much so, in fact, he had arrived for it ridiculously early and was, for quite some time, the room's sole occupant.

His solitude was interrupted first by a couple of lesser Vice Presidents, neither of whom looked particularly happy to be there. Glum, was how the Head Human Resources Honcho would have described them. These were followed by a few of the company's somewhat more prominent Senior VPs, who ignored the others, and, finally, by the CEO and EVP, who ignored everyone else in descending rank order.

Seats were taken, papers were duly shuffled, and pens were nervously fiddled with until the CEO conspicuously stopped moving. He looked over at the Executive Vice President and nodded once, executively. The latter got right down to business. He addressed the Head Human Resources Honcho, who was sitting opposite him smiling absently.

"We have, I believe, discussed the Moskowitz situation *ad nauseum*, so I won't waste anyone's time by re-covering unnecessary background. You," he said, pointing menacingly in the direction of the HHRH, "were given responsibility for getting Myron Moskowitz back to work. I don't want to hear any excuses. I don't want any long explanations. Yes or no: *did you get it done?*"

The Head Human Resources Honcho had been marveling at how much a newly-appearing cloud resembled the profile of George Washington. It took a moment of strained silence before he realized he was expected to say something.

"Oh, um, hmm?"

The EVP repeated his question with obvious impatience and less-obvious glee.

"Oh. Yes. He starts back a week from Monday."

All eyes turned in on the Executive Vice President, including his own. His expression at that moment comprised the best features of stunned, embarrassed, livid, and about-to-detonate.

The HHRH went back to looking at his cloud, which now resembled a giant cow. The meeting adjourned without him.

Mike was a new Moskowitz.

He had emerged from his little coffee klatch a lighter, happier being. Mike nearly skipped the short distance from the coffee shop to his car, but he wasn't quite *that* new a Moskowitz. It seemed as though a sixteen-ton weight had been lifted off him and, if he concentrated hard enough, he just might be able to fly. Being somewhat on the order of skipping, however, he didn't attempt to do that, either.

Practically another hour of relief-inspired bliss enveloped him before it dawned on Mike that he was not

nearly out of the woods yet. Sure, he had gotten through
Phase One relatively unscathed. But this was mere child's
play compared to Phase Two. Phase Two! That was where
Phase One would probably go to die. His future rested on a
dangerously tottering house of cards once it entered the
Phase Two Zone, and Mike could swear he saw funnel
clouds lining up in tight formation against the horizon.

He had not spoken with Dan in several days. This had
seemed like a good thing, in a no-news-is-good-news kind
of way. But now Mike was having serious doubts. *Really*
serious doubts. Staggeringly serious, not to put too fine a
point on the matter.

He dialed the number for Dan's cell phone, silently
urging the ringing to end with its owner picking up, and
sighing with an audible "huff!" when the call instead went
to voicemail. Mike hesitated so long trying to decide what
message to leave that he missed the window for providing
one. Fortunately, the voicemail service had features for
reviewing and, if desired, re-recording messages. He
nearly missed that second window, too.

Dan would have been more than happy to answer
Mike's call when it came in, but this had been one of those
occasions when the vibrating in his pocket and the buzzing
in his ears were happening in an alternate universe.

A still somewhat out-of-body Dan returned that phone
call a short time later and assured Mike that things on his
end were progressing exactly as expected. He neglected to
mention that those things were expected to end in complete disaster since Mike seemed to believe...well, just
believe. This whole enterprise had been so thoroughly

fraught with buzzkills that it seemed downright cruel to heartlessly heap yet another one onto an already over-stacked pile. Better to let Mr. Moskowitz enjoy a little short-lived encouragement, Dan reasoned. Because when the sledgehammer eventually dropped, encouragement might not be the only short-lived thing in the room.

The cubicle-like area that passed for Dan's office at the Itinerant Life & Casualty Company was graced by the presence of Jackie who, as already mentioned, was pretty hot in a geeky sort of way. She'd become concerned when Dan failed to respond to a single one of her texts, so when her afternoon break came around she ventured off in search of him. Jackie found her cell leader either contemplative or just pretty much out of it. Whichever it was, he appeared to be breathing on his own. She took that as a good sign.

"Dan!" she called out excitedly, startling the bearer of that name into seeking a position of relative safety underneath his work station.

Climbing back out, slowly, he was within inches of reading his visitor the riot act. But it was Jackie, and she was kinda hot, and his mother hadn't raised any dummies.

"Jackie! What a, um, pleasant surprise." Which was at least half-true.

He got up, found his chair and stood next to it, alternately resting his hand on the seatback and taking it off, occasionally causing the chair to roll and himself to roll with it. Hands often held a slightly awkward dexterity for him. Sometimes it was hard to know just what to do with them when they weren't specifically required.

"Where have you been? Oh, never mind that, now that I know you're all right. I've just been going over your implementation sequence, and it's brilliant! I don't know how you figured all that out, but I think it could really work!"

This was news to Dan.

"In fact, I'm so excited right now that, if we weren't at work, I'd probably kiss you!"

Dan, he told himself, whatever you do, don't mention Kermit.

"What about Kermit?"

Why'd he have to mention that?

"I doubt Kermit wants to kiss you. Or me either, right about now."

Dan glanced around his cubicle.

"What are you looking for?"

"The hidden camera."

Jackie got it. But then, she generally did.

"Let's get everyone together tonight over at my place. You can stick around afterwards."

Dan got it. Or at any rate, he sincerely hoped he might.

Chapter 30

Time is a funny thing, Mike observed. It was difficult to get time just right. He was his own case in point: having been burdened for far too long with far too much of it, he now sat bleakly despairing its impending loss. Or maybe, Mike reasoned, time was always the same and it was only people's perceptions of it that wavered. Mike was, in other words, enjoying the sort of thinking that only someone with an excessive amount of time on his hands would ever even *think* of thinking about. All that notwithstanding, he seriously wondered whether he had just made the biggest—no, make that the *second* biggest—mistake of his life, by getting his old job back.

"Mike? Are you home?" rang Christine's decibel-enhanced voice.

Nope. It wasn't a mistake. Or not one quite so high up on the list, at any rate.

"In here."

"What are you doing home?" Christine thought she might have stumbled onto something revelatory. You would have thought she'd know better by now.

"I decided to take a few mental-health days."

"Are you mentally under the weather?" his wife asked, seriously.

"No more than usual," Mike replied, somewhat less seriously. "I thought a little down time might be good for the ol' psyche."

"Oh, well don't get your hopes up too high. I don't think even a *lot* of down time would help that ol' psyche all that much."

It hadn't so far, he agreed somewhat moodily.

They stood facing each other, Moskowitz-a-Moskowitz, neither sure what else to say at that moment but not feeling any strong compulsion to take themselves elsewhere.

Whatever you do, thought Mike, don't suggest doing something together.

"So, as long as I'm home, do you want to go any-where?"

Oops.

"Together?"

Okay! A chance to weasel out of it.

"Why not?"

Paradise lost.

Christine acquiesced so quickly she caught even her-self by surprise. Mike acquiesced too. Or, more likely, just quit before he could dig himself in any deeper.

Their first port-o'-call was the neighborhood multi-plex. Mike couldn't remember the last time he and Chris-tine had gone to a movie together. It had to have been fifteen years ago, at least. At first, they could never agree on any one movie each was willing to sit through. Eventually, different tastes gave way to downright obstinacy. Nowadays, if the two felt like watching a movie together, they did so on separate television sets.

This time they had no trouble finding common ground film-wise, and the buttered vs. plain popcorn debate was solved with equal concord. There were no sour grapes.

Mike considered making an attempt at slipping away during one particularly dull patch in the film and placing a surreptitious call to Dan. But the action on-screen became interesting again, and before long he temporarily forgot that Dan even existed.

Dan, on the other hand, had not forgotten about *him*. His thoughts were inextricably Moskowitz, and not even a smiling Jackie or scowling Kermit could derail that train.

The cell was gathered at Jackie's apartment to put the finishing touches on the plan, and concord was not reigning supreme there. Rather, it was concord's cousin, discord, who was holding court at the moment. The cell members seemed deadlocked, unable to agree on just about everything.

Well, that wasn't entirely true. Dan was in complete agreement, as was Jackie. Kermit, however, was vociferously not on the same page, and was making a point of being as patently disagreeable as his capabilities allowed. One or two of the others, believing Jackie was treating their friend more meanly than even someone like Kermit deserved, took his side; and while they thought Dan's plan was brilliant, they were determined not to give him the satisfaction. What they gave him instead was a migraine.

"I don't know why we're even wasting our time talking

about this," Kermit insisted. "It's not like it can possibly work."

"That's why we're talking about it," answered Dan, his exasperation seeping out through his pores. "The object of the exercise is to figure out where we need to tweak the thing."

"*Scrap* the thing, you mean. Your plan totally sucks."

"So you keep saying. But *where* does it suck? How? What am I missing? Give me at least *one* specific, for crying out loud!" Dan's head was throbbing so loudly he was sure the people in the next apartment were wondering where the noise was coming from.

"The plan is perfect. You're just peeved because you didn't think of it yourself!" Jackie told Kermit in her un-happy voice.

"Hard to think up something when nobody consults you about it first!" Kermit retorted, in his whiny, *nyah-nyah* voice.

"Kermit, you're an ass!" Jackie paused a second. "And that didn't even make sense!"

"Oh, yeah? Well, you..."

The throbbing in Dan's head began to form words at this juncture. When he cut Kermit off in mid-comeback it was in a voice that would have had Darth Vader looking around for an exit door.

"We'll proceed with the plan as it stands. Each of you knows what he needs to do, and I expect you to get it done. Well? What are you waiting for?" The air-being-breathed-through-a-heavy-black-mask sound effects were completely gratuitous.

When everyone else had gone, Dan got up to leave, too.

"You're leaving?" asked Jackie with evident disappointment.

"I have things I need to do. I need to call Mr. Moskowitz and—"

"Too bad. I was really looking forward to having you alone for a while."

Well, after all it was Jackie, and she was kinda hot, and Dan's mother hadn't raised any dummies.

The next morning, a much more optimistic Dan reached out to a much less domestically discontented Moskowitz. The latter had been having a pleasant couple of days with Christine. And the former, well, suffice to say that Jackie had been exceptionally encouraging.

"Hey, Mr. M. Just checking in. A 'Mike' check, you might say."

"Why might I say that?"

"Um, not important. So, is that head HR guy on board and ready to go?"

Mike knew there was something he had meant to do.

"Uh, yeah...not as such."

"He won't do it?"

"Well, to be honest, I haven't quite gotten around to discussing your plan with him yet."

After everything he'd been through, this was not the sort of news Dan was especially keen to hear. But the Jackie effect was strong, and thus he refrained from reaming Mike a new one right there over the phone.

"Cutting it a little close, aren't you, Mr. M?" he said, instead of what he really wanted to say.

"Yes, I suppose. Unintentionally, though. I meant to deal with that a few days ago, but it sort of slipped my mind."

The Jackie effect was strong, but even *it* couldn't keep Dan from beginning to lose his cool. Mike sensed he'd just prodded a proverbial hornet's nest, and added: "I'll call him as soon as we're off the phone."

Dan stopped seething long enough to give Mike all the relevant details. Just for spite, he made Mike write them down and repeat them back to him. Twice. If there had been a blackboard handy, Mike would have spent a period in detention filling it.

Realizing he had forgotten to call the Head Human Resources Honcho had caught Mike almost as much by surprise as it had Dan. All the time he'd been spending with Christine had kept him so distracted that, until Dan mentioned it, he hadn't thought about going back to work even once. Freaky, really, considering it had become his life's foremost preoccupation since bordering on forever.

He wondered if he'd been in denial, but denied that was it. The truth was, and he could not believe he was saying this even to himself, Mike had simply been enjoying spending time with his wife. This would not have seemed so unusual if that wife had been anyone other than Christine, a woman who seemingly avoided joy like it was some sort of large, highly venomous reptile. But for the past few days, at least, there had been no sign of that person. The one Mike had been hanging around these past few days had actually been fun to have around.

Which, while it may have explained why he hadn't called the Head Human Resources Honcho before, it did not explain why he *still* hadn't placed the call. Mike didn't have any answer at all for that one, so he picked up the phone and dialed the company's number.

The HHRH, who had been elevated to a state approaching human resources nirvana, was only too happy to take a call from the guy who had single-handedly helped him get one over on his old, corporate nemesis. His gusto began to wilt almost instantly, however, as words like *complication* and *potential problem* began bombarding his ear canal from the other end of the receiver. These were not good words. They were bad words. Unhappy words. Troublesome ones, if they were true.

The Head Human Resources Honcho cast furtive glances around his office as if expecting something nasty to leap out from behind one of the filing cabinets. As it happened, something large and insect-like roughly fitting that description *did* scurry out from behind one of the filing cabinets, but it was on the floor, where the HHRH wasn't looking, so he missed it. Which was probably just as well for everyone concerned, the bug most of all.

He agreed to meet Mike right away at the usual place, though the last thing his jangled nervous system needed right about now was another high-octane coffee-based beverage.

Chapter 31

Their usual table was waiting for them as if they'd made a reservation ahead of time. The Head Human Resources Honcho arrived a minute or two before Mike and scouted around for any place to sit that *wasn't* their usual table, feeling at that moment just the teeniest bit superstitious. But whether the feeling passed or the HHRH was simply surrendering to his destiny, he plopped his posterior down in familiar territory. Mike's own posterior was right behind him.

The two men exchanged brief acknowledgements, then Mike launched right into the business of explaining everything that had happened to him leading up to their present vis-a-vis. It took a while. Ironically, had the Head Human Resources Honcho listened to Mike when he first had the chance the whole thing would have taken practically no time and everyone would have been spared a great deal of grief, instead of turning into the plot device for a Marx Brothers movie.

"They wiped you off the computer?"

"Yep."

"*Which* computer?"

"All of them."

"*All* of them, all of them?"

"Every last one."

"But how—"

"The whole thing's beyond my comprehension. Apparently, you have to have an exceptionally gifted intellect to accomplish something that mind-bogglingly stupid. Otherwise, I suppose, everybody would be doing it."

"So you've been off the grid for... this whole time?"

"Um hmm."

"Really? Wow. What's it like?"

"It's sort of like the introduction to *A Tale of Two Cities*. And I've always hated *A Tale of Two Cities*."

"Wow. I mean, why wouldn't somebody in your situation just buy a motorcycle and ride off into the sunset?"

"That's Plan B."

"Fascinating. So what, exactly, do you need me to do?"

"Again, I don't understand all the mechanics, but somehow my name and various other things need to be entered by a lot of people into a lot of computers at the exact same time. You, or someone in your department, has to be one of those people."

"I can do that." The HHRH was relieved. This sounded easy enough, and Executive Vice President-proof, too. "And then you'll be back on the grid?"

"Beats the hell out of me. Seems to be the prevailing theory, though."

"Maybe I ought to talk to...those people?"

Mike thought that would be about as good an idea as giving matches to children and telling them to go play.

"Sorry, no time for that. So much to do. You understand. Can I tell them you'll do it?"

"What? Oh yes, of course. Whatever you need."

Mike was relieved. He crossed his fingers he had reason to be.

The men parted, shaking hands so vigorously that, under different circumstances, the act might have seemed a little weird. The Head Human Resources Honcho high-tailed it back to the office. Not to get back to doing anything important and work-related but instead to look up *Myron Moskowitz* on the internet. His search engine of choice completed the task almost before it had begun.

Mike was going home, but first he needed to bring Dan up to speed *in re* the company's human resources department's commitment to cooperate. He probably wouldn't phrase it quite that way when he got Dan on the phone.

For Dan, this was the last card on an already over-stacked house of them. When the news finally reached him, Dan was relieved. He crossed *his* fingers he had reason to be.

Somehow, Dan had succeeded at roping in everyone he thought he could possibly need for this grand experiment of his to take wing. This was really saying something since the plan required a veritable cast of thousands, each of whom would have to be ready and willing to perform his or her part according to a critically precise schedule. Fortunately, most of the volunteers already had a sporting interest of one kind or another in the outcome, so their participation had not required an excessive amount of arm-twisting.

As a special, added feature, not a few of Dan's Little Helpers were, in fact, employees of some of the very same entities Mike's data needed to be submitted to, and were thus uniquely qualified to do the entering. There were still a few wildcards, most notably wherever government agencies were concerned (and that was assuming their computer systems would even be working that day), but Dan was cautiously optimistic. The Jackie Effect again, no doubt.

And then, there was Kermit. He had his own version of the Jackie Effect, which to all outward appearances was the polar opposite of the one making Dan such a happy camper. Kermit could wind up being the biggest wildcard in the equation, though for all practical purposes you could not really describe him as wild and he was by no means a card.

Sure, he *had* taken to grinning fiendishly of late. But Kermit had always been a bit skewed toward the over-ly-dramatic, so for all anyone knew this might be just an-other one of his stupid phases. Besides, Dan assured himself, if it turned out to be anything else Jackie would take it as a personal responsibility to get even with Kermit herself. Sort of like delegating only without actually hav-ing to, which was just as well. Dan didn't even have the energy to tell somebody else what to do, lately.

Celia was feeling neglected. She did, sometimes. Proba-bly more than sometimes, when you got right down to it. Usually she merely shrugged the feeling off as part of any unappreciated mother's lot. But there were times when she thought her flesh-and-blood was behaving more ungratefully than he normally did, and her present disposition left little doubt to the initiated that this was one of those times.

Her Myron, for whom she'd (fill in the blank) had not been around to see her in over a week, and hadn't so much as picked up a telephone, at least as far as Celia was concerned, in considerably longer than that. Figuring he must have been in an accident or, God forbid, something worse, she had finally broken down and called him herself.

Imagine her disappointment, then, when Celia discovered that the fruit of her loins had not only *not* been in an accident or, God forbid, anything worse, but had instead been busy doing things with his wife. That explanation required more suspension of disbelief than a home-made Godzilla movie; and, between the two, Celia was more inclined to believe Godzilla.

"Myron, if you didn't want to talk to me, you should have just called and said so. After all, I'm only your mother."

"It wasn't like that, Mom." Not exactly.

"And another thing. Next time at least come up with something a little more convincing than hanging around with that wife of yours. I mean, really! Who are you trying to kid?"

"That wife of mine has a name. And we weren't just hanging around. We were out, doing things. Going places. Having a good time, if you really must know."

"Spending quality time together?" Celia asked, sounding unconvinced.

"Yes, Mother. Spending quality time together."

"Myron! Don't you know it's wrong to lie to your mother? It's even in one of the commandments, I think, about respecting your parents. And I'm your parent!"

Apparently. So was *Thou shalt not kill*, thought Mike, suddenly understanding why certain rules needed to be spelled out clearly like that.

"Honest, it's not an excuse. I mean, it *is* an excuse, only an honest one. I...oh, for crying out loud! I'm telling you the truth. Christine and I have been on the go constantly, lately. We've hardly been home."

"'Hardly' would be the word for it, if you've been spending that much time with that woman."

"It's been...nice, surprisingly. Quite nice, as a matter of fact. Sort of like it was back when we were still dating."

"The two of you couldn't keep your hands off each other when you were still dating. I walked in on you that one time, remember? Oy! Such an image a mother should never have!"

Mike remembered. But, as he'd reasoned at the time, when you come home a lot earlier than you were supposed to, you had to allow for the occasional element of surprise. Of course, he was much younger and more sure of things back in those days. "I said it was *sort of* like when we were dating. And I see your memory is every bit as good as it used to be."

"Myron, you know my memory was never as good as it used to be."

Say goodnight, Gracie.

Chapter 32

The Executive Vice President was mad. Not crazy, mad-scientist mad, though a strong argument to the effect would have probably found at least a few sympathetic hearers. He was, rather, angry-mad. And the EVP was just the sort of person who, when angry-mad, generally found himself inclined to do something about it.

He'd been smoldering ever since his last encounter with the Head Human Resources Honcho. While no actual smoke had, technically speaking, wafted from his ears, it was not unusual lately for those seeing him to sneak a second look, convinced they had noticed something very much resembling it.

That meeting had been planned meticulously: he would walk the HHRH down the path and straight to the unemployment office. Perry Mason couldn't have planned it better! It had taken every bit of self-control the Executive Vice President possessed to maintain any sense of decorum or professionalism in the process. But the CEO was watching, and these things had to be handled with a certain degree of ceremony.

And then, just as he was about to close in for the kill,

the damned guy had the nerve—the audacity!—to duck. The Head Human Resources Honcho walked away without so much as a wrinkle on his reputation. *He*, the EVP, on the other hand, had stumbled out of the Hibachi Room looking like an absolute moron. An exceptionally dim one, even by moron standards. The memory still smarted.

The CEO hadn't helped alleviate the pangs of utter debacle, either. He'd simply shrugged his shoulders admonishingly and given his that's-why-I'm-the-CEO smile. As if nepotism was some sort of acquired skill! The senior man didn't even say anything. He hadn't needed to. That thought really *did* send small puffs of smoke trailing from the EVP's ears and out into the unlit office.

Such an affront could not, in the Executive Vice President's opinion, be given a free pass. Aside from the personal animus aspect of the thing, there were other factors to consider. People could get similar ideas, for example, and start pecking away at his authority like chickens in a barnyard. Or a chicken-coop. He wasn't all that clear on the subject of chickens. Then there was the not-to-be-forgotten personal animus, which was formidable enough in its own right to launch more ships than Helen of Troy, if only just to get farther away from it.

This called for some serious nipping in the proverbial bud. His ability to intimidate underlings was the foundation of the EVP's management philosophy; once fear went, respect would surely follow. And that, he knew, was no way to run a company. It was called leadership.

And the one thing capable of turning that leadership into an endangered species was called Moskowitz. *Myron*

Moskowitz, as if merely being Moskowitz wasn't enough. The Executive Vice President could not, even in his wildest dreams, have ever imagined his career dangling within the tenuous grasp of a Myron. And he'd had some pretty wild dreams in his time. No, he had successfully remained Myron-proof this long, and he fully intended to keep it that way.

It would have been one thing if this Moskowitz was important, or even just powerful. But he was a nobody! The EVP couldn't so much as find a trace of the man on the internet. Not even using the *I Feel Lucky* feature. Myron Moskowitz did not exist, according to the world-wide web, and the internet supposedly knew everything.

Well, the elusive Moskowitz may have been snared, and he may even have agreed to rejoin the company. Until he was officially back on the payroll, however, there were still plenty of opportunities for things to go wrong. And the EVP would see to it that they did.

Mike was having trouble sleeping. This is slightly misleading, since for someone to have trouble doing something there must be the underlying presumption it can be done. In the case of sleeping, and as it applied to Mike, and, in particular, now, any possibility of sleep would have been entirely out of the question.

Apart from his usual chronic insomnia, tonight was merely a sheer curtain separating him from the events of tomorrow. Tomorrow was "the day." Either everything would happen according to plan and he'd be once more back among the Googleable, or he'd be measuring himself for a motorcycle helmet and yelling for Paco to wait up.

Then, Christine had rolled over onto his side of the bed. *Way* over. He was already scrunched about as tightly as his distressed skeletal system would allow, having shriveled into himself like a heavily over-cooked sausage. Christine had not trespassed this far into Mike's own territory since at least a couple of Presidents ago. She'd done such a good job of avoiding it, Mike suspected his wife might have been aided by GPS. But there she was, at angles not even a seasoned jigsaw puzzle designer could have dreamed up, and out like a light.

Mike wondered what had prompted this unexpected side-of-bed invasion. Admittedly, the pair had been spending an unusual amount of time together, talking and doing things beyond the typical sharing of common breathing air. Still, that didn't explain violating her long-established policy against physical contact. At least, Mike didn't think it did. What Christine might have been thinking...well, who knew? She made an art form out of not sharing that sort of thing. Maybe if he nudged her and asked...but where *that* could lead was far too scary to contemplate.

Mike considered getting out of bed, figuring that being anywhere else could only be an improvement. Getting out of bed and doing *what*, however, was more than he had the concentration to decide. Instead, he just lay there shifting and yielding as many of his body parts as the laws of physics were willing to let him.

Dan slept like a baby. In other words, he woke up crying about once every hour. Not literally. His traumatic freak-out was somewhat more age-appropriate. But only somewhat. Even Jackie, whose apartment they were currently in, was bouncing off the walls a little, though in a geeky-cute sort of way.

"What is there left to do?" she had asked, with a mixture of reassurance and exasperation.

"Nothing," Dan had replied, still feeling like there had to be something. There was *always* something. Perfect plans were notorious for it. That he had not yet worried himself into figuring out *what* only worried him even more.

He tried to forget about it. So did she. Both trying to forget about it only reminded each of them what it was they were trying to forget, which in turn only guaranteed that neither one possibly would.

The Head Human Resources Honcho slept like a man who had no conceivable idea of what the following day had in store for him. He would remember this interlude of carefree slumber fondly, barely twenty-four hours later.

Chapter 33

The Executive Vice President had had a late night.

When he was but a young boy, his mother frequently found herself wondering if the apple of her eye kept himself awake all night thinking up ways to drive her crazy. He considered that idea preposterous, since thinking up ways to drive his mother crazy rarely took more than two or three hours at most. Besides, to his way of thinking, she already had a significant head start in that direction. A lifetime of practice had honed his abilities to where a mere thirty minutes would have gotten the job done while also allowing sufficient extra time for a bathroom break and a quick snack, too.

This Moskowitz matter was proving to be a tricky one from the prospective misadventure perspective, however. There were an unusual number of variables to account for, for starters. Individually, none were particularly formidable, but collectively, they formed a mosaic of bricks high enough to build a wall, with a *No Trespassing* sign posted too prominently to ignore.

It had kept him up late. When the EVP's head finally hit the pillows, though, it was a happy head. If people hated Mondays before, it assured itself, tomorrow was going to make every Monday that had ever been seem like Christmas. Or in this case, Hanukah. The Executive Vice President was nothing if not equal-opportunity.

The CEO had temporarily forgotten all about Myron Moskowitz and was oblivious to all the Moskowitz machinations taking place behind the scenes. On the whole, he much preferred things that way.

*D*aybreak seemed an exceptionally appropriate way to describe what kicked off the following morning. The day broke. It dawned first, of course, rather pleasantly, as these things go. The sun rose, the birdies chirped and the all's-right-with-the-world checklist showed a long column of neatly ticked boxes. There was nothing in any way unusual about the dawn. In places where the name Myron Moskowitz was not yet a household word, the day was coming up roses.

In places where Myron Moskowitz *was* a household word, however, the day was giving way to the aforementioned break. It began like an earthquake that hasn't happened yet but that everyone is expecting to at any moment, and remained that way until the pavement underneath the world's feet went into full frappé mode. Figuratively speaking.

For Dan and his Itinerant Life & Casualty Company cell, Monday morning debuted while the roosters were

still heavily in REM sleep. A contingent of around twen-
ty-odd twenty-somethings arrived practically *en masse* at
Jackie's apartment, which would have no doubt concerned
the neighbors if they'd been awake at the time and were the
type who became concerned over that sort of thing. The
assembled were surprisingly perky in a sleepy sort of way,
as folks in that general age bracket can be. Dan, already in
his thirties, both appreciated the fact and hated them for it.

There was, of course, nothing for anyone to do there.
But since companies like Itinerant Life & Casualty did not
just hand out their building keys to every Tom, Dick and
Kermit, it was necessary to wait until their respective office doors officially opened for the day. And since they
had to be somewhere, Jackie's place was as good as any.
Plus, she was kinda cute, in a geeky sort of way.

"Everybody know what they're supposed to do?" Dan
asked for the eighty-second or -third time.

No one answered. They'd stopped answering somewhere back around time fifty-four or -five.

"Any questions?"

Apparently, there were not.

"I feel like we ought to be doing something," Dan
sighed exhaustedly. Everyone *was*, in fact; though playing
video games on their cell phones probably wasn't what
Dan would have had in mind, if he'd had anything in mind.
Once again, nobody even acknowledged him.

The clocks—Jackie had several—ticked away ener-
getically if not synchronously, but as far as Dan could tell,
the time never changed. He was beginning to regret having
the operations group departing all at once from Jackie's

place, but at least that way he knew they'd all be present and accounted for when zero hour came around. There was some consolation in that, Dan tried desperately to convince himself.

The Head Human Resources Honcho awoke, stretched and abandoned bed and bedclothes with a deep sense of regret. This was separate from the deep sense of dread that came on him suddenly, the origin of which presented him with something of a mystery. Today was the day Mike Moskowitz re-joined the firm, saving the HHRH's own bacon in the process. And while there were several more mundane matters on his agenda to be dealt with, none of them were likely to prove particularly traumatic in any foreseeable way.

Still, he could not shake the sensation that a large weight was dangling directly above his unprotected cranium, at the end of a very short and tired thread. Had he held even a tiny clue as to what the Executive Vice President had in store for him, that thread would have snapped long before he'd had a chance to notice it. And one can merely speculate as to the havoc an imaginary weight could wreak on a real human cranium. Fortunately that intelligence had yet to be gleaned, so the imagination could safely sit this one out.

He arrived at the office as he did every weekday morning, sat down at his desk and proceeded to do absolutely nothing. It was not unusual for the Head Human Resources Honcho to begin his workday sitting at his desk doing nothing, but today he seemed to be doing more of absolutely nothing than was usual, customary, or reasonable. The specific mechanics by which he didn't do anything, however, remained more-or-less unchanged.

Mike practically sleepwalked out of bed, sleep-ate his way through a modest breakfast and sleep-drove in the direction of his once and future place of daily toil. He was feeling just a bit on the tired side this morning.

By habit he pulled into the strip mall housing the coffee emporium in which he had practically become a shareholder, nodded at the young server behind one end of the counter and had his usual coffee-based beverage waiting for him at the other end. Henry Ford would have been impressed with efficiency like that, even if he was not making any money from it. Mike then assumed his practically rightful place at his practically reserved table before remembering he was supposed to be somewhere else.

And it was then that it occurred to him: he really did not want to go. Too late to get out of it now though, he brooded. His timing had always been pretty lousy that way.

Raising his still-un-tasted coffee-based beverage in the air like it was the Olympic torch, Mike sprung up out of his adopted seat for what he guessed might well have been the very last time. Bowing and scraping to the oblivious coffee delivery mechanism behind the counter, Mike backed his way exit-ward. He was shaken out of reverse after colliding butt-first with a professionally dressed woman whose complete line of sight extended no farther than the cell phone she held balanced vice-like between her hands. She glanced up in annoyance at Mike, but her thumbs never stopped moving.

He successfully navigated the remaining few feet to the sidewalk without any further mishaps, and paused there to collect himself for a brief moment. He cast a symbolic gaze street-ward then beyond, seeming to scan the horizon for the old, familiar landmark that would be this morning's final destination. A whole lot of other mornings' final destination, too, if Dan was a lot more competent than he looked. Mike had to admit that, in all probability, Dan would pretty much have to be.

As a final symbolic gesture, Mike turned to face his as yet un-sampled cup of coffee-based beverage and, bidding it farewell, proceeded to dump it, its contents intact, into a nearby trash receptacle. The act seemed an appropriate, if unnecessarily messy, end to an era that would otherwise not be too sorely missed.

Mike's drive the rest of the way to the company's parking lot progressed in slow motion, as if out of a movie whose director didn't know how overused that cinematic gimmick appeared to audiences nowadays. Even the radio seemed to be playing in slow motion, though this was somewhat understandable as it was tuned to NPR.

His thoughts, however, were a different story. They were racing along at better than Formula One speed which, for Mike Moskowitz, was considerably faster than he was used to. A whole lot of people had to get a whole lot of things absolutely right in order for the exercise to work, and Mike really needed the exercise to work. More to the point, *he* really needed to work, so everyone involved in making that happen had to be on their toes. Perhaps we should have said it was more to the *pointe*.

The Head Human Resources Honcho sat at his desk, his head sandwiched between two damp palms. He had just received a call from the Executive Vice President's Executive Assistant directing him to proceed forthwith to the Hibachi Room, without either passing *GO* or collecting $200.00. It was a phrase the EVP had something of a workplace monopoly on.

This was no way to start a Monday, and this Monday most of all. Myron Moskowitz was due any minute now. The HHRH was half-surprised Mike hadn't beaten him in that morning. His own plan had been to corral the man of the hour safely inside his office, and keep him there until the whole, complicated on-boarding process was a *fait accompli*. After which, the Head Human Resources Honcho fully intended to throw the man out of his office on his ear and hope he never had to lay eyes on him again.

But there was no sign of Mike yet, and the HHRH was faced with something of a Hobson's Choice: either ignore the summons Hibachi Room-ward and give the EVP grounds for making trouble; or obey the summons, prevent Mike from escaping cyber purgatory and rejoining the payroll, and give the EVP even *more* grounds for making even *more* trouble.

This *really* was no way to start a Monday.

The man of the hour could, around this time, be found dawdling behind the wheel of his car, which had found an unusually good spot close to the building. His palms were damp, too, and other prominent sweat centers were in the throes of catching up with them. This was never a very auspicious way to start a workday, especially a Monday, and even more especially, *this* Monday. The unwanted bodily moisture was particularly hard to explain in light of the fact that his circulation had earlier retreated to parts unknown, leaving him chilled nearly to shivering. And he couldn't blame that on NPR.

After sitting there until the posture risked becoming permanent, Mike tugged on the lever of the driver's-side door and, in a sudden burst of vitality, shifted his body quickly to the left, with the obvious intention of extricating himself from the driver's seat. He had, however, neglected to release the seatbelt first, and as a result wound up being slammed like a crash-test dummy into the head and backrest. This *really* was no way to start a Monday.

Mike bravely half-swaggered toward the entrance with his head held high and his chest thrust slightly forward. It was the best impression of dignity he could muster. He looked so convincing that, observing his reflection in the door glass, he nearly believed it himself.

Chapter 34

Mike made his way down to the Human Resources office which, as they frequently are, was buried in an out-of-the-way basement corridor. He wasn't sure why companies relegated their HR departments to the lower depths, though he thought he could probably venture a pretty good guess.

The Head Human Resources Honcho's assistant was anxiously awaiting his arrival, but did a marvelous job of pretending not to be when Mike finally made his way into the department. Her feigned surprise could have won an Oscar, but that last bastion against intrusion by troublesome employees was otherwise at a loss. Her boss had been practically climbing the walls anticipating the now-present Moskowitz. Yet, following an unexpectedly early phone call, he had suddenly vanished without leaving her any explanation or instructions.

The assistant found herself in the position of having to improvise, but other than coming up with creative ways of putting people off, she'd had very little practice at this sort of thing. She also, without knowing exactly why, understood that getting Myron Moskowitz back on the payroll was somehow critically important to her boss. And keeping the HHRH happy was way up at the tippy-top of her job description. In bold letters and italics, no less.

Figuring a good offense was the best defense, she decided to strike first.

"May I help you?" she asked, brandishing a telephone receiver. There was no one on the other end of the line; but company policy prohibited her from brandishing anything more useful, such as baseball bats and samurai swords.

Mike was amazed she needed to ask, all things considered.

"I have an appointment."

"An appointment with whom?"

The office was home to only two people, fifty percent of which was sitting at her desk asking stupid questions. The process of elimination should not have posed an especially high degree of difficulty. Still, the assistant did not appear to be embracing the task.

"Your boss," Mike answered patiently.

"And your name, sir?"

"You *know* my name. I used to work here, remember? I'm supposed to start working here again. I assume someone's probably mentioned it?" Mike replied a lot less patiently, his vital signs having returned to their normal, frustrated levels.

"Let me see...Mr. Moskowitz, isn't it?" She was stalling, and floundered slightly as her gatekeeper reserves noticeably dwindled.

"You say you have an appointment?" she asked, falling back on an old stand-by.

"Yes, I have an appointment," Mike repeated. The accompanying sigh sounded remarkably like that of a sizzling ember burning its way along a lighted fuse.

"Let's just have a look," the assistant said, turning to face her computer. This was yet another comfort prop, since she could stall more-or-less indefinitely while pretending to look things up on it. Pretending, because she had so far not gotten around to booting it up yet.

"It's a little slow this morning. Probably hates Mondays as much as the rest of us!"

"You might find it'll run a little faster if you turn it on," Mike suggested, pointing to the power button. "They usually work much better that way."

The assistant was slipping rapidly into panic mode. She could feel her skin constricting into shrink wrap around her head and face, and only hoped her teeth weren't showing. They were clenched rather severely, and she thought it would be better all around if they remained safely out of the public domain.

Mike tried very hard not to stare, but the challenge proved too difficult. The assistant's face appeared to be morphing into...well, it was hard to say what, exactly. Somebody else's face? A poorly-executed balloon animal? Mike couldn't be sure. But whatever it was, it was pretty fascinating to watch.

Finally, whether through complete exhaustion or unconditional surrender, she slumped back into her desk chair. The chair was considerate enough on this occasion to refrain from sliding away inconveniently as she did so.

"Look, he was here earlier, okay? But then he got a

phone call, and shot upstairs like a bat out of hell," she blurted.

"What's upstairs?" Mike asked.

"*Everything* is upstairs. We're in the basement, re-member?" Her thumb was pointed downward and bob-bing, as if there might be something even lower than they were. The thumb was just being ironic, since it knew perfectly well there wasn't.

"I mean, do you have any idea *where* upstairs? You know, was he going outside to look for me, or did he get called into a meeting—"

"How should I know? I'm just the one who's supposed to keep everything running around here. Why on Earth would he tell *me* anything?"

"I guess I'll have to just sit here and wait for him then, would you say?"

"Please yourself. I'm going topside for a smoke." This unprecedented explosion of brutal honesty had a powerful, liberating effect on the HHRH's assistant. She felt a sud-den urge to learn how to operate a parachute. And take up smoking.

Mike's attention followed the plane of her back out through the office door and into the corridor. It lost interest in plane watching as she turned out of sight, presumably heading down the corridor, and engaged itself with a bank of chairs lined up neatly against the rear wall. His attention then followed Mike into one of the chairs, whereupon it immediately began scouring the area for a magazine.

The Head Human Resources Honcho sat alone and uncomfortable within the confines of the Hibachi Room. At least some of his discomfort was a result of the room's temperature, which, on this occasion, at least, was due less to any potential grilling than it was to the Executive Vice President's having tampered with the thermostat earlier that morning. Every thirty seconds or so the HHRH cast a nervous eye in the direction of his watch, noting that very little appeared to have happened there movement-wise in the preceding interval.

He shifted his gaze to the open door, with its view of the adjacent hallway. There was nothing to suggest any executives were already working their way toward the room, or that any of them had even arrived for work yet. Myron Moskowitz was probably downstairs by now, waiting in his office and it occurred to the Head Human Resources Honcho that he'd forgotten to tell his assistant what to do with their guest. Well, he assured himself, she could certainly string him along if need be. She was good at that.

Back in his own office, the Executive Vice President was experiencing a sudden case of stage fright. The plan he'd embraced with so much confidence on the road to evil dreamland last night was not passing quite the same muster in the light of day, and it was now approaching show time. He paced back and forth across the floor of the office, though only mentally since he could not summon enough motivation to get up from his chair and do the pacing himself.

It was an extremely simple plan, as these things go:

Prevent the Head Human Resources Honcho from putting Myron Moskowitz back on the company roster. The plan was a tad light on details as to exactly how he was supposed to accomplish this, but he had a knack for figuring those sorts of things out on the fly. Unfortunately, however, his normally keen business mind was at present off minding its own business somewhere else. *Leave a message,* it was telling him, *we'll get back to you.* And there are few things worse than a mind that won't take your phone call.

The minutes fairly galloped past as the EVP tried to coax his executive backside into gear. His intended stress-inducing-late entrance was quickly giving way to an anticlimactically boring one. If he did not leave soon, the Head Human Resources Honcho would probably start dozing off. It had become a battle of mind over matter, and mind was currently in the process of getting its butt kicked.

The Head Human Resources Honcho glanced at his watch one more time and realized he needed to be back in his office, fingertips poised at his keyboard, in fewer minutes than he'd had just a few short minutes earlier. Which made sense, if you stop and think about it.

He made a decision, and hoped like crazy it was the right one.

"It's show time!" the Executive Vice President's inner voice announced to the rest of him for its eighth repetition. Eight was apparently the lucky number, because his hands suddenly began pushing his torso upwards off the desk and his legs took over the load from there. Forcing a grin of total corporate condescension, the EVP launched his trademark strut through the office door and toward the Hibachi Room. I can do this, he told himself as he went over the top.

The EVP fought his way across no-man's land only to find that, when he reached the enemy trench, it had been completely abandoned. He plopped himself down in his customary seat at the table, and held court anyway.

Across the half-vast Diaspora of Dan's chosen people, an orchestra of lap- and desktops was warming up. Everyone was in his or her place. Screens were open to the sites and pages they needed to be. Where applicable, passwords had been correctly entered. Few among them wore watches—analog time probably read like a foreign language to most—but those who did had them synchronized to the atomic clock. The rest had simply brought the atomic clock itself up in a corner of their screens, effectively cutting out the middle-man. One way or another, each was synchronized to everyone and everything else.

Even Kermit was ready to go, in spite of himself. It takes a big man to realize when he has lost; in Kermit's case it had taken a formal intervention and being called a clueless jackass a couple dozen times by Jackie to convince him he was better off playing for the home team. After all, he may have been clueless, but he wasn't stupid. Not really.

All systems were *go*. Instructions were hung from the monitors with care, in the hope that Mike Moskowitz soon would be there. In virtual iteration, that is.

Celia Moskowitz was distraught. She had just come to the realization that if she disinherited her son for completely ignoring her, he'd never even notice.

Chapter 35

Mike's attention was nearly going out of its mind when the Head Human Resources Honcho quickstepped past him, and the rest of Mike was not very far behind.

"Where have you been! Sheesh! Talk about cutting it close!"

"Sorry. I'll explain later. Or not. Maybe. Where's my assistant?"

"She mentioned something about sky diving as she was tearing out of here. Come to think of it, she was moving so fast I thought she was about to go airborne. I'm not sure if they're connected. Anyway, you can worry about your assistant later. C'mon! We're burning daylight!"

The Head Human Resources Honcho headed straight to his office without adding to the repartee, and discovered his door had been left unlocked. This was a serious breach of protocol, leaving everything unattended and open to just anybody, especially with a department outsider hanging around. He would have to have a stern conversation with his assistant if he ever saw her again. Or, if it turned out the oversight was his, he'd have to have a stern conversation with himself. He often found a good, self-delivered rebuke therapeutic.

The computer was up just as he'd left it, all the necessary documents lined up neatly and precisely nearby in typical Head Human Resources Honcho fashion. Mike pulled an uninvited chair around to where he could get a better view. The HHRH appeared too preoccupied to notice the trespass, or even care.

There was a clock on the wall directly above the door frame, and two sets of eyes watched it with an intensity worthy of something considerably more important. Seconds ticked by loudly in an otherwise silent room. At the two-minutes-and-counting mark, Mike asked: "How accurate is that thing?"

"You're only thinking to ask that *now*?"

"Well...yes!"

The HHRH compared the reading on the clock against the expensive piece of Swiss chronometric jewelry on his wrist. They were pretty darned close. This did not necessarily mean his watch did more than an average job keeping time, but it had been very expensive, and to the Head Human Resources Honcho, that was good enough.

"Shouldn't you be doing something?" Mike asked.

"Like what?"

"I don't know. Typing? Clicking? Whatever it is you're supposed to do for this thing."

The Head Human Resources Honcho considered this. It was probably not a bad idea. Theoretically, he could be entering data by now. A contemplative glance at the clock: less than one minute to D-Day. D-Hour. The HHRH began his D-Entry.

The D-Entry was on the cusp of completion when, according to the big timepiece on the wall and its much smaller, wrist-borne counterpart, the moment of truth arrived and then quickly passed into history. The *submit* button received its final mouse-click early within the space of that brief interval.

Immediate effect came there none. Anti-climactic did not begin to describe the pall of uneventfulness that descended, blanket-like, over the two observers. It didn't help that neither man had had any idea about what to expect. Whatever it was, however, nothing at all wasn't it.

Nothing continued happening at a leisurely pace, and went on not happening for who-only-knew how long. Time had apparently left the building, without bothering to forward its calls first.

When time returned, which wasn't altogether that long afterward, changes were afoot out in cyberspace. The world-wide web hiccupped once or twice. It made a funny gurgling noise and coughed. Then a single alliterative name began popping up in computer systems and databases throughout the land, including territories and some of the more remote protectorates. That name, Myron Moskowitz in case there was any doubt, was followed quickly by lines and lines of identifying numbers and personal information. This, in turn, was followed almost immediately by the eager keystrokes of hackers in former Soviet republics, who it seems are exceptionally enterprising for a generation only once removed from former Communists.

The email lottery scams and appeals for bank accounts to transfer vast sums of non-existent money into were not to appear for another couple of days.

Neither Mike nor the Head Human Resources Honcho could have known all this, of course. All they saw were the words, *New Employee Data Accepted* appear unceremoniously on the screen.

"Well then. That's done. Welcome aboard, *back* aboard, that is, Mr. Moskowitz. Now if you'll excuse me, I have other things I need to do."

Mike was still staring trance-like at the screen.

"Hmmm? Oh, uh, thank you. I'll just go back to my old spot then, right?"

"I'm not really sure. Probably not a bad place to start, though."

Mike scooted his chair back and replaced it in its rightful spot across from the HHRH's desk. He half-waved, half-saluted as he dazedly made his way out of the office and into the reception area beyond.

When his not-quite-new employee was safely elsewhere, the Head Human Resources Honcho got up out of his seat and closed the door. He made it back to his chair just in time to collapse into it instead of face-down on the floor. His recovery was hastened by a call from the EVP's assistant, who didn't even try to disguise her displeasure at having to make it.

As for the numerous other data-enterers, a.k.a., Dan's people, the moment it became obvious that the operation was a success they let out a collective "Yeah! Cool!" and went back to screwing around on their respective cell phones.

Chapter 36

Paco was savoring a rare private moment away from his radar-resistant retinue. They were far fewer in number than he had, perhaps, led Mike to believe; yet there always seemed to be at least a few of them around when you didn't really need one. *Me* time was a tricky enough proposition for Paco, and when he threw Herman Rabinowitz into the mix the whole *me* business could become downright complicated.

The pretense under which he had stolen himself away from his fellow Bedouins concerned matters of motorcycle maintenance. Not in any mechanical sense, of course, since, despite Paco's façade of technical bravado, Herman could barely tell a screwdriver from a socket wrench. Both personas, however, were crackerjack in the art of cleaning and polishing. The act of detailing his bike had nearly evolved into a form of spiritual meditation for him. Besides, the gleaming chrome and sparkling, metallic rest of it made an impression on everyone they came in contact with, which was about as close to being noticed as either Paco or Herman ever wanted nowadays.

The main reason for spending as much time as he

possibly could engaged in prettying up his motorcycle, however, was this: as long as he was busy wiping and shining, he wasn't riding. For, as awesome a spectacle as the massive Harley might have been to look at, bouncing around on it day after day had turned the machine into a torture instrument of practically medieval proportion. Herman could still feel his internal organs vibrating like fruit in a blender long after the kickstand had made its final landing every evening. Then, of course, there were his back, hips, knees—every bone and joint in his body, in fact. He'd be paying *that* particular piper for as long as the *corpus Hermanus* remained planted on the right side of the turf.

Paco covered up for Herman's train-wreck of a carcass by scowling as menacingly as any Rabinowitz ever possessed the wherewithal to do. Above all, he never complained. None of the other Bedouins ever complained, which of course did not necessarily mean anything. For all Paco knew, they were each just as miserable as he was. At first, Herman had searched their poker-like faces for any signs of pain. Lately, he'd been searching those same poker-like faces for any signs of sanity. The noise factor alone was enough to seriously mess with a guy's mental state, all those revved-up, muffler-less road monsters unleashing their endless cacophony morning, noon and night. Maybe he was just as crazy as the rest of them by now, though he took at least some consolation in the knowledge that he still had enough sense to worry about it.

Hardly the sort of thing someone with two master's degrees would have ever imagined for himself.

Then, there was seeing his old pal Mike Moskowitz again. Truly the man had it all: off the grid, a steady paycheck and a real car to get around in, like a normal person. Paco/Herman sighed with a slight twinge of friendly envy, just picturing all the possibilities.

Mike throttled up the Harley Fat Boy as the giant motorcycle slipped smoothly into third gear. He could feel the wind blowing what was left of his hair straight back, despite its being encased in a helmet potentially more suitable for an average moon landing. Of all the model names listed in the company's online catalog, Mike had chosen the Fat Boy above the rest because it positively *screamed* with attitude. It was a biker's bike—or at least, it sure sounded like one. The perfect road-mount for any warehouse-sized, patch-wearin' Easy Rider.

Cruising fast but in no obvious hurry, Mike took note of everything there was to see along his route: buildings, trees, mountains, lakes and rivers, even the ocean; while back at the Moskowitz house Christine took note of her husband lying sound asleep on the sofa, his arms elevated slightly Frankenstein-ward. He looked thoroughly contented, however, so Christine was not unduly alarmed. Her threshold for unusual Mike-behavior lately was a relatively high one, and she could discern no angry mobs on the horizon brandishing anything close to either torches or pitch forks.

A mere few weeks had elapsed since Mike and the Head Human Resources Honcho sealed their deal over expensive coffee-based beverages, and he was already settling back into his former old work routines. It was unsettling how settled in again Mike was becoming, and how very quickly. For all intents and purposes he might never have been away. Other than something having to do with someone called Howard that no one at the company seemed willing to talk about, the place was exactly the same as it had been when he'd left it.

Since his return, Mike had only seen the HHRH once. But the other man had seen him first and high-tailed it purposefully in the opposite direction. Apparently Head Human Resources Honchos don't bond, as his former assistant could readily attest if anyone ever manages to locate her.

He was really looking forward to retiring someday.

Mike still began most work mornings at his usual table at that same, on-the-way coffee emporium. This was the one routine he still managed to find strangely comforting, a sort of bridge between alternatives. Mike knew he had picked the right one, in the end; but the little daily reminder didn't hurt any. Nor did the large shot of caffeine he ingested to help jump-start a few of his more important vital signs.

He had taken to carrying his spiral notebook in with him, and as he sat sipping Mike occasionally jotted down incidents from his journey into off-the-grid limbo. Maybe there would be a book in it someday, something hovering in that gray area between memoir and science fiction. Or horror: dystopian, or even non-topian, if there was such a thing. Published under a pseudonym, of course, because Christine could never be allowed to find out about any of it.

Mike was on the phone with his mother.

"Myron, are you telling me that wife of yours *still* doesn't know about—*it*?" Celia tried her best to sound incredulous. But after having asked the same question the same way so many times by now, she no longer had any incredulous left in her.

"That is exactly what I'm telling you, Mother. That wife of mine—still Christine, by the way—has not yet been apprised, and I see no good reason to change that particular state of affairs now or ever. A lot of really bad ones, yes. More bad reasons than you can shake a stick at, as a matter of fact. I'm perfectly content to let igno-rance—hers, in this case—be bliss. Mine, that is."

Celia wasn't going to argue, for a change.

"Okay, so like always my lips are sealed. Say, Myron, what's with your voice? Are you coming down with something?"

"I hadn't noticed, but you're right. I do sound a little froggy, now that you mention it."

"I hear there's something going around. Maybe you caught it. If you're sick, you know, you should..."

Mike did not hear what came next. The Himalayas had already hung up.

About the Author

Joel Bresler Joel Bresler was born and spent most of his life to date in and around Cleveland, Ohio. After earning a degree from Skidmore College, he worked briefly in social services before entering a niche field of business consulting. His first published work, *Letters to be Read in a Heavily British Accent*, established him as a humor writer with a unique voice. In the tradition of such heavyweights as P.G. Wodehouse, Evelyn Waugh, and Douglas Adams, Bresler holds his own writing to a very high comedic standard. Which is not to imply that he is above throwing in any moderately-interesting pun that might find its way from pen to paper. Lately, he can be found deep in the desert Southwest, dodging snakes and cactus spines and ducking the "dry" heat.

A sneak peak at *Sunderwynde, Revisited:*

Chapter 1: Jerry

It was raining.

Looking out from his office window on the forty-first floor of Cleveland's Exceptional Techno-Corporation Building, Jerry could see droplets of rain bouncing off a sizeable portion of downtown. In a rare, philosophic mood, he wondered if the rain might not be symbolic of something, in a meaning-of-life sort of way. Then, re-membering how extremely often it seemed to rain around here, Jerry decided that it probably wasn't. After all, a symbol had to have at least *some* element of the unusual about it, or else how would you ever notice it in the first place? Feeling he'd satisfied his minimum daily require-ment of deep thought, Jerry turned his attention back to his desk and the more mundane matter of trying to figure out just what in the hell he was doing there.

It wasn't that he was *dissatisfied*, exactly, with his life at Exceptional Techno-Corp., dubbed ExTC by the Cleveland business press, and Ecstasy by those employees who'd discovered a way to make their work day just a little more interesting. How could he be? His tenure with the company read like a condensed version of *How to Succeed in Business Without Really Trying*, with only slightly fewer musical numbers. Launching his career in a four-person cubicle down on the third floor, it was practically no time before he was kicked up to seven, then eighteen, then thirty (that brief stint on eleven during a remodeling wasn't even worth mentioning). And now here he was, sitting pretty way up on forty-one, in an office roughly the size of Armenia.

Even the firm appeared to be prospering, in spite of itself. Their slogan, *Technology So Advanced Not Even We Know What to Do With It!* (trademarked, no less), hardly seemed like the sort of thing to inspire confidence in the hearts and minds of prospective customers. Yet, contrary to all common sense, it had somehow managed to achieve a nearly pop-culture status. Buyers would jokingly ask "So, have you guys figured it out yet?" as they signed contracts for multi-million dollar orders. Jerry wasn't sure if the company had the most brilliant marketing department in corporate America or just the luckiest, but results had a funny way of keeping the higher-ups from asking all those terribly inconvenient questions they didn't really want to know the answers to. Where ignorance is bliss...

In Jerry's own case, however, increasing success left him feeling increasingly unsettled. With each new elevator button came a sense that he was leaving something of himself behind. Not in terms of his weight, of course--if anything, he'd managed to put on a few new pounds every time he changed offices. It was more like pieces of his composure that he saw gradually slipping away. Confidence, sense of purpose, whatever you want to call it, Jerry's was clearly waning. Or perhaps it had already waned.

"Wane, wane, go away. Come again another day!" Jerry began singing. His executive assistant, who had chosen that particular moment to enter the room, turned an immediate about-face and walked right back out again.

Jerry knew it had gotten out of hand when, as of his last promotion, he didn't even have a job title. New office, nice pay raise, stock options that were practically obscene—and no title. If Jerry seemed just the slightest bit confused over exactly what constituted work for someone in his position, whatever that position was, of course, well, he felt he could be forgiven. A consoling thought, that, but one which did absolutely zilch to alleviate the pangs of uneasiness collecting in the pit of his stomach over the firm belief that things couldn't possibly go on this way indefinitely. Outside of government, anyway.

His boss hadn't helped matters much, either. After heartily congratulating Jerry on his latest promotion, he had made a brief ceremony of test-driving Jerry's new office furniture, concluding with the ritual pat on the back and the admonition to keep up the good work.

"And precisely what good work will I be doing from now on, Chief?" Jerry had remembered to ask.

"Why, your *job*, naturally," had been the reply, with the unmistakable overtone of surprise that the question had even come up.

That was six months ago.

In the time since, Jerry had made quite a show of being a guy who knew what he was doing and did it with authority. He looked prudently contemplative at meetings, joked about the workload with colleagues over the executive urinal, and was appropriately condescending to all the right people.

When he wasn't doing these things, Jerry could usually be found hiding within the protective confines of his office, pacing the vast floor (he'd logged so many miles that his suits now felt loose on him), signing his name to things his assistant occasionally placed in front of him and, weather permitting, watching raindrops bounce off the metropolis below. Occasionally, just to break up the routine, Jerry would move the stack of papers from one side of his desk to the other, then back again, or check his computer for new emails. Now and then he even stopped to *read* some of them. He couldn't understand why everyone marked their own messages *URGENT!* when most weren't even worth the bother of sending in the first place. Those little emoticons were still good for an occasional chuckle, though. Performing these little tasks being somewhat normal things for one to do in one's office, they usually helped relieve some of the anxiety Jerry experienced when he wasn't busy doing them.

As he was trying to decide whether that stack of papers over here might not be more comfortable over there, Jerry noticed an envelope he hadn't recalled seeing on his desk before, addressed to him and marked, *Personal & Confidential*.

"Now what in the world could this be?" he wondered,

4

as he picked the envelope up and tried to open it. Unfortunately, Jerry had never quite gotten the hang of envelopes, and after several unsuccessful attempts to tear neatly along the flap he finally managed to destroy the wrapper sufficiently to extricate the prize inside.

> *Jerry:*
>
> *This is to acknowledge outstanding performance of your work. You consistently demonstrate a level of professionalism and dedication which stands as an example to the rest of the company. I am especially pleased with the way you've adjusted to the rigors of your new position. Commendation is hereby given. Copy to Vice President, Human Resources.*

It was dated nearly two weeks ago and signed by his boss.

"Perfect," sighed Jerry. "Just what I needed! A commendation. For what? I've done approximately nothing for the past six months, and now I'm on track for Employee of the Year!"

Jerry paused and tried to recall if perhaps he had, in fact, done anything even the slightest bit noteworthy, which might have slipped his mind. A brilliant report, perhaps? Good suggestion at a meeting? Nope. The only thing he could even remotely think of was that he'd managed to make it into the office on time every day.

"Terrific," Jerry concluded. "Honey? Kids? Guess

what! Daddy's just been named this year's Poster Child for Attendance and Punctuality!"

Turning his chair and attention once again to his wall-length bank of windows, Jerry studied the Cleveland skyline, which appeared as it often did against a backdrop of varying shades of gray. When he was little, his mother used to smile and tell him that inside every cloud was a silver lining, and if it never rained there'd be no rainbows.

Yeah.

www.ingramcontent.com/pod-product-compliance
Lightning Source LLC
Chambersburg PA
CBHW021408110726
47901CB00008B/2108